SEE NO SEA

NO SEA TRILOGY - BOOK ONE

Happy Birthday Addie!

Hope you have a wonderful day
+ a better year!

R. M

Roslyn McFarland

www.RoslynMcFarland.com

See No Sea / Roslyn McFarland—
1st Edition, June 2013
Current - 2nd Edition, October 2015

ISBN-13:
978-1518756795 (Createspace)

ISBN-10:
1518756794 (Createspace)

[1. Supernatural—Fiction. 2. Camps—Fiction. 3. Interpersonal—Fiction. 4. Ability—Fiction.]

Cover design by Roslyn McFarland.

Stories by Roslyn McFarland

Paradisi Chronicles

Light the Way
(Find the Way)

No Sea Trilogy

See No Sea
Hear No Sea
(Be No Sea)

Para-Rom Shorts Collection

Soldier Boy
(Crystal Clear - a No Sea story)

Roslyn McFarland

For my family.
You stuck with me through years of a disabling illness, never
resting until we found the cure, and encouraged me in my dreams
despite it all.

CONTENTS

Our job in this lifetime is not to shape ourselves into some ideal we imagine we ought to be, but to find out who we already are and become it.

- Unknown

1

Accidental Rescue

DERISIVE FEMALE LAUGHTER erupts around me as my teammates trickle into the locker room, succeeding at breaking my concentration.

"…imagine the Stork going to homecoming next fall?..."

"Going? Why don't you just put her on the court!"

"…you just see it?"

"…who'd escort her?"

"We couldn't hang streamers, the stick would hook 'em with her head…"

"Hysterical!"

As I wait for them to get gone, I keep my eyes on the shiny metal seating around me, my face burning hot, never to be cooled by the tears I won't let them see.

In an alternate universe they'd probably call me the *Anti-Drama Queen.*

I hate drama.

Probably because I have it thrust upon me on an almost daily basis, thanks to Belinda Schneider and her gaggle of followers.

I take a deep breath, focusing on exhaling out all of the darkness that tries to invade my brain during run-in's with

Belinda. Be in there? Now? No thanks. Locker room hazing, lunchroom ambushes, monikers like "Scarecrow" and "the Jolly Joke Blonde Giant" echoing through school corridors. I'd had enough years ago.

Inserting my chicken scratches, I stick strictly to swimming skill evaluations and recommending individual events. More often than not, Coach John takes my suggestions, a happy bonus to my un-official assistant position. Mainly, I'm choosing avoidance over confrontation.

Shifting the clipboard, I try folding my extra-long legs under me in an effort to find a more comfortable position on the metal bleachers. You'd think my crazy height might deter bully-wanna-be's – I hit six feet at thirteen – except my stick limbs are about as intimidating as a willow-wisp, blowing in a light breeze.

Another peal of laughter erupts, making my teeth gnash. I focus on the task at hand in a vain attempt to block it out, jotting down another note before writing my own name into the second string relay.

I never, *ever*, win races anymore. That's what started this whole mess years ago. Miss Popular Belinda never forgave me for beating her out of her gold medal back in grade school. Whatever. It was *grade school*, for crying out loud, at a swim-for-fun-summer-camp, no less. That girl simply does not like to lose…at anything. If a little drama (or a lot) gets her what she wants – leveling unsuspecting innocent bystanders in the process – so be it.

The thing is, water is my only refuge. Its blanketing, flannel-soft embrace calms my otherwise jaggedly-raw nerves. I'd be in the water twenty-four hours a day if anyone would let me. Yeah, like that's gonna happen with my practically water-phobic parents. Those two are a match made in uber-perfection heaven. Don't ask me how their DNA managed to merge into a genetic polar opposite. I'm not the one holding multiple doctorates or charming heads of state and foreign dignitaries.

See?

Polar. Opposite.

The next best option to getting the pool time I crave is participating on a team running before and after school practices. Unfortunately, the best team in town with (more to the point) the best training facility, features Belinda and her flock of flunkies as my ever-so-supportive teammates. As a permanent resident on their poo-list, I can pretty much count out any potential friends here, or at school, which they'd taken over by fourth grade.

Double-checking the opposing teams stats, my shaking hands (courtesy of suppressed anger and frustration) calm enough to allow me to insert another name.

What's really crazy is I don't even care about winning. Being in the water is what counts, what I won't give up. Second or third place is enough to keep me on the team and off Belinda's radar...mostly.

I so don't need the drama.

"JULIE!!!"

The piercing shriek rips past my ear, spiking my heart rate. My head whips up in surprise while my darting eyes find, not the source of the scream...but the cause. The team schedule drops from my limp fingers, bouncing unnoticed through the steel stadium seating like a misshapen ping-pong ball.

At the far end of the building, my coach's two year-old daughter – visiting for the day with mom before they're all supposed to go out to dinner – teeters on the edge of the dive tower's second tier. On all fours, peering over the side and giggling like a mini-maniac, her mother's cry (and getting busted in an off limits area) startles her.

"Mama?..Wha..whoa!" Her little tow-head jerks up as her weight shifts fractionally, enough to loosen her grip on the ledge. Balance lost and losing her hold entirely, she tumbles forward with a shrill cry of terror.

I watch, eyes frozen wide, my stomach plummeting the 24 feet with her.

With no conscious thought of moving, I hit the deck of the Olympic sized pool at a run, just as the smacking sound of her frail little form impacting the water echoes through the cavernous building.

At least she didn't hit the pool deck. The thought flashes through my brain as my body moves of its own volition, propelled purely by instinct. *I can GET to her in the water!*

Her desperate father, Coach John, shoots himself off the edge of the pool at the same time as me, his flip-flops leaving him mid flight. We pierce the water at almost the exact same moment, but there the similarities end.

Now, my coach looks like your average, ordinary guy. As an ex-Olympian for the U.S. swim team, not so much. Fear for his daughter drove him to swim faster than ever before.

He was no match for me.

Entering the water with barely a splash, I use my own dolphin kick variation to shoot forward, not breaking the surface again until I'm about halfway across the pool. Hydroplaning for the briefest of moments, the water propels me forward as I dive back under, straight at the point where little Julie splashed down...and where she has yet to resurface.

Kicking hard, my heart hammering wildly in my chest, I ignore the stinging foulness of the opaque water in my wide-open, goggle-less eyes. Mentally cursing the pool technician, I put on another burst of speed as a small form emerges out of the gloom. Drifting, totally motionless.

Oh God, I pray. *What if she inhaled a bunch of water? Please no!* It wouldn't take much to drown such a tiny

4

body. *What if the impact broke her neck?* These thoughts barely flash through my mind before I reach her.

Quickly bracing Julie's head and neck, I kick for the surface with all the force I can muster from my legs. The sound of her tiny, choking gasp as we sail into the air and come down with a massive splash, floods me with relief.

Securing my grip, I quickly locate Julie's parents. Coach John barrels towards us, an angry sea serpent reclaiming its young, as Mom (Jill) races around the edge of the pool at a dead sprint.

"That's all we need," I grumble to my passenger, trying to relieve some nerves and slow my own heart rate via sarcastic distraction, "your mom slipping and cracking her head open. *That*'ll help." I may whine about the pool rules at times, as required by teenage law, but they were put in place for a reason.

Julie's response is to smile her perfect white baby teeth at me. Giggling delightedly, she cries "Fun! Again, Lee! Again, again!"

Before I can tell the little stinker what I think about her idea of fun, her dad is upon us, his features a battle of conflicting emotions. I can read his face and body like subtitles as they practically scream at me, *Hand over my baby!!!...but make sure she's okay first!*

"How are you feeling, tadpole?" he asks her instead, his voice impressively calm as his hands shake, keeping himself from snatching his daughter out of my secure grip.

"Daddy! Again Daddy! Lee an' me go again!"

Coach John shot me a look that was a cross between gratitude, fear and something else. Evasive maneuvers!

"Ah, how about you let your daddy make sure you're okay? Preferably before your mommy jumps in with all her clothes on, hmmm?"

"K!" she replies, giggling at the idea of her power-suited and high-heeled mommy all wet.

A quick first-aid check and tugboat ride later, Coach John hands Julie up to her weeping mom. Joining his family, Jill clings to them both, oblivious to the water soaking into her designer silk suit. Julie simply looks bewildered by all the fuss.

Pulling myself out of the pool, I attempt to fade back into the background. Any extra attention pretty much paints a big fat target on my forehead. Credit for rescuing coach's kid? The girls would be beyond ticked, making my life generally unbearable – even more than it already is – for an extended period of time. No thanks.

Jill, however, notices my not-so-stealthy try at escape and somehow pulls me in to the hug, exhibiting tremendous strength for such a petite person. "Thank you, Doralis," she whispers, using my full name (pronounced Door-ah-lee). The fact that it loosely means "Golden Lily" in French makes it appealing to her. I think the more understated "Lee" fits me way better.

Nodding back, uncomfortable, I'm a bit choked up myself.

Within a few heartbeats Jill morphs back into Supermom, all business and organization as she carries her wet child around the pool to get her changed into something dry.

Turning back to my coach, taking in his expression, my happy bubble goes *Pop!* Gratitude now set aside, his head is practically flashing with shots of insight. My throat constricts, suddenly dry as desert sand, as I realize why.

Coach John—retired world-class athlete, Olympian, and all-around-driven-individual—has just been beaten across the pool, by me—a low-to-mid-level ranked, couldn't-get-more-average-if-you-tried, high school swimmer. And by a significantly large margin. There's no freakin' way he's letting this go without a fuss.

Whoops.

So much for avoiding drama.

Roslyn McFarland

2

Oh, Canada

STROKE…STROKE…STROKE…breathe…

Stroke…stroke…stroke…breathe…

Bubbles of air swirl around me. The slap, slap, slapping of my arm strokes are muffled by the warm embrace of the liquid joy surrounding my head, shoulders and body.

Breath in…tuck the head…bunch the stomach muscles…roll…twist… flip…leg muscles tense…feel the gritty-smooth texture of the pool wall on my feet…push off strongly…twist…flip…push…I rise to the surface, slowly completing a lazy dolphin kick and preparing my arms for their opening strokes.

I'm at the Prince George Community Swimming Pool, trying out my new prison…er, home away from home.

After my little lapse in mediocrity, my coach ambushed me at home. Waxing eloquent about my rescue of his daughter, a minor how-was-your-day-detail I neglected to mention to my parents, he adamantly insisted that I receive special training over the summer.

Not interested. Thanks, but no thanks. Have a nice day and don't let the door hit you on the way out. Not included in that particular adult conversation, however, my desire to be bored at my own home never came into consideration.

And where, you might ask, would this proposed fun-fest be located? Hawaii? Florida, maybe? Not a chance. My luck tends to run more towards the depressingly ironic. No, he meant here – Prince George, British Columbia. Also known as the-middle-of-nowhere Canada. Coach John's buddy here is some sort of renowned, world-class swim coach, who's expected to train the will to win into me. Yeah, good luck with that.

Now, did the little slice of crazy stop there? Oh no. Of *course* not.

My mom, brilliant and gorgeous Ph.D. that she is, received an invitation to present her eco-minded bio-engineering program to a University in—yep, you guessed it—the same, never-heard-of-it-before town. My publicist-extraordinaire dad practically pounced onto the promotional possibilities for his talented wife. Not to mention, as Coach John spun his over-the-top tale, I could practically watch Dad's brain ratcheting through the possibilities of what he could do with a gold medalist daughter. *Right.* Like that's gonna happen.

So *voila*, welcome to our fun, family working vacation. Nice.

We left my home in Oregon as soon as I finished the last final exam of my sophomore year. Yay, roadtrip. After caravanning two cars 800 miles up the I-5 and BC-01, I can honestly say that my mom's little Japanese car is not designed for anyone over five feet eight, to spend extended periods of time in anyway.

All that fuss to get here and I'm not exactly impressed yet. The community center building is a monument to poured concrete, including the three rows of bench seating for pool spectators, with retro metal accessories. I can't even think about complaining though. As my only source of swimmable water more for the next *three months* (ugh!), a pool so remarkably clear and low in chemicals hits well above my ungraciously low expectations.

In my peripheral vision, the lifeguard is getting down from his perch to pull in the cracked-yellow floating lane lines. Time's up.

Finishing my lap, I leverage myself up and out of the pool, settling down on the ledge with a quick twist of my torso. Yanking off my goggles, I shake out my long, dark blonde hair ("dirty" blonde according to some), letting it hang free past my waist. Swimming since the age of three and competing since seven, I still can't bring myself to cram all of my hair into one of those stupid plastic caps, unless forced to during a swim meet. Wearing a suit so tight you almost paint it on is one thing, but I'll never get used to the process of wrapping lengths of hair round and round my head in order to wrestle on a latex sheath. All for the sake of a split second or two in a race...that I didn't need, or want.

Idly, I watch the lifeguard finish tucking away the twenty-year-old lane equipment into its precariously tilting metal rack. There's a girl stretching in a nearby corner. Possibly the aqua aerobics instructor, as I note elderly ladies wearing oversized suits and obnoxious swim caps emerge from the locker room. While not much of a fashion plate myself, the various floral motifs still trigger my "ugh!" reflex. Those colors should never, ever be in the same room together, let alone on the same ugly plastic cap!

A voice from behind interrupts my introspection.

"Planning on joining us today? Or simply too oblivious to care about taking your own...sweet...time...getting out of the way?"

Whoa! That tone! Diamond hard, razor-edged and coated in poisonous honey. About as welcoming as an Orca's jaws to a seal. The aqua aerobics instructor managed to sneak up on me while I'd been distracted by the plastic flora. Shorter than me by at least five inches, her palpable arrogance more than made up the height difference. In her late teens or early twenties, I guessed, the glare blasting its way through her dark brown eyes marred her otherwise obvious beauty. I know the look.

11

Great. My first day here and I manage to find Prince George's version of Belinda Schneider.

Completely flabbergasted I freeze, my natural instincts battling: fight or flight. Stand up for myself, or just get gone. Per usual, evasion wins. "Um, no...th-thanks, I'm done." I finally mumble, hastily pulling my dripping feet from the pool. *What the heck did I do?*

The flint-eyed girl doesn't look away or lighten up an ounce until I'm backing towards the locker room, at which point she very deliberately turns her back on me, gracefully diving into the pool. I don't wait around for her to resurface.

What the heck is her problem? Safely inside the empty locker room, my face burns as my body shakes with repressed reaction. Rehashing my less-than-eloquent performance, I'm unimpressed with myself. *No comeback, Lee? Really? You* know *that type of girl is everywhere. They'd probably import one if the locals hadn't grown their own. Get a grip!*

Stripping down, I crank the concrete walled shower up to as hot and hard as possible. Of course the ancient nozzle hits me about shoulder level, the maximum temperature reaching lukewarm at best. The water pressure, almost high enough to peel paint, saves the experience from being completely miserable. No push for water conservation in the 60's I guess. Gratefully, I let the intense spray of water pummel some of the knots out of my back.

"This place is SO completely messed up!" Now I'm talking to myself in public. Not a good sign.

My sullen acceptance of a few minutes ago is taking a complete nosedive into full-blown self-pity. With my new coach (Tim-something) on vacation this week, my relatively peaceful, for-me-only pool time that I'd been counting on is effectively ix-nayed due to some snarky local she-beast. That just plain sucked. I figure that gives me the right to take five and pout like a five- year-old in the safety of an empty locker room.

After 10 minutes of pounding water on my back and pounding thoughts in my brain, I decide I've been sufficiently pounded and it's time to get a grip. Ducking my head down to wash my hair, the water chose that moment to instantly transform from lukewarm to ice cold. Shrieking bloody murder I reflexively jump, cracking my suds-filled head into the low-hanging nozzle in the process.

"CRACK-A-FRICK-TASTIC!" What I wouldn't give to have a full trucker's grammatical repertoire readily accessible at this point, but it just isn't me. Standing outside the rushing spray of glacier runoff doesn't get me any less soapy, or alleviate the ache from my head, so I finally grit my teeth and stick my head under the freezing water to finish the rinse.

Warming myself with friction, I towel off with lightning speed, redressing in my standard summer gear of shorts and a tee. "Ow!" I complain, as my head throbs at the touch of my hairbrush. "This is so not my day." Giving it up as a lost cause, I grab my hastily repacked swim bag and escape outside.

My new bike, chained to a post in front of the building, awaits me. I won't turn sixteen until the week before school, so manual transportation it is. Oh, well. Shiny lemon yellow, multiple gears, tires small enough to be sorta light while tough enough for some easy off-roading. It's a nice enough bike, if you're into that kinda thing. At least my commute covers only a few easy miles.

Anyway, the extra exercise doesn't bother me. The air does. Internet research told me Prince George, originally a mining and railroad pit-stop, now harbors pulp mills, sawmills and an oil refinery. All those emissions get contained within the valley, creating some of the most polluted (some argue lethal) air in the world. I've always been sensitive to smells and here I can practically taste the nastiness. The locals say it smells like money. Who are they kidding?

It takes a few moments to convince the touchy combination lock I have the right numbers, adding another dose of frustration to an otherwise *peachy* day. Freeing my bike from the post, I mount it no less awkwardly than everything else I do out of the water, pedaling away.

The rental house nestles on the edge of town, in a little cul-de-sac, surrounded by other homes exactly like it. It's amazing how my parents found a rental just as boring as our own home and neighborhood. You know, uniform landscapes, neutral colors…the kind of place that makes you sleepy just looking at it.

Upon arrival, I stash the bike in the garage by expediently tipping it over in a corner. Now what? My parents are already working, of course, and I don't feel like hanging around manor humdrum or riding the bike anymore. Exploring it is.

Our cul-de-sac, branching off a main road, lays claim to a small park on the other side of the street, including a kids' playground and tennis court (which doubles as an ice rink during the winter) surrounded by an endless ocean of dark, dull, unhealthy looking grey green. Looking both ways for nonexistent traffic on the "main road," I cross the street without seeing anyone.

Pretty basic and older than me, I survey the chain link swings with cracked used-to-be-black plastic seats, the scratched and warped metal slide, sagging monkey bars and, the pièce de résistance, an imbalanced merry-go-round. All of the equipment is a matching shade of dull silver metal. Grazing my hand over the nearest sagging testament to childhood as I trudge past, my fingers skitter on the uneven texture, dislodging specks of dull red from the generous splotches of rust, any paint worn away years ago by the weather. My shoes squish in the field of soggy bark chips, the moisture wicking in and making my feet feel clammy. Yuck-ola. Feet should be wet on purpose.

With not a soul to be seen I gingerly sit down on a pie-like wedge of the old merry-go-round, laying back on the cold steel and using one leg to propel myself around. The green of sickly trees and scrub brush blur together with the cookie-cutter housing as the metal sucks the warmth from my back.

Thrilling.

Closing my eyes, I listen to birds chirping, mingling with slight rustling and buzzing noises emanating from the bushes, mostly obscuring the weak, neighborhood sounds of daytime television. Taking measured breaths, in and out, my mind and senses drift and I feel...not *happy* per-se, but more relaxed than I've been since leaving home. It feels nice. Especially considering my bunk morning.

"What's she doing?"

A male voice interrupts my reverie. Flinching slightly, my skin tingles as if grazed by electricity. Very weird. His tone is unusual, nearly tangible. I don't open my eyes, even if the guy *must* be talking about me. Who else?

"How very odd. She's obviously too old for a playground. It's comical, really."

My face burns hot, my nails digging gouges into the dirt-covered hunk of rust I rest on, as I refuse to look at the opinionated and obviously obnoxious boy. He blithely continues talking about me, like a roadside billboard put up for public display.

"Definitely new to the area. I would have remembered seeing *her* before."

Oh nice, the neighborhood census taker.

As he appraises me like a new cow to the herd, I notice the schmuck's accent – like French, but not. Off somehow. My dad's French, so I should know. French-Canadian maybe? And sexy. Undeniably masculine. I unwillingly wonder if the rest of him matches, blushing harder, the blood rushing to my face, fueling my temper and provoking another internal brat-or-bail moment.

"Huh, I can't quite tell from here, but she must be pretty tall. Just look at the size of her foot!" He chuckles. Not maliciously, but definitely at my expense, snapping my brain out of it's melodic-voice induced haze.

Brat it is.

"That does it!" Sitting up quickly, I try to orient myself on the still spinning merry-go-round. "Enough already!"

"Oh sh…she heard me!"

"Well no kidding I heard you!" Thoroughly ticked off and unwilling to back down this time, I pull myself to my feet. Shaking my head to clear the residual spin, my mass of hair whips wildly around me like Medusa's dreadlocks.

Orienting myself towards the backside of the park near the tennis court, where the voice, *his* voice, seems to be coming from, I prepare myself for a nice little "chat" with Mr. Tactless. I may avoid drama as a rule, but I refuse to be a pushover. Especially after Miss Manners used up the last of my patience this morning. Nuh-uh! No more!

Stomping my evidently big feet through sodden wood chips to the corner of the back-courts, I only find a narrow trail and a hill, covered in a sickly green blockade of prickly bushes and trees. No breaks at all. No one there, nowhere for anyone to go.

Where did he go?

Am I going nuts? Does pollution affect people so quickly? Coolio. Not only am I stuck here for the entire summer, this place is making me certifiably crazy on top of it. Straightjacket please, order for one.

A flash of movement at the edge of my vision catches my attention. Spinning quickly, I try to catch the intangible creep, finding only a couple of big puddles. The murky surface of one is rippling. Teasing me. *What the...!*

Grrrrr! The jerk must know a way out of here I don't. No fair!

Not about to give him the satisfaction of wasting any more effort, I kick a pile of soggy bark chips and gravel at the offending puddle, just to make my own ripples, before turning and stomping off, my head held high.

What WAS it about this place? I'd met (sort of) all of two people here and they'd both been completely horrible.

Bite me, nature boy.

***

The next morning the sun peeks its orange-red head over the tree line as I pedal away from the rental. Reaching the main road I take a left by the park, a reminder of yesterday's events. The memory of *his* voice elicits an unwanted current of emotion, jolts of mixed-message electrical charges, running under my skin and leaving me totally on edge. Why am I so affected? Between mystery boy and the inexplicably hostile girl at the pool, this place is turning out to be just plain foul—and not only the air.

I keep pedaling.

More homes begin appearing, the endless stretch of forest soon left behind me. Suburbia slowly starts to be infiltrated by more commercial buildings. Not exactly high-rise, but commercial. Mom-and-Pop shops, warehouses, a major chain store (looking distinctly out of place), grocery store and pharmacy, and of course the cement jail block...um, community pool. My destination.

Perusing the messy public board, I'm ignored by the administrator manning the mustard colored front desk, who looks like he needs another cup, or pot, of coffee. Bright orange, yellow and green flyers overlap garage sale notices and ten-year- old ads for swim gear. Victory! The monthly calendar and class schedule. Double victory! Aqua aerobics doesn't immediately follow the open lap swim this morning. Not quite up to confrontations this morning, I sigh with relief.

Changed into my comfy suit, I slip into the water in the lane closest to the spectator benches, furthest from the locker rooms and the zoned-out lifeguard, immersing myself completely before standing to fit my goggles on my wet head. I don't really need them. The feel of the water here is indescribable. Ironically, despite the foul air, it's pure and clear, practically chemical free. I take my time to enjoy the liquid silk sensation on my skin.

Goggles firmly in place I submerge, casually pushing off the wall, letting the tranquil energy of the liquid guide me to the surface before settling into my rhythm.

Stroke...stroke...stroke...air...

Stroke....stroke....stroke...air...

Lap after lap I swim, no pauses or breaks, the familiar exercise finally easing my tense muscles and mind. In my own little happy place, as the pool populates around me. Eventually the outside world forces itself past my mental bubble.

Whooomp!

Awareness crashes over me – literally – as another person, previously somewhere on the pool deck, suddenly lands in the pool...right on top of me!

Total surprise, combined with the weight of the body on top of me, forces almost all of the air out of my body in a whoosh of bubbles. Water madly churning like a heavy duty wash cycle, pain flaring on my left side as a stray elbow digs in—a spectacular bruise-to-be, I'm sure – I instinctively curl into a ball to protect my head. Holding what little breath remains in my lungs I wait, the large mass of flailing human being pinning me down. I should probably be scared, or something close to it. I'm wedged against a concrete floor getting road-rash while my oxygen supply slowly dwindles to nil. Irritation flares instead.

Whoever it is finally manages to get a clue and, more importantly, gets off my back. Floating in my protective sphere, I wait patiently for an opportunity to get away. Despite the lack of oxygen I still feel fine, lungs tight yet uncomplaining. The product of a lot of training, I guess. The next thing I know someone is roughly grabbing me around the waist, yanking me to the surface. Breaking though in an explosion of crystal droplets, I barely take a breath of processed pool air before...

"WHAT THE HELL..?!"

For a second I blink, staring stupidly at the burly blonde boy in the lane with me.

Wait...what?

For some reason I cannot fathom, *he* is yelling at *me*, taking my shocked silence as an invitation to continue his sputtering rant.

"I mean seriously (blah, blah, blah) a total accident! (blah, blah, blah) ...Levi's fault really. (blah, blah, blah) ...anyway, *why* would you stay on the bottom for so long! I thought I *killed* you!"

As my brain finally kick-starts back into motion, four things occur to me almost simultaneously.

Observation #1: This guy valiantly rescued me from the bottom of the pool, not the middle-aged, m.i.a. lifeguard. Granted, the help had been totally un-required and he *had* been the one to put me there in the first place, but...whatever.

Observation #2: Whoever he is, he's really, really good looking! About my age, maybe a little older, light blonde and square jawed with milk chocolate eyes. Totally the kind of guy every girl in my high school would drool over, yet less than 5% of the female student body has an actual chance with.

Observation #3: His anger isn't anger. More like total panic, probably because he *genuinely* thought he'd killed me. I could tell him it takes a lot more to hurt me in the water, but...

Observation #4: He's still yelling at me. Rescuer or not, panicked or not, cute (and I mean totally cute) or not...NOT cool! For the second time in two days, my internal switch flipped to fight instead of flight.

"SHUT...UP!"

He actually did.

I inhale deeply, if not so steadily. Now what? Since the blonde hulk is still gaping at me, speechless, I go with the first thing flashing into mind.

"So, besides the fact that *you* tried to drown *me* in the first place," I jab my finger at him accusingly, "how do YOU get off yelling at ME!"

He doesn't know me. For all he knows, I really *am* this tough and outgoing. So I go with it.

Staring at me like a deer in headlights, water drips from his hair and into those distracting eyes. His muscular bare chest heaving in the water with each heavy breath, I wrench my gaze away long enough to realize he actually tops me by a couple of inches.

Oh...*my*...!

"So are you going to say something or what?" I demand. Okay, more like choked out, *and preferably before I lose what little cool you think I have here.* My wildly beating heart feels like it might try to escape my chest as I consciously reminded myself to breathe.

Salvation comes via a whoop of male laughter behind me. The blonde hottie blinks at me twice before switching a glare to his buddy on the pool deck.

"Shut up Levi!" he bellows, "It's your fault anyway!"

I turn towards the still chuckling Levi, grateful for a chance to collect my wits and somehow keep up this charade.

"Y-eep...!" The squeak escapes my lips before I can

clap my hands over my mouth to stop it.

Dang it! Levi's looks are above average too. As in *very*. Light brown hair, with a slimmer musculature than his friend, though still totally ripped. His mischievous hazel eyes and warm open smile ensnare me.

Whoa! Sensory overload! Boys don't notice me. They don't. Like, ever! It's a simple fact of life. My experience maxed out at holding hands with a guy…in grade school. Suddenly and acutely aware I'm wearing my old comfy swimsuit, I flush beet red, hoping they'll assume my face naturally turns that shade after a near drowning.

The aqua-linebacker's buddy stops laughing long enough for introductions. "As I'm sure you've guessed, I'm Levi." He stretches out his right hand to me. I shake it, applying just enough pressure. Introductions to all of my mom's intellectual groupies paid off, I guess. Looking moderately impressed he continues with a cocky grin, motioning at the still glowering boy in the pool. "And this justifiably embarrassed friend of mine is Bryan."

"Yeah, uh, hi." Bryan sounds about as stunned as I feel and doesn't offer his hand to shake, thank goodness. *Awkward* didn't quite cover it. He recovers quickly though. "Hey, I'm really sorry about the whole falling on you thing. Levi thought he'd be funny and trip me into the pool. Didn't see you there I guess."

Yeah, right. I raise one eyebrow at him, placing my hands on my hips in what I think could be a jaunty pose. "Look, I know I don't really shout for attention, but I'm not exactly tiny enough to miss." I gesture at myself, emphasizing my six-foot frame, something I'd never imagined doing even in my nightmares. There really has to be crazy juice in the water. "Especially in a pool this size."

"Um, I guess we weren't really paying a lot of attention," Bryan admits, ducking his head in embarrassment. "You're new here though, right? Are you here to train with Tim?" Deftly switching topics, he names the dreaded torturer…um, coach.

"Yeah, I am. You guys?" They move like swimmers, not to mention the whole rockin' physique thing. I took an educated guess.

"Yup!" answered Levi. "This is our third summer here under the old guy. He's pretty cool, and there's a lot of stuff to learn from him. Beats the local camps at home anyway."

"Oh. Yeah, I mean…I sort of thought I'd be training on my own…" How stupidly pompous can I sound? "Don't get me wrong! I'm actually really glad it's not going to be just me. It's sort of a relief."

"Hey don't worry about it! I think that's Tim's standard m.o.. He's pretty selective, doesn't work with very many swimmers at a time, and really good. You almost think you *are* the only one in the pool sometimes. Are you staying on the University campus?" he asks, switching topics on me again before continuing on, without waiting for me to come up with an answer. "Bryan and I are sharing a dorm room. No one's really there during the summer, so we kind of rule the place. I guess it's good practice for next year, eh, amigo?"

"Oh yeah! California, here we come!"

Ah. Seniors this year.

What do I do now? To me, boys are like some sort of exotic creature you see in a zoo or something—wonderful to look at, great to study from a distance, and totally unapproachable. They also generally ignore all spectators—like me.

"So where are you from?" I ask, attempting casual conversation while avoiding the living arrangement question. While not really a big deal, my being here with my parents, it felt sort of weird admitting it to the un-chaperoned.

"Minnesota." Bryan pipes up. "Our dads swam together as kids. Tim's a legend, from even way back then. What I wanna know though, is why couldn't we train in Hawaii?!"

"No doubt!" Levi agrees, smiling at me again, making my knees perform some sort of weak jiggle thing. "Bryan and I started swimming together as kids too, though he'll never admit I'm better," he adds, a mischievous glint in his eye. Bryan answers back with a cocky grin of his own, both boys posing and presenting their well-formed muscles like peacocks flashing their rainbow tails, fanning and fluttering, a non-verbal duel for dominance.

"Let me guess," I offer, trying to think past the obviously practiced (though no less distracting) show, and make use of my hormone flooded brain. "Bryan usually wins on the sprints, while Levi usually takes anything longer than a...200? At least in freestyle."

Two sets of jaws drop open. Sa-wish and score for me.

"Wow! That's awesome! You got it exactly. How did you know?" Bryan asks, smiling enthusiastically. His previous embarrassment at nearly drowning me, and frustration at his buddy's needling, are obviously totally forgotten.

"Just something I'm used to looking for I guess. I help my coach at home with the scheduling sometimes." I can feel my anxiety creeping back. Time to excuse myself while I'm still able leave them with a good impression. Taking a not-so-subtle look at the clock, high on the cement wall over the administration office, I don't even notice the time. "Hey, I gotta get going. I guess the lane's all yours."

Easily pulling myself out of the water, I stand to go. Now next to Levi on the deck, I notice he also tops me by a couple of inches.

Fabulous. *There're two of them!* Two tall, especially

gorgeous guys, in one remote town and in close proximity to me. Heaven on Earth for any normal girl my height. Me? I fight off panic attacks while racking my brain for witty responses, while attempting to look all casual of course. Emphasis on *attempt.*

"Are you coming back tonight, for the evening open swim?" asked Levi.

"Uh, yeah. I'd been planning on it." *I am now, anyway.* My thoughts, briefly flitting to the aqua aerobics instructor I hope to avoid, veer back as both boys look genuinely happy about my response.

Um, *wow.*

"Great!" Bryan enthused, "I guess we'll see you then!"

I nod back with a small smile, hoping it didn't look as overwhelmingly fake as it felt. Doing my impersonation of an awkward saunter, I feel two pair of eyes traveling over me as I make my escape to the locker room. I really need to get a grip before seeing them this evening, *so* not used to this kind of attention. It's a total head rush! Making my escape without breaking into a very uncool run or falling on my face, the door closes behind me and I don't know whether to break into a happy dance or collapse from an overdose of nervous energy.

I'm meeting cute boys tonight!

Roslyn McFarland

3

Pete

BACK AT THE house, my mind is awhirl as I contemplate what to say and how I should act tonight.

Should I go with the uber-confident-yet-blatantly-false *"Hey guys, I'm kind of a big deal, as if you hadn't noticed"*, or the more-conservative-yet-flirty *"Why don't you find out what kind of girl I am?"* Hmmm. All of these options require my mouth to work.

Ugh! I can do this!! They're only guys (really, really hot guys) BUT JUST guys!! What if I say something stupid?...or I forget to talk? I can be cool. And I know just the outfit I want to wear. It's hanging in the closet at home...in Oregon. The top's tight enough to almost be too slutty anyway. Maybe they like slutty. Should *I* like guys that like slutty? *AARRGH!*

It felt like cramming for a life-altering important test.

Taking advantage of my better than usual mood, I decide to distract my brain by spending some time taking care of the chores that I had grumped-out on and avoided before, like unpacking.

Most of my clothes still reside in my suitcase, so I start pulling stuff out, finding temporary homes for everything. When I get to my swimsuits I stop. Looking at each suit carefully, remembering what it looks like on me, I try to determine if any are flattering. None of the excessively used, washed and faded suits seem to fit into any category, other than functional. And barely that. Maybe I can get my mom to take me shopping for a new suit or two. Do they even sell suits here?

I sigh. If I'm shopping with mom, I may as well review my outside apparel as well. Not a long review. More of a caption really. Here again, the concepts of "basic" and "functional" rule, with force (I only own the one slutty top). My style borders on nonexistent, which never bothered me before. Why start now? I know, flushing at my own memory. Specifically, they're called Bryan and Levi.

With nothing else to do regarding my clothing, barring major damage to my parents' credit card, I move on to putting away my bathroom stuff.

While in the startlingly white and pale blue, closet-sized space, I take a moment to scrutinize my face in the mirror above the sink. *What do boys see?* It's something I've never bothered asking myself before. Mirror time is meant for averting obvious embarrassments, like something huge and green in my teeth.

Really looking sort of takes me aback. My long, thick and surprisingly-dark-for-a-blond-ish-girl lashes frame my funky green-gold-copper (a.k.a. hazel) eyes, making them stand out like some bizarre emerald-opal combination. My thick long hair, while still mousey, glints as if flecked with gold. My toned and firm body, the direct result of spending every moment possible in the pool, features unusually clear skin with a natural flush to my cheeks...or am I blushing at my own reflection. Sheesh.

Overall, though, not too bad. Not the flawless make-up, perfectly styled hair, painted-nails-with-matching-accessories stylish look, but pretty much okay. I decide I can live with my natural non-style, a new concept for me. Being comfortable in my skin *outside* of my bathroom...well, baby steps.

Closing a drawer full of the last of my unmentionables, I hear the front door open and close downstairs.

"Lee?" My mother calls from the bottom of the stairwell.

"Here! Coming!" I call back, already walking out of the bathroom. My workaholic mom, home in the middle of the day? Should I be thrilled or really suspicious?

"Hey Honey! Your dad is busy organizing, so I get some free time this afternoon. I thought we could grab some lunch...and maybe do a little shopping?"

She looks so adorably hopeful. Parents can be so cute when they think they're asking for the moon. If only she knew. Her timing couldn't be more perfect.

"Sure, sounds like a great idea to me." My attempt at nonchalance failing miserably, Mom actually freezes for a moment, her face an advertisement for "Stunned" by designer Will Notshop.

"I need a couple of new suits before mine fall apart," I add, smothering a laugh behind my hand. No need to get her hopes up too high. How much shopping I can endure, easy-on-the-eyes guys or not, remains questionable. Unbidden and unwanted, mystery voice boy floats to the forefront of my mind...I mentally smack myself back to the present.

Mom nods and smiles. *This* is the daughter she knows and loves, only eager to shop when swimming related items are involved. Giving me no chance to change my mind, we head straight out.

By the end of our spree, my wardrobe has increased by three new shirts, two pairs of shorts and my first pair of real jeans since grade school. Long enough to wear with very low heeled shoes—coincidentally, the only type I own – they actually fit in all the right places. As for swimwear, two new one-piece suits and, most surprisingly - a bikini - come home. I grudgingly admit that I look pretty good in the two-piece, despite the expected bruise forming on my left side, courtesy of Bryan's elbow.

After grabbing some to-go Chinese from the food court, my mom drops me at the rental house before heading straight back to the University, a box of orange chicken in her lap and a fork in the hand not steering. The fork waves at me as she drives away.

The afternoon beckons – sunny, seventy degrees and as bright as it ever seems to get here. I don't want to spend it inside, so I stash my new clothes in the front entryway and grab my take-out to take out…side.

My feet unconsciously point me towards the park, the only place I can think to go, though my stomach clenches with anticipation. Would *he* be there?

Tough nuts! My mind tells my overreacting body. *If I want to eat outside, I darn well will eat outside. He can go find a lake to jump in, for all I care!*

Luckily the park remains empty, my resolve untested. Settling myself on the end of the doublewide slide, my food cartons next to me on the comfortably warm spotted metal, my view of the trail around the tennis courts is totally clear. No one's sneaking up on me this time.

About halfway through my meal, taking a moment to sip on my drink, my mind drifts toward fashion and boys. Leaning back against the sun-warmed slide I relax, closing my eyes, enjoying the nice day.

"Um…Hello."

Startled, I spring upright, my pop sloshing down my blouse, a neon orange map to my lap, as I try not to choke. *Him* again! "Good thing this isn't new," I mutter, glaring down at my Fanta-splattered attire before looking up.

Any words lodge painfully in my throat as I take in the guy lounging against the tennis courts. He…he's…*unreal*! The only word that makes total sense, and no sense, all at the same time…and fits him perfectly.

At least six and a half feet tall, his perfect muscles ripple under a skin-tight tee and shorts. And believe you me, I've seen my fair share of nice muscles at the pool, Bryan and Levi being especially nice examples. They don't even come close to the vision of male perfection before me now. His longish black hair accents a strong jaw and striking cheekbones, with silky tendrils flipping into his eyes. And those eyes! I've never seen anything like them. Silver! Not grey or blue-grey. Pure, liquid *silver*. Immersed in their pools, it never occurs to me to respond to his greeting.

"I said hello. I believe the proper response is to say hello back?" His full, perfect lips half smile, half smirk at me.

Bad idea. A flash of indignation releases me from his spell. Wrenching my eyes free, utilizing a lot more effort than I want to admit, my mouth regains the power of speech. "Yeah, whatever, hi." Time to go on the offensive, preferably before I fall back in. "Look, I think you've proven you can sneak up on people. Congratulations."

"I apologize for startling you," he looks more amused than apologetic, "but you couldn't exactly see me coming through closed eyes."

Oh, yeah. Details, details. Not enough to let him off the hook yet.

"Sure, convenient explanation. So what about yesterday?" My eyes touch his and I'm helpless to look away again. That current of energy I felt around him last time? It's definitely there again, and apparently hardwired to my mouth, shorting out my verbal controls. It takes every ounce of hard-headed will I can muster to regain some semblance of control. "You think you can make all the crude observations you want, right in front of me I might add, and then waltz in here with a simple 'hello,' bat your eyes, and I'm supposed to swoon and be thrilled to meet you?" I fake a pathetic swoon to emphasize my point...and to keep my freed gaze otherwise occupied.

"Yeah, sure, *that's* going to happen!" Okay, it so *might* happen. I try a peek at his expression, using my peripheral vision.

"I really am very sorry for my behavior." He drops his gaze for the first time, his massive shoulders hunching in embarrassment. "You see, I didn't think you'd be able to hear me. No offense meant. I was just sort of…making observations to myself."

"Why wouldn't I hear you?" I huff, not yet mollified. "Do I look hard of hearing or something?"

"No. Um…" He pauses, taking a deep breath, making his muscular chest rise and fall in an interesting way. *Snap out of it Lee!* "No. It's rather, um…complicated."

Oh-kee-doh-kee.

"Hmph. What's so complicated about knowing whether or not I can hear you? Sounds more like a judgment call to me, one you quite obviously screwed up."

"Yes. I did. I also apologized." His disconcerting gaze flashes back up to meet mine, so quickly I missed my chance to look away. *Aw, shoot!*

"Oh…yeah." I manage to choke out. Not normally the vindictive type, and firmly held by his gaze, I feel sheepish… a little. "Okay, apology accepted then," I grumble, less than graciously, dragging my eyes away with effort.

Silence. Now what?

After awkwardly staring at the ground for a minute, my foot tracing patterns in the moist soil, I notice he hasn't moved. Like at all. My jumbled brain registers the unusual *lack* of movement. His back rests on the chain link wall of the tennis court, feet braced, knees slightly bent, while his arms, crossed over his broad chest, strain tight as drawn rubber bands, ready to fire. Zero relaxation. Almost like he's *afraid* to move…

Guh! Earth to Lee? Don't be ridiculous.

"Sooo...do you live near here or something?" My attempt at civility sounds more like a really bad pick-up line.

He laughs, mesmerizing me again, via sound this time. It's hard to describe, like a songbird symphony...if the songbirds had really deep voices.

Focus, focus, focus!

"Not really. I come here to get away. My family doesn't really...understand me." While he struggles for words, part of me is constantly battling against the distraction presented by his eyes, body and voice. "You could say I don't want to go into the family business... among other things...." He looks so unhappy, the depths of his shimmering eyes pools of sadness. My squishy heart can't take it. There must be *something* I can say or do to help him, right? So much for my tough act.

"Ooo-kay. Don't want to work with the 'rents. Check. I understand, I guess." Sorta, kinda, not really. I try to empathize, though. "I'm not much like my parents either. I'm an only child, which you'd think would add pressure. They're pretty okay though, other than making me come here anyway." I gesture to the mossy-grey expanse around me, grimacing.

"Why are you here?" Deftly switching the subject back to me, his sterling gaze pierces through me like a visual saber, demanding a truthful answer.

Taking a shaky breath, I give him the edited version. "Well, I swim on a team back home. My coach thought I could do better and talked my parents into bringing me up here to train with some uber-coach during the summer. A good business opportunity for them popped up at the same time, so the next thing I know it's a done deal. And no one ever asked *me* if I even wanted to come," I whined.

Sulking is not my best look. I know that. I'm also not used to having someone to talk to, venting some of the frustration I typically bottle up. Expecting some form of commiseration, his next question takes me completely off guard.

"So is your coach right? *Can* you do better?"

No one's ever asked me straight out before. It shocks me into more honesty.

"Well…yes."

"I see. You could do a lot better." A statement, not a question.

"Yeah, so what? What does it matter to any of *them* how fast I can swim, or what place I take in a race?" My voice hardens as I straighten my posture defiantly and glare at a rock by his foot. For some inexplicable reason I can't bring myself to glare at him. "It's supposed to be *my* life, right? What about what *I* want?"

"Do you know what you want?" He shoots back. "Are you even old enough?"

"Whoa! Look who's talking?" *Arrogant, ridiculous, know-it-all….* "And *YES*, I know what I want. I just want to *swim*. Period. End of story!" Running out of steam, I succumb to his eyes again. *Frick!* Fumbling, I try to better explain. "I—I've never been more happy than when I'm in the water. I can't *be* happy without it. Not really. I just…I just want to do it *my* way." I sound ridiculously immature. I can't help it.

Giving me a chance to mentally regroup before replying, his expression is calculating, thought not unkind. "Will you believe me when I tell you…*I* understand?"

Well, that was unexpected. And, for some crazy reason…"Yes. I…I believe you." And I do. Every fiber of me tells me he's not playing me, not now.

So why am I responding to this random, gorgeous, strangely immobile guy this way? It's inexplicable. Like some bizarro-me took over as soon as I switched countries. No denying it, though, something's there – in his molten

34

eyes, in his liquid voice – like he asks himself some of the same questions I ask myself. His palpable magnetism entrances me, almost intoxicatingly, tangibly pulling at me as the moon pulls the tides.

Now what? I have no idea what to do or say. What's new, right?

The quiet is broken by a whisper. "What's your name?"

"Doralis," I whisper back, forgetting for the moment I always tell people *Lee*.

"Doralis," he repeats. The way he says my name—like turning the blandest ingredients into the most mouth-watering, omg-worthy concoction—makes me shiver. Lee-schmee. His eyes, so warm and liquid in his otherwise still-as-stone bod, caress me. "It suits you. I'm Petoile d'Angelus. You can call me Pete if you'd like." Definitely a French accent. Originating from…well, somewhere.

His full name almost soothes the senses. So lovely, it seems such a shame to Americanize it, or Canadianize it, or whatever. Then again, I don't think I'll ever pronounce it as beautifully as he does. Better to stick with the easy version. "Sure…Pete."

He's smiling at me, a glorious sight, bordering on dangerous, like staring at the sun. I have to wrench my gaze away, blushing furiously and nearly hyperventilating. My teeth worry the inside of my cheek as I try to control my own expression. Lost in my tumbling thoughts, I nearly jump out of my skin at the blast of a nearby car horn.

It's my dad in his flashy blue Jaguar.

"Hey Lee!" he calls out over the rumble of the extra-large motor. "You going back to the pool this evening? I'll drive you! Meet me at the house!" He grins and waves, gunning the loud engine as he pulls away. The neighbors are going to hate us.

Looking up at the sky, I finally notice how far the sun

moved. I never even finished my food. Very unlike me.

"Hey, I gotta run, Pete. Will you be here tomorr...ow...?" My voice trails off. No one's there. "Pete?" No response. For a guy who barely moved a muscle during our whole conversation, he sure bolted like lighting when my dad showed up.

As I turn to go, strangely reluctant to leave, I catch a flash of movement out of the corner of my eye. Looking back towards the tennis courts, nothing's moving but another ripple in the large puddle by the woods.

How does he DO that?

Mentally setting the mystery aside, for now, I hurry off to meet my dad. After all, a teenager without a license, or car, never turns down a free ride.

***

Dad drops me off at the pool just in time for the evening open swim session, with "tons to do" before the incoming intellectuals arrive this weekend.

Note to self: Be elsewhere. I so don't feel like playing the well-behaved-yet-mute daughter for a bunch of snobby strangers.

In the locker room I change into one of my new suits— a Manchester green, like part of my eyes. Wondering if the guys are here yet, my heart and mind sprint in anticipation. I felt like I'd made a good impression this morning and I so, so, *so* wanted to keep it up. Pete's overpowering image pops into my head unbidden and I shove it roughly aside. I know I'll be spending the summer with Bryan and Levi. Pete remains a mystery...one that's consistently frustrating, irritating, or both.

Flip-flops on, I head for the pool, my scanning eyes spotting Levi and Bryan quickly. They stand in the same far lane where I first "met" Bryan, talking to another girl. Her back to me, dark brown, almost black hair fell straight and smooth to her shoulder blades, emphasizing a traffic-stopping figure. I guessed the face matched, considering how much attention the guys are lavishing on her.

My budding ego takes a direct, wilting hit as I absorb the change in my evening plans. A sliver of hope revives, however, when Levi sees me, the smile blooming onto his face speaking volumes. *He looks legitimately glad to see me!* I smile back, immensely relieved, as I continue towards them.

Just then, the other girl notices Levi's inattention, turning to see the cause of it. I literally trip on flat concrete, stumbling like a fool before recovering my balance. The glaring eyes and darkly pretty face belong to my new nemesis, the aqua aerobics instructor!

Oh, Great! Fabulous! Just *swell*!

I feel like I've been sucker punched in the gut. Gritting my teeth, I keep walking, resolving not to back down from her acid remarks this time. Because there *will* be remarks. No doubt about it.

Stammering a hello to the guys, I avoid the girl's sharp eyes. Bryan and Levi laugh at my display of clumsiness, otherwise clueless of the building tension.

"Hey, maybe you should get in the pool before you fall on someone!" Bryan jokes.

"That's your job," I throw back, grinning at him, both surprised and proud of myself for keeping it together.

"Hey, Lee!" Levi jumps in. "You meet Crystal yet?"

I take a deep, shaky breath, trying to act casual. "Yeah, sort of. Yesterday, right? I didn't catch your name though." I pretend the daggers shooting from her eyes wouldn't skewer me.

As she turns back towards the boys, her faced morphs into the picture of calm interest. "Yes, I believe I *did* see you yesterday. You're the *new* girl, huh? I hardly recognized you out of that raggedy suit you modeled for us yesterday. Got yourself a new one, eh? Lucky us." Her voice gushes enough syrupy sweetness to flatten a pancake house as she tries to embarrass me.

Fortunately, sort of, this isn't my first ridicule rodeo. Shoving down my surging anger, I do my best to mimic her false smile, not bothering to respond to her double-edged inquiry. Definitely older than me, and obviously used to getting things her way, I still can't grasp what her problem could be. I don't even know her!

Finally catching on, Levi gallantly jumps in to save me.

"This is Lee, by the way, Crystal." He turns towards me, slyly winking. "Want to share a lane Lee? Crystal and Bryan can use this one." He suggests, propelling himself towards the other lane even as he speaks.

I nod, beaming him a genuine smile before letting out the breath I never realized I'd been holding. How long had that been going on? I give Bryan a quick smile also, as I start toward Levi's lane.

Crystal makes a small noise (*did she just snort?*) behind my back, getting into the pool with Bryan. "Come on Minnesota, let's see if you still got it."

As she pushes off the wall, Bryan right behind her, I study her strokes out of curiosity. Definitely an accomplished swimmer, I don't bother guessing her events, still resentful of her unfair behavior towards me.

"Crystal's been Tim's pet for three years running," supplies Levi, being helpful. "She's 18, just graduated and kicked butt at Nationals this year. With an ivy-league scholarship next year, this will be her last season training with Tim. He only works with kids he thinks he can help further."

I stop my examination of Miss Nasty to turn my attention back to Mister Accommodating, daring to ask the obvious question. "So if she's the Queen B around here, what's her problem with me? She went from zero to nasty at warp speed."

Levi actually laughs.

"It's just Crystal's way of welcoming new girls. She likes all of the attention."

"No, really? Thank you Captain Obvious."

Chuckling at my sarcasm he continues, "On the bright side, if you make Tim's cut and come back next year, she won't be here." Come *back*? I had enough to worry about making it through *this* summer. "Anyway, I thought you handled yourself alright. What are you, 16?"

"At the end of the summer," I admit, flushing.

"See, you did great! No problem." He confidently smiles at me again, leaning in a little. Was he…flirting? I've never seen flirting aimed directly at me before, especially not from a guy who could give the football captain a run for his money, so I can't be sure.

"Um, sh-shall we swim?" I suggest, groping for a more neutral topic.

"Okay," he agrees, laughing. I think he recognized my attempt at evasion, since I'm about as subtle as a battleship in a duck pond, but was not a bit bothered by it. "How about I take point and you follow. Don't want to crowd you or anything, " his grin playfully mocking.

"Oh, I think I can handle it," I retort, feeling my competitive nature kick in, responding to his veiled challenge. Immediately I sink underwater and push off the wall. Let's just see how well *he* follows *me*.

I feel good, strong and invigorated. *Oh yeah!* The water here can only be described as fabulous. I can feel he's pushed off after me, but with no intention of either waiting or letting him catch me, I push on.

We swim a five hundred, standard warm up for someone well trained. I keep my pace even with his, slipping through the water in effortless joy. Feeling more than seeing his location, I don't let him fall more than half a length behind me. When I notice him starting to flag a little I stop.

"Wow," he's gulping air like a fish out of water, "we're just…(gasp)…warming up here, you know…(gasp)…not racing."

"Sorry," *Whoops!* "I thought I'd set a healthy pace for an accomplished distancer like you." My mind is racing, frantically calculating what to do now.

"Yeah, I…(gasp!)…like the five…(gasp!)…though not at a two hundred pace usually."

Obviously, the shorter the race, the less time there is to win and the faster you swim. I hadn't been working particularly hard, though my competitive side did reign free for a while there. Levi's macho side obviously wouldn't let him slow to his normal pace either. I can tell he'll blow out soon – like a tire on a racecar meant for twenty laps and pushing thirty.

"How about a stretch break?"

He grabs at the offer like a lifeline, still posturing to look nonchalant and tough. "Yeah sure,…(gasp)…I'll just tell Bryan…(gasp)…in case he wants to come." Pretty funny, really. Especially considering how awe-struck I'd been of both him and Bryan. Did I meet them only this morning? *Huh.*

Not sure how Levi can get Bryan's attention, he solves the riddle by picking up a foam kickboard and hurling it at his friend like a misshapen Frisbee. A good shot, the board bounces off Bryan's head with an audible *thwack* before continuing its flight back onto the pool deck.

"Not your first throw?" I wryly observe, watching Bryan come to a sputtering halt. A quick glance at the lifeguard says he can't care less about the boys' antics. Very professional.

"What the…!" Bryan glares at the gleeful Levi, knowing very well the culprits identity.

"We're taking a quick stretch break," I pipe up. "Wanna join us?"

"Already?" Bryan's stunned expression switches to me. "I've only gone about three hundred, and I usually do five before breaking."

"Well we *have* done five hundred, so catch up already will ya?" The smug look on Levi's face effectively masks his fatigue. He must not be used to beating his sprinter friend during warm ups, because he sure reveled in it now.

Bryan's jaw drops open just as Crystal's sleek dark head surfaces next to him.

"What's the hold up, Minnesota?" I honestly don't know how she makes such a simple question sound so demeaning. Is it only me who heard that?

Audibly snapping his mouth shut, Bryan abruptly turns and pushes off to finish his opening laps, his pace faster than before. Crystal spares a glance for Levi, and a glare for me, before gracefully following. We both laugh, mine laced with the slight tremor of nerves, as we turn toward the benches.

"Man, I don't know if that was your norm or if you're just trying to show off, but you'll sure give Crystal a run for her money! Woo-hoo! I can't wait to see what happens when Tim gets here and we start racing!"

In the process of reaching his arms over his head to stretch towards his toes, he thankfully misses the panic-stricken look taking over my face. Leaning down into my own legs, I hide as I fight my misbehaving facial muscles.

He thinks what? Attempting to de-throne the current queen pretty much torpedoes my no drama rule. The girl already doesn't like me, for crying out loud. I don't need to give her *cause!*

Roslyn McFarland

4

Bug Bites

MY HEART RATE increases, tap dancing rapidly on my ribs in conjunction with my escalating anxiety. *"Groan!"*

Levi looks up at me, grinning broadly, probably making assumptions I don't plan on correcting. "You pushed it too hard, didn't you?"

I just grimace, unable to make myself otherwise respond to this hottie who is somehow smiling *at me*, wishing I could disappear into the concrete below. Let him think whatever he wants. The swim had been fine. It's the pool-school politics I'm drowning in.

"So, you and Bryan are going to school in California next year?" I ask, changing the subject with no subtlety whatsoever.

"Yeah!" He seems happy enough to comply. "We've both applied for a couple of scholarships. No official word yet, but my dad knows a guy." His grin is totally smug.

"Wow, congratulations. Really. You guys must be pretty good."

"We do alright," he replies, oozing false modesty. "We both placed at Nationals last year. I'm hoping Tim can whip us into shape for the World Championships."

"Boy, aim high much?" I tease, impressed despite myself. The World Championships is like the off-season Olympics, every 4 years, and a very big deal in the sport of swimming. I momentarily forget I just wore this guy out on a warm up.

"I don't expect to win or anything," he adds. "Even making the team would be great!"

I can't disagree, even if I've never pursued any real goals with my own swimming. Nationals or the World Championships seem really far removed from my world. For the first time in my life, I wonder why that is…

"Shall we get back to it?"

"Sure." I agree, taking a final swig from my water bottle. "How about you lead off this time, so I don't overdo it trying to show off anymore." It's not *my* showing off I'm worried about. Outdoing one of the top swimmers in the *country* sort of blows out my carefully cultivated façade of mediocrity. Anyway, I kind of like the view from back here. *Blush!*

Bryan and Crystal are just getting out for their stretch break as we splash back in. I avoid looking at them, focusing on the pool water.

"Boy, did you see the look Crystal gave you? She is really threatened! Wooooooo-hoo! This should be an entertaining summer!" Levi submerges, big bubbles exploding with his bellows of laughter.

Not. Funny.

Fortunately, we spend the remainder of the evening swimming, not talking. With me following Levi's lead the whole time, we switch strokes from freestyle (front crawl) to breaststroke, to backstroke, to butterfly and back to freestyle. He definitely proves his endurance when setting his own pace, and I'm enjoying matching him. Some time later, a mid-breath glance at the wall clock tells me Dad should arrive in about fifteen minutes. Finishing my lap, Levi notices my absence behind him and turns around mid-lane.

"What's up? You're doing great! Getting tired?" His eyes sparkle, despite some underlying fatigue.

"Actually my ride will be here to pick me up soon. I

gotta run."

"Oh," his face fell fractionally. "Boyfriend?"

"No!" *Me? Boyfriend!* Blushing hard, my brain as scrambled as I like my eggs, I avoid looking at him. "It's just my dad. He and my mom are working here this summer while I train. I don't, uh, have a boyfriend."

Bryan stops at the end of his lane, overhearing me.

"Well all right then!" he throws in, a bit too loudly. "You gonna be here in the morning?"

"As always," I force cheer, a small nervous laugh escaping. Seven days a week for me. A no brainer to anyone who knew me even a little bit.

"It's my turn to trade laps with you tomorrow. Deal?" He informs more than asks, ignoring the dirty look Levi is aiming at him at him.

"Sure," I reply lamely. "We'll see how well *you* keep up then." I add, attempting to recapture my long-gone air of cocky confidence.

He laughs and waves before pushing off to continue his workout, buying it completely. Levi laughs too, a bit more knowingly, returning to his swimming as well.

How bizarre to meet people—muscular, um, *interesting* ones—who like to swim as much, or maybe even more than I do. Okay, not likely more. They just aren't on the clock like me tonight. Surfacing out of nowhere, I randomly wonder if Pete likes to swim. Shaking the silly thought from my head, I head for the locker room.

Once there, my thoughts veer towards a more immediate problem. Crystal sees *me* as competition? The very idea is unreal, absurd even. The girl epitomizes the total package – gorgeous, talented, older than me, complete with a shwanky swim scholarship! Average, not-yet-a-Junior-who-never-finishes-over-2nd-place *me* competing with *her* goes beyond crazy. It's downright insane!

So why does one, niggling, totally out of character

question keep popping into my brain, staying with me despite all of the overwhelming logic?

What if I *do* decide to truly compete with her?

The person I've cultivated is physically plain (okay, not entirely honest with myself there), no competition in the pool (by choice) and not otherwise noticeable (especially by boys).

Suddenly I'm turning into a person who banters back and forth with hot guys (*three* of them here in Hicksville! What are the odds?), sort of cares about what she looks like (a work in progress), attracts the undying animosity of the designated popular girl (okay, nothing new there) *and* (this is where it gets *really* crazy) is actually considering taking on the challenge.

I must be mental.

***

The next morning my head remains filled with leftover dreams. Nothing tangible really—I never fully remember my dreams, just swirls of color and emotion—yet I distinctly recall the sound of a beautiful voice...lilting, with a soft French accent.

Pete's of course.

Why am I thinking about Pete? Gorgeous or not (the word gorgeous hardly covering it), he's some random guy I met him in a deserted park, which *should* ring some mental psychopath-stalker-warning bells or something, right? My brain just won't go there. Logically, the two obvious hunks from Minnesota should star in my dreams. Especially since, for some reason I can't fathom, they seem to sorta like me. If I'm not crazy yet, I'm well on my way.

When I reach the pool, it's deserted. A note taped to the inside of the door explains an "unexpected closure" for some "required maintenance." Yeah right, like what? The water's good, could they be changing the air filter? While "sorry for the inconvenience," they hope I'll come again soon. Duh! Of course I'll be back soon. Tomorrow, in fact. What else is there to do in this town?

I don't know exactly where Bryan and Levi live, and we haven't exchanged cell phone numbers, so I can't give them a heads up about the pool closure. Lamenting my lost chance to try out some flirting, I get back on my bike with a sigh and start pedaling. They'll just find out the hard way, like I did.

Back at the house, I drop my swim bag by the front door, plopping down on the lumpier-than-it-looks rental couch. Staring out the window, at the endless expanse of blah, my emotions roil. Frustration, confusion, anxiety, and other sensations I can't quite pinpoint. Sticking around probably isn't the best idea. When I don't get my swim time, my mood is less than sparkling. Dad just assumes "horror-mones," but mom can match me mood-for-mood if she's so inclined, and her "horror-mones" outrank mine. Bottom line is, I *need* my pool time.

For today, a bike ride will have to suffice. Pedaling to the end of the cul-de-sac, I consider going to the park for one brief moment. Hoping to talk to Pete again borders on ridiculous, considering the drool-worthy alternatives. Completely out of my league, no doubt, but at least I'm familiar with them, or their type anyway. And yet...the mystery of the boy with the silver eyes and hypnotic voice has me totally hooked. My skin almost tingles, thinking about him. Exposing Pete to my current mood? Baaaaad idea.

I take a right at the main road instead. With all day to burn, I may as well explore.

Cookie cutter suburbia flashes by on my right, with trees, trees and more trees on my left. Eventually I come to a section where the houses stop and walls of trees now line both sides of the road. Great.

Later rather than sooner, assuming I'm not heading

completely away from civilization, I pull into a parking lot at what appears to be a trailhead. What I can see of the trail, before it disappears into the forest, looks pretty easy. With energy to burn, I decide to give off-roading a try.

Amongst the trees it's really lovely, surprising me. The light filters down through the branches and leaves, nature's canvas of light and life, highlighting colors and details of the forest. Between the beauty around me and the exercise using up some of my extra energy, I feel some of my funk burning away with the cloud cover.

The sun feels warm on my back. Flowers fill every open space, their sweet scents combining to form a rich perfume I inhale gratefully. It's as if everything knows the time to bloom, pollinate and grow is limited. Life simply explodes all around me.

Unfortunately, that life includes the biggest mosquitoes I've ever seen.

"Dang it! Ow!" I exclaim, smacking my body repeatedly in a futile effort to drive the buzzing monsters off. Every time the path strays into a shady area, they come at me in droves, big enough to carry off small kittens. And here's me, a tasty treat without my super-strength bug spray.

Pretty soon, every uncovered part of my skin (and most covered spots too) looks like a bad case of chicken pox and I'm decidedly uncomfortable. The trail continues on, no end in sight. The heck with that. I turn around and head back the way I came, avoiding the shade as much as possible. Either this tactic works, or the local mosquitoes filled up on *Chateau de Doralis* during my first time through, because I receive far fewer bites on my way out.

I reach the parking lot with relief and immediately start back. The score stands at Mosquitoes : 100, Lee : 0. I know when to call it quits. Hopefully I can find something to put on the already red and swelling lumps peppering my skin.

By the time I reach the house, my parents are thankfully gone. Being eaten alive effectively ruined any chance of bettering my mood. Both cranky AND itchy now, at least I can be grumpy in peace.

I rummage through every cupboard and drawer I can think of for anything helpful, with no luck. Not even a thousand mosquito bites can convince me to look in my parents' bathroom. Frankly, I don't need to see what *other* things may be in their love nest.

Now what do I do?

Trying to distract myself with some mindless television lasts all of about three minutes before the bites are louder than the blaring antique box on the table. Getting up to pour myself a drink, I grab an unread magazine. Maybe if I keep my hands full and my body moving I won't scratch. The idea seems sound enough.

Five minutes later I'm dashing upstairs and jumping into a cool shower. The cold water sooths the hot red bumps. Not a permanent solution, I use the respite to think.

Hmmmm. On the return ride, the bumps being hit directly by the sun didn't itch as badly, as if the sunlight burned the insect venom away.

Unable to stay in the shower 24x7, I decide to test my theory. Turning off the water and toweling dry, immediately triggering a new round of intense itching (*Grrrr!*), I hurry to my dresser, pulling out the bikini my mom talked me into buying. Sure, when we bought it I would have sworn it'd never again see the light of day, no matter how cute on. I've never been so happy to be wrong. The less fabric touching my tender skin the better.

The backyard of the rental enjoys its own mini grove of towering trees, completely covering it in shade. I wonder if a swarm of the little vampires live there too. I ix-nay the front yard too, since it actually sees more traffic than the park does.

Sigh. The park.

As much as I literally dreamed of talking to Pete again, somehow the idea of doing so while flouncing around in a bikini, covered in bright red mosquito bites, never entered the picture. A truly horrifying thought, the desperate drive to find a way to calm down the bites completely crushes any sense of modesty. Tossing on a pair of shorts over my bikini bottoms, I grab a large, worn out beach towel and dash out the door.

Reaching the deserted play space, I pick out a small patch of prickly, brownish-green grass between the swings and the merry-go-round, untouched by a single shadow. Laying my towel down and pulling off my shorts, I settle myself face up. Arms, chest and thighs practically screaming at me, I close my eyes, willing them to cut me some slack and be quiet already.

"Wow! Doralis!"

My heart leaps at the unwanted (only because of the bites and bikini combo) yet subconsciously longed for sound of Pete's voice. Blushing scarlet, I quickly sit up to find him in his spot by the tennis courts. A stray beam of sunshine emphasizes his perfect musculature, his hair shines and his silver eyes are practically alight. My breath catches, my heart beating and stuttering wildly as I assume he's commenting on my bikini-clad form...

"What on earth happened to you?" he continues, his eyes widen in easy to read horror, bringing my own ogling to screeching and embarrassing halt.

Ugh! My bikini-clad form isn't enthralling him, probably the opposite. It's all of the hideous red spots, fully revealed on my (apparently) less than awe-inspiring body. *Awkward* simply doesn't cover how I feel right now, as elation spirals down towards humiliation.

"A whole fleet of mosquitoes attacked me," I snap at him, attempting to cover my disappointment and shame.

"What does it look like?" Plopping back down I re-close my eyes, futilely trying to ignore him and the unexpected pain.

"Oh, mosquitoes! I've heard of those!" he exclaims.

"Wait a minute, *heard* of those? How in the world can you *not* know about mosquitoes?" This unreal revelation is enough to briefly distract my self-absorption. Cracking an eye open to check his expression, it doesn't look like he's messing with me. *Seriously?*

"Um, well…we don't exactly have them where I live, so I've never seen one before." Looking away from me, he appears embarrassed. Mister Super-Hotness is being super-weird.

"Again, *HOW*? I thought you live around here somewhere. I mean, how else can I be talking to you every day?" My roller coaster emotions are cranking up again.

He won't look at me. "I guess you could say I live nearby, at least close enough to get here every day. It's sort of a matter of perspective."

"Perspective? What the hey? Either you live around here or you don't. Either way, mosquitoes are everywhere!" Irritation on its way, he'd better start making sense soon, over-the-top-gorgeous or not. My eyes close again, distracted from Pete by my own plethora of problems. "Ugh! I'm too itchy to figure you out right now. It's infuriating."

"What do you mean?" He sounds concerned.

"What, infuriating? You know, frustrating? Annoying? Able to drive people crazy in a single sentence?"

"No," he calmly replies, not allowing my sarcasm to bait him. "I refer to your comment about being itchy."

I sigh dramatically. No one can possibly be this dense. Especially after being particularly observant just the day before. "Okay, mister I've-never-seen-a-mosquito. Itchy refers to fact that all these little red dots are not just a fashion statement, and are, in fact, slowly driving me crazy! It almost feels like I'm still being bitten, they're so bad. The only reason I'm lying here barely clothed, not like you noticed, is because the sun makes them feel better. A little, anyway."

"Oh."

Ever-so-eloquent response, Pete.

No one says a thing for a while. I'm just starting to rethink snapping at him when he asks, "Is there anything you can put on those to make them stop hurting?"

Nuh-uh! He did *not* just ask that!

"Now why didn't *I* think of that?" My sarcasm shifts into overdrive, fueled by mosquito venom and emotional overload. "Oh, right, I can't happen to find anything in our house despite looking everywhere, or I just *may* have used it. And unless you happen to be carrying around a lifetime supply of the stuff yourself, I'd appreciate a change in topic. Thinking about it only makes it worse." Cleary over my emotional limit, the bites have driven me batty. I should tell him to go away, get out of range of my horror-mones, but for some reason I can't.

He sits quietly for a moment, saying nothing. I can feel his gaze on me, almost tangible again. I want to squirm right out of my itchy skin as it tingles under his scrutiny.

"I may have something for you!" he suddenly exclaims, excitement ringing clear. "Hold on, I'll be back!"

"Like I'm going anywhere," I grumble quietly, repressing a flare of hope, but the lack of tingle tells me he's already gone.

After about ten minutes, my bad attitude is fading.

After twenty minutes, I start to feel guilty for how I spoke to him. I'm not usually such a rude person and it doesn't sit well with me. The air pollution must be messing with my reactions.

After thirty minutes goes by, I feel terrible, wondering

if I chased him off for good. Maybe he won't come back? With a harpy like me waiting, I wouldn't blame him if he bailed. I even go so far as to get up and walk over to the tennis courts, testing the wall of impenetrable looking foliage here and there. Though I didn't expect to actually find Pete crouched behind a bush, or something equally ludicrous, finding nothing more than wilting greenery still stings...on top of my bites. Trudging back to my towel, guilt weighs on me heavily.

After about forty-five minutes, I'm contemplating a jump into the deep end of depression. How pathetic can I be? A gorgeous guy talks to me—okay, he's sorta weird, overall pretty nice, and altogether too intoxicating somehow, like a shot to my hormonal system—and I tell him off the first chance I get. I just answered my own question. I'm *totally* and *completely* pathetic.

About an hour after he left, I've flipped onto my stomach, my face buried in my arms, wallowing about what a miserable person I turned out to be. I'm desperate to apologize. Something about Pete makes it vitally important. I can't explain why, not in any sensible way. I'm not crushing on him (there's too much confusion interlaced with the cuteness), and it definitely can't be love at first sight (I don't believe in it), it's like...I *know* he should fit into my life somehow. Laughable, I know, but the shell I become simply contemplating his absence proves it.

Then the idea of losing him for good – okay, driving him away – hits me hard. *Really* hard. I imagine a punch in the gut is much more comfortable.

"I got it!"

Pete! He's back! My eyes fly open as my heart soars, freeing my self-mangled soul. And there he is, standing awkwardly in his usual spot near the tennis courts, gazing at me with the strangest expression. Still, he's *here*. Everything else is totally irrelevant.

"Pete? Pete!" I sit up quickly, drinking in his presence, not about to let him get away again. "I'm so sorry I was rude to you! You don't deserve it. I'm usually not this awful of a person. Honestly! I just don't know what got into me. Well I know what got into me, mosquito juice, which is totally beside the point. I'm really just so sorry for being so...so..." Knowing I'm babbling doesn't make it stop.

"Doralis, Doralis!" I *love* the way he says my name. "There is *nothing* to be sorry for. You are obviously uncomfortable. I should take more care with my own observations and words," he soothes.

Now I really feel like a schmuck. Like somehow, in any way shape or form, he is at fault here? I'm utterly happy he came back, and not mad at me...but I'm still a schmuck, a big one.

"To be honest, I sort of liked the way you spoke to me. It's not what I'm used to at all. So direct. I found it quite entertaining."

"Yeah, that's me. Heading for Broadway," I quip lamely, sagging with relief. He smiles at me though, his sincere eyes pulling me in, forcing my own lips to twitch tentatively. Being direct isn't my usual thing, but boys here sure seem to like it. I'll never understand them.

"Anyway, what's important now is you put some of this on your bites. It should soothe and heal them."

"This? This what?" Help for my ferociously itching body? My heart rate shifts up a gear or three, as he takes a careful step towards me. His fitted clothes leave little to the imagination. For a moment I'm so busy staring at his massive, perfectly sculpted body, I don't notice his hand reaching towards me until it's right in front of my face. Startled, I gasp, my breathing ragged in reaction to his closeness.

Uncurling his long fingers, there's some sort of

container resting on his enormous palm. Leaning closer, I try to figure out what it could be while slowing down my breathing. I'm not feeling screamingly uncomfortable wearing only a bikini, only hyper aware of *him*.

"What is it?" It appeared to be some kind of jar, but like nothing I'd ever seen. Small and round, with vertical stripes in cream, light pink, dark rose and an almost black maroon. He held a sea urchin shell. I'm sure of it. Fired with a coat of clear glaze, or something like it, protected the pattern, making it as smooth as a glass paperweight. Some sort of a lid attached by a hinge, and a small tulip shell on top doubled as a handle.

"Wow!" I exclaim. "It's so pretty!"

"I'm glad you like it," he murmurs. "Your enjoyment, while a happy side effect, is not really the point now, is it?" He hesitates a moment before sitting down next to me— almost falling down, truth be told—my heart-rate increasing with every inch of gap he closes. Then he uses his other ginormous hand to tentatively grasp the delicate shell on top, very carefully opening the lid.

Inside is a light pink substance I guessed to be some kind of cream. Clearer than the ones I'm used to, it's closer to an opaque gelatin than hand lotion. He doesn't move a muscle as I dip in a cautious finger. Cool, soft and sort of slimy, it absorbs into my skin quickly and cleanly, without residue. "Cool."

"It's for your red bumps, not your finger." Pete's amused voice breaks into my fascinated examination, with barely controlled laughter.

"Ha, Ha, Ha." Bantering's good. It feels normal, lowering my blood pressure. "How do you keep doing this? You disappear and come back without a sound. I don't even catch a glimpse! Where do y-...Oohh...my...!" I've dabbed some of the "cream" onto a tortured area of my skin as I speak (rant). It absorbs just as quickly and cleanly as on my fingers, but the treated spot cools immediately, healing the area almost instantaneously and feeling better than good. I close my eyes, enjoying the sensation. It felt like tasting the best chocolate dessert ever…and I'm a big time chocoholic, so I should know.

Now he really laughs at me, a wonderful sound—like a burbling waterfall with a clarinet or oboe or…something, playing in harmony. The icing for my cake of feel-like-heaven bug bite soother.

"I'm glad you like it," he demurs between musical chuckles.

"Like doesn't even cover it!" I regain my use of speech with some effort, greedily applying the healing stuff to every spot of red agony, and feeling better by the second. "Thanks again! Really, *really* thanks!" My eyes meet his, shining with pleasure. "Where did you get this anyway? I've never seen anything like it."

"It's just a standard first aid remedy from home," he replies, instantly guarded.

"Standard? Some sort of Canadian thing then? Well, trust me, this would sell like crazy in Oregon! It's *amazing!*" My distracted brain veers back to something he'd said. "Now wait, you said you got it from *home*? You left for over an hour. Do you live so far away? You never really told me before."

He paused. "Um yes, you could say that."

Evasive and cryptic again. Ugh! Which question did he answer? Fortunately for him the bug bite cream made me a momentary softie.

"Okay, okay. I can tell you don't want to talk about home. Who does? I'm only letting you get away with it because you brought me heaven-in-a-seashell though."

He seems to accept my offer to change the subject, his expression warming again, but he doesn't laugh. "I'm glad it's helping you. You can keep the jar by the way, I have many others."

"Really? But this is so beautiful! I've never seen anything like it!"

"It's nothing, really. My sister makes them, among other things." He looks away, melancholy for some reason.

"Oh. Well, thanks again." I continue my happy dabbing. "Wait, aren't you avoiding the family business?"

"Good memory," he murmurs, not any happier, or answering my question, *or* looking at me.

My heartstrings tug, breaking through the bite-cure-bliss. His obvious sadness feels just...wrong, for some reason.

"I wish you could talk to me," I almost whisper. "You...you've been sort of a...a friend to me. I want to be your friend too."

"I'd like to be," he almost whispers back. "I just don't think it's possible."

Wrong answer. My haphazard emotions flare.

"What do you *mean*? Who says? I know you want to be Mr. Anonymous. Okay fine, I get it. *I don't care*." I scrutinize his face, hoping to spot something, anything, to tell me more about what's bothering him. "What I *do* know is you've listened to me. You're perceptive and you went out of your way to help me when you didn't have to. There's something about you...I dunno. I can trust you." Something flickers in his expression, some emotion. It fled too quickly, and he didn't say anything.

Okay, soul baring time. I take a deep breath. "Look, I don't have a lot of close friends. Not just here, back home either. I sort of...hide myself from everyone, I guess. When I focus on my swimming, it doesn't matter what the other kids might think of me." Tentatively I reach out, touching the tips of his fingers with mine. So warm and smooth, unlike anything I've ever felt. He freezes. "You...you called me on it, didn't let me get away with my usual...er, stuff. I *appreciate* it. Now, I don't know what your situation is, but I *do* know how to listen. I can be an ear for you…be your friend."

Silence. I drop my hand, unsure of his reaction to my impromptu little speech, or how I'd even made it. Somehow I know I need to wait for him to talk first. Twisting my arms around to my back, I try to reach the elusive spots still flaring between my shoulder blades with the roll-your-eyes-back-good lotion. Noticing my efforts, he thaws a bit.

"Here, let me." He's already dipping one large finger into the small container. I pull my hair over my shoulder and turn my back towards him, waiting for him to say more. When he touches me though, I forget all about talking, or even how to talk. The warmth of his fingers contrasts with the cool of the salve, the combination sending my nerves into ecstasy overload as he slowly caresses my heated skin.

"C-can I think about this a while?" he asks tentatively, as he finishes his ministrations. I don't want him to stop, ever. "You…you don't know…I don't know…I-I really appreciate the offer…I just need to think."

I turn to read his face, a mask of warring emotions piercing straight to my heart. Clearing my sensation-filled brain, it also confuses me. What could be so hard? Even if he were black, me white, and it was the era of slavery, I wouldn't care. Religious differences, maybe? I can't fathom what his problem might be. Unlikely to get any answers from him now, I let it go.

"Sure. Take all the time you need."

"Thank you." Relief relaxes his whole body. "Are you coming to the park tomorrow?"

Not actually thinking beyond this moment, his eyes make my answer obvious. "Yes, of course. I usually swim in the morning." I hastily add, remembering my normally iron clad schedule belatedly. "Today the pool's closed, sort of an exception, so I won't be here as early."

"Okay. I'll be here."

And he vanished.

I don't know how he did it. I'd hardly blinked. One minute we're talking and the next I'm suddenly alone. As alone as I've ever been or felt. The only sign I haven't experienced a very lucid dream is the urchin jar, sitting where he'd once been.

"See you then," I whisper under my breath.

Collecting my things, I carefully cradle my jar of miracle cure, making my way back to the house in a daze. Tomorrow seems far too far away.

Roslyn McFarland

5

Past vs. Present

I MAKE IT to the pool before Levi and Bryan again. The schedule says Crystal's class is later and I fervently hope she'll skip the open swim. Miraculously, and very thankfully, the wonder-goo healed my bites completely, making my skin as unblemished as usual. Crystal doesn't need more ammo for snide comments.

I'm already in the water and warmed up when the guys show up, plenty of time to get my head together, sorting out my confusion about the interaction with Pete yesterday. I was emotional, PMSing, my reactions were totally off and it really wasn't as intense as I imagined it to be. That's what I'm telling myself anyway.

Levi and Bryan are elbowing each other, messing around as usual.

"Hey, Oregon!" Bryan calls. Apparently, state names are how one identifies others when in a foreign land. "I hear you're going to give me a run for my money!" Both boys grin widely, and for completely different reasons.

"Oh really?" I shoot Levi a look. "I guess we'll just see."

Bryan tosses his towel to a bench and jumps into the lane next to me.

"Let's do this!"

"N-now?" *Seriously?*

"Why not? No time like the present right!" His eyes sparkle—rich milk chocolate with flecks of golden toffee. I think I like silver better. His grin gushes cocky confidence.

The cockiness allows my brain to override my wandering thoughts, snapping me out of my daze.

"Ooo-kay. What's it gonna be?"

"200 I.M.," he responds promptly. He's obviously given this some thought. "On Levi's mark."

The 200 I.M. combines all the strokes seen in a typical swim competition. Back, breast, fly, free, fifty meters each, which in this pool means once down and back. The higher the level of swimming, the faster this race becomes. It's pretty well classified as a sprint category by the time you reach upper state and national levels. I knew Bryan fit as a sprinter. His choice of events tells me he probably picked his best race. Hence the über confidence.

I shrug and nod, sparing one last glare for Levi. I don't see a way out of this, with testosterone-fueled competitiveness involved, so I go with it.

Starting block platforms are bolted into the end of each lane, the bars on the front designed specifically for starting backstroke events. I grab the bar on mine and pull myself up into position, feet gripping the textured wall, body curled and tense, ready to launch.

My body is still. My mind is racing. *What am I going to do? I can't possibly beat him. I mean, I might be able to, but do I want to deal with the repercussions? Nope. So how bad do I lose?* ...On and on it goes.

Perma-grin Bryan gets himself into position as well, while Levi, openly laughing now, steps between our two starting blocks. He doesn't waste any time.

"Mark...set...SW-"

"HEY! What you kids *doin'*?"

Startled into almost losing my grip on the bar, I look up to see an older man (sixties maybe?) walking toward us from the direction of the office door. He's wearing battered jeans, a worn flannel shirt, and tennis shoes older than me. His wild hair shines almost pure white, and his scruffy unshaven jaw looks like he's just found his way back after being lost in the woods for a week. Not a big stretch around here. A ruddy complexion, his ice blue eyes flash bright and very alert, a direct contrast to the impression made by the rest of him. He doesn't look like he misses much, or puts up with much either.

"Tim! Hey man! Great to see you!" Levi enthuses, walking towards the man and extending his hand to shake.

So this is the infamous swim coach. The guy who'll train the will to win into me? I relax fractionally, putting my feet back down on the pool floor.

Yeah, good luck buddy, I think to myself.

Bryan gets out of the water to greet him as well. "Yo, Tim! How'd your year go, man? I thought we wouldn't see you 'til Monday?"

Coach Tim's smile feels warm enough, but controlled. After shaking hands with both boys, clapping them affectionately on the shoulders, he finally turns his sharp gaze on me. "I got back a bit early, thought I'd stop by an' see who might be serious this year. Mayhap you gen'lemen like t' introduce me t' this young lady?" his gravely voice rasps.

"This is Lee," pipes up Levi. "I think you're going to like her. Crystal's already threatened, so major plus, right!" He laughs at his own joke.

Bryan joins in as well—his grin *huge* now. "He's just never gotten over the fact that Crystal doesn't find him nearly as charming as he thinks he is!" he semi-whispers to me, conspiratorially winking over his fuming friend's head. "She never lowers herself to date younger guys when there are older ones available," he adds, salting Levi's wound.

I stand my ground, trying to control the hot blush I feel creeping up my neck into my cheeks. Who the guys did or did not date, and whom Crystal does or does not like, is totally none of my business.

Thanks guys. I think at them, furiously. *Tell my new coach his pet prima donna doesn't like me because of a nonexistent threat I pose to her social calendar. Great first impression.* I keep my eyes locked on the coach during the whole scene, trying to ascertain his reactions.

Tim's eyes narrow ever so slightly, studying me studying him. "Well it's nice t' meet you, Lee." He doesn't comment on the Crystal drama.

"Um, yeah. Nice to meet you too, Coach Tim."

I don't extend my hand to shake and he doesn't offer his. Something about him throws my perceptions off. He feels closed somehow. I can't really read him.

He finally breaks eye contact first, looking back at the boys. "You didn' answer my firs' question gen'lemen. You plannin' on racin' withou' me?"

"Well yeah, Tim! You see, Lee here put Levi through his paces the other day. Wore him out pretty good as a matter of fact." He nudges a scowling Levi in the ribs for emphasis. "I just wanted to see what she's made of, see if she could take on a real swimmer!" If possible, his cocky grin expands yet again. Levi won't look at me.

"Did she now?" Coach Tim studies me again. Calculating. "Well, I guess we'll jus' see what we see. Training starts Monday though gen'lemen, an' I'd prefer no informal racing afore I'm here to…supervise. We'll let you see wha' this young lady can do then."

"Lee." He makes a sort of slight bow to me, simultaneously gesturing with his hand, somewhere between a salute and tipping an imaginary hat. Turning back to the guys he again does the bow-gesture thing ("Gen'lemen") before walking away and letting himself back out through the administration door.

My breath exhales in a whoosh. I'd been holding it again. Tearing my gaze away from the now closed door, I look over at Levi and Bryan. The latter's self-satisfied smile and barely contained laughter contrast nicely with Levi's fuming, ready-to-beat-or-tackle -someone expression.

"Wore me out did she? I'll show you worn out!" And then he *does* tackle Bryan into the pool.

I dive out of the way as eight tangled limbs splash down right where I'd been standing. If I didn't know better, I'd think they were aiming for me.

Glancing over at the lifeguard, I expect a whistle blow at best, or the guys getting kicked out of the pool at worst. He just sits there, looking bored, disinclined to move. I shake my head in disbelief, turning back to supervise the aqua wrestling. A short time later they break apart, both grinning ear to ear now. I don't know who, if anyone, won. Neither seems to care.

Differences finally settled (somehow) Bryan turns to me. "So, you still want to swim?" he asks. "We shouldn't race, because Tim knows *everything* going on in his pool."

"Sure, sounds good," I agree, quite happy to be doing something other than avoiding two overgrown children. "It's what I'm here for after all."

Bryan imperiously waves me over to his lane, taking the lead without a word. I raise an eyebrow at Levi briefly, before starting off myself. His bark of laughter follows me, echoing throughout the cement hall.

Bryan sets a good pace and I keep up easily. We finally stop after about 1000, Bryan somewhat disgruntled to find me still right behind him.

"I'm already warmed up, remember?" I point out, trying to sooth his obviously ruffled feathers.

"Yeah! Right!" He brightens considerably. "Back in a few!" He calls over his shoulder, leveraging himself out of the water and heading for the men's locker room.

Levi arrives at the end of his lane then, grinning at his friends retreating back. "I think you wore him out more than he wants to admit. He almost never does such a long first leg, or at that pace. Probably pushing it for your benefit, I think. I *told* him!" He crows, looking very pleased with himself.

"What *is* it with you guys? Is it your job to test the newbies or something? I hope I passed because I don't think I can take much more of this." Despite my irritation at being used as some sort of masculine pawn, I fake heavy breathing, as if Bryan's pace taxed me as well...which it didn't.

I'm totally fine. Ready for round two as a matter of fact. Self preservation tells me to keep one step – or stroke in this case – behind these guys. My pride refuses the idea of backing down, though, because they've been so cocky and ready to show off by beating me. Simply put, emotionally I'm conflicted.

What's new, right?

On top of all that, how am I supposed to know if they're doing more than usual? Flying under the radar is a lot tougher when you don't know where the ceiling is set.

Levi grins at my sharp comment. It's kind of nice to be around someone who smiles at me so much. "Nah, we don't mean anything by it. Last year 10 tried out and only 5 made it through the first week. Two of those guys graduated last year, and you've met the rest of us: Me, Bryan and Crystal. We sort of wondered if you'd make the cut or not. Don't want us to get too attached and have you sent home, now, do you?" His hazel eyes sparkle merrily. "I think, with our help of course, you'll be fine."

My answer is a splash of water in his face.

Too attached my...

"Wait! What do you mean, *make it through the first week*? No one told me about try-outs." I'm not being told a lot lately. I go from erroneously thinking I have a private coach, to then discovering we have try-outs, in just days. I don't know whether to be pumped up, freaked out, or irritated beyond belief. My teeth grind together and my hands are shaking. Not my best moment.

Levi doesn't seem to notice. "Don't worry about it. I said you'd be fine didn't I?" As if he's the one calling the shots. "The others should arrive sometime this weekend, and it'll be easy enough to pick out the one or two who'll make the cut, other than us four of course."

He's counting me as a part of the group already? I know I should feel grateful or thrilled...not dread. I can't help it, and I need to get away. I need to process.

"I...I think I'm done for now. Tell Bryan keeping up with him made me too tired, will you? And, see you later?" I quickly slip out of the pool.

"Sure thing!" he says, winking at me as I make my retreat. "And yeah, we'll be back for the evening swim. You'd better believe it with Tim back. He'll be previewing the *newbies*."

"O-Okay, see you then." I wave clumsily and hurry away, my feet scraping on the rough flooring.

"Wore you out, did I?" mocks Bryan, emerging from the mens room before I can fully escape.

"Yeah, you did." I try out my best deflated look. Wouldn't want to burst his puffed up little bubble. "I'll see you later though."

"Later, Oregon!"

My thoughts are roiling as I shower and change. *What is my problem?* I've tried out for teams before. Granted, never as prestigious as this group, but whatever. And I'm not upset about sharing my "personal" coach. Quite the contrary. Other swimmers take the focus off of me. It can't be Crystal. She's just the same kind of snotty uptight girl as back home, nothing new there. So what?

Stuffing my things back into my swim bag, I fling it onto my back before heading outside to my bike and my maliciously difficult lock. By the time I talk it into releasing, with a great deal of gratuitous banging, I'm practically growling.

Back to suburbia, up the hill and onward, I pedal harder and faster than normal. It's almost 70 degrees today, hot for this area. Sweat is trickling down my back in no time.

Before I know it, I'm passing the lonely little park. Without even thinking I veer towards it, barely missing a rare and unexpected vehicle. The driver swerves like a madman, blaring his horn. I don't care. A sudden, almost overwhelming desire to talk to Pete consumes me. I want to tell him everything, let him sort it all out for me.

Pulling up, I jump off my bike – not exactly nimbly, more like a controlled crash. My face flushed from riding, my heart pumping at an abnormally high rate, I call for him.

"Pete? PETE?" I wait. Not my strongest skill. *He can appear out of nowhere, right? So appear already!* The seconds stretch as they tick on, taking hours.

He's not around. My shoulders slump dejectedly. Trudging over to the merry-go-round I sit, elbows on my knees with my head in my hands.

What is the big deal? Why am I getting so worked up over such a dumb thing as tryouts? I go over everything in my mind again, attempting to sort out my feelings. Unfortunately the more I think about it, the more anxious I become. Closing my eyes, I concentrate on my breathing, soaking up what little rays I can and trying to relax.

"Doralis? Did you call me?"

Pete's voice floats over me. I don't (quite) jump for joy at the sound, but I can't help the involuntary shiver of pleasure running down my spine. Opening my eyes, I look at the tennis courts. Sure enough, there he is. Adonis in a fitted tee. Smiling...at me.

He's *here*.

"Pete! I'm *so* glad you came!" I gush. "I really need to talk to someone...to you, I mean. There's just so much...I don't know what...ugh! Now I can't even speak right!" I furiously blink my suspiciously moist eyes. Where did this crazy emotional thing come from? What happened to unflappable Lee?

Holding up his hands in the universal gesture of peace, he stops my jumbled flow of words. "It's *fine*, Doralis." Concern mars his features, even as his voice sooths. "*You're* fine. How about you start from the beginning. I'm here. I'll listen."

I can't remember such simple words ever sounding so good.

Another shaky, cleansing breath, and I start talking. And I mean *talking*. It all pours out of me.

I tell him how as a child, I'd always been drawn to water. And despite my parents' aversion (they're practically water phobic), I managed to learn how to swim.

I describe how I've been taller than everyone in my class for years, awkward and unsure, learning to make myself almost invisible. A chameleon. The downside is, when you don't stand out anywhere, you don't really fit in either. Hard to find friends that way. Impossible for me.

Then there's my brilliant parents. I'm proud of their accomplishments, really, though I'd never dream such high goals for myself. They love me too, maneuvering to spend the summer here for me...and for them.

I tell him about the accident with Coach John's daughter Julie, and how he made it his personal mission to see me elevated in my swimming career, my feelings never considered.

I explain how I expected to be coached alone, and it turns out I'm trying out for a small group of elite, nationally ranked swimmers—a title I'd be horrified to consider claiming for myself. Not to mention I'm stuck in the middle of nowhere with my parents all summer, team or no team.

I can't look at Pete when I bring up Levi and Bryan, and how friendly they've been. How I'm not used to it at all. Not really a great topic to tell another guy, but if I'm laying it all out there, the subject has to be included. I can't stop the honesty now.

Almost eagerly, I move on to Crystal, about how she hates me on sight. Not the newest of experiences, but it's hard to deal with such immediate and intense dislike. I can practically feel the red and white bull's-eye stamped to my forehead.

In a nutshell, swimming is my piece of happy in an otherwise crazy world.

And for the first time, ever, I confess my biggest secret to another living being. I admit how I consciously curb my swimming abilities, so as not to garner too much attention.

Talk about a serious data dump. The poor guy never knew what hit him. After expelling the avalanche of words and feelings I feel deflated, yet already better somehow. I've set my load down where I can see it, even without any answers.

I've avoided looking at Pete the whole time, focusing instead on the puddle next to him, so as not to be distracted (a.k.a. lose my nerve). He listens with extraordinary patience, not interrupting once. Now I glance up, letting myself fall into his silver pools, ready for him to tell me what I've been missing…make me feel better.

By now I should know better.

"What's so wrong with winning?" While not asked in a mean way, he's disarmingly direct. "I thought people aspire to being the best? Am I wrong?"

I sit there staring at him, stunned. Of all the stuff I told him, the drama of my whole life, *that's* what he picks up on?

"Well?" he continues, all business. "I don't see anything wrong with you. Quite the opposite actually." Did he just blush? "So why should you be hiding behind others who don't deserve what they win? If you ask me, and I'd like to remind you, you *did*, you're being a coward."

"*Excuse* me?" It came out in a huff, like the breath had been knocked out of me, which is exactly what it felt like. I bare my soul to this guy and he's calling me a *coward*? My shock morphs into anger. "I am NOT a coward! You don't *know* what it's been like to be the class freak! And *you*..."

"Are you the tallest in high school?" he cuts in calmly, stopping me mid-rant.

"Wha- what? Well, no." I admit, grudgingly. "There are a couple taller people in the upper classes. Only guys. But..."

"Are you the ugliest?" he persists, his eyes narrowing, daring me to lie.

Despite my lack of overwhelming confidence, he has me there.

"Um, no...b-"

"The meanest?"

"No..."

"The weirdest?"

"No!"

"The dumbest then?"

"NO!"

"So what's your problem? What's holding you back? You don't strike me as being any of those things, and I can't imagine what could make you feel like you deserve less than anyone else."

Ugh! How dare he not commiserate with me! I'm shaking so hard it's a good thing I'm still sitting down.

"I DON'T feel like I'm any less! I am NOT any less of a person than THEY are! I'm actually BETTER!" I blast back, glaring at his ridiculously handsome face.

I'm yelling. Yelling at the world I hide from. Unleashing something kept under lock and key for a really long time. Primarily, I'm yelling at *him*—the beautiful boy who ticks me off when he should be comforting me instead, who doesn't allow me to wallow.

"So why won't you win?"

I stop short, blinking stupidly. Such a simple question, yet no simple answer. The anger drains out, leaving me cold inside, hollow. A familiar feeling. Maybe there's an answer after all.

"It's...easier." I speak so quietly it's almost a whisper, especially compared to my last fury filled blast. "No one can make fun of you...hurt you, if they don't know you exist."

"They can't befriend, encourage or love you either."

Something hot and wet is making tracks down my face. I touch a finger to one, holding my hand out to look at it. I haven't cried in years. I never saw the point. It doesn't help anything, and I'm the only one miserable. The tear triggers an old memory.

"You know, I think the last time I cried was right after a swim meet. I won all of my races and a group of kids cornered me in the locker room. They called me names, told me what a freak I was, pushed me around when I tried to get away. Girls from my own team. They told me it didn't matter how many times I won, I'd always be a loser." I took a deep breath. "It got worse. At school or the pool—I could always count on someone there spreading the latest gossip about the 'Jolly Joke Blonde Giant'. After that, everyone avoided me. Probably afraid of getting teased too, guilt by association and all. I was eleven years old." I pause to wipe my eyes, trying to get a firm mental grip on myself while I'm at it. "I never came in above second again. It worked, too. When I stopped winning, they backed off. Problem solved." A depreciative chuckle escapes me.

"But it's not, is it? Your solution is hurting you now." His voice is a soft caress as he points out the flaw in my reasoning. I thought he might come over, try to hug me, or something. He looks like he wants to, but doesn't. Maintaining his awkward distance, his eyes bore into mine.

"Yeah, I guess it is." My lashes glisten with leftover tears as I force my eyes away. "It's just become such a habit. I don't know how to do anything else."

"Do what you've been born to do. Even I, who knows you so little, can tell you are meant for more. Feel the water, swim fast and free, and don't let anyone tell you who or what you are."

"What if *I* don't know who I am?" Part of me wants to live in the dream he's weaving for me—a lovely, enchanting, entirely unrealistic fantasy. Most of me is just plain afraid. I pick up a dry brown leaf, idly stripping it down to the stalk.

"Find yourself. I know you can. You will!" he encourages. "People like your old teammates, like this Crystal, they are powerless over you. Not unless you give them the power."

"Yeah, sure, piece of cake. Ignore the entire student body population. Why didn't I think of that?" My sarcasm is weak. What he says makes sense...sort of.

"I'm sure you did. Maybe you just need to find your courage. Your *real* courage...your you."

"You know, I've never met anyone who speaks 'cryptic' as its own language. Do you go to school for that?" I'm trying to switch to a lighter subject, mostly to cover my blushing discomfort. Crumbling the stripped leaf bits, I let them fall to the ground.

"Yeah, well I'm not sure if I can say more anyway...I know you'll figure it out..."

Finally, the comfort I've been looking for the whole time. When I look up to smile my thanks, the park is empty.

"Pete? Pete, are you still there?" He doesn't answer, gone. "Dang it! What is with this guy and his disappearing act?"

Somehow, though, I'm not mad. Not at him anyway. I also realize our strange connection is getting stronger.

Pete is unnerving, irritating when I want empathy and consoling. No pity party provided. Then he disappears. And I'm drawn to him more than any other guy I've ever met. I am a nut.

Standing up and wiping the remaining tears from my blotched and puffy face, I dust the dirt off my backside and pick up my much-abused bike. Pete's given me a lot to mull over. Back at the rental, I fully intended to do some serious thinking.

I need to make some sort of decision, or emotional resolve, or both. I just hope I'll be able to do it before trials start on Monday.

6

The In Crowd

THE NEXT COUPLE of days solidify my place with Bryan and Levi as our own mini team, training together daily. Crystal sort of comes and goes as the mood takes her, totally confident in her place with the guys if ever she should want it. Me she simply ignores. It's odd to feel like a key member of a group. A first really.

During the remainder of my breakthrough afternoon, I made the decision to be more proactive. I'm finished being content with anonymity and passivity, which hurts me almost as much as those cruel teammates. No one to blame but myself now. This team—league, summer camp, whatever you want to call it—is my place to start. It might mean more drama, but I'm ready.

As Levi predicted, the other swimmers began arriving Friday night.

The first, joining us at the pool on Friday evening, is Duane. A California golden boy, bleached blonde hair with a perma-tan and celebrity parents we've never heard of. He stayed barely long enough to get wet.

The next morning came Reg, a Canadian boy. Though very friendly, I can tell after the first lap his strongest gift isn't swimming. He'd be great at sales though.

Saturday evening adds two more to the open swim—Joseph from New York, and Kari Ann from Boston. The east-coasters have arrived.

Joseph is tall, dark, and nasty. Big money. Bigger

attitude. Teeny tiny talent. He won't be joining us long.

Kari Ann is the total opposite of her fellow Atlantic-an. Petite, cute as a button with dark hair and wide, crystal clear blue eyes. Her huge smile envelopes everyone, her obvious good will an instant and welcome fit to our group. Though smaller than most successful swimmers, she moves through the water like a minnow. If she swims as fast as she talks, I can see her making it through the trials no problem.

Sunday morning add one more girl and boy.

Kym from Washington, sports a thick head of cinnamon hair and warm brown eyes. In great shape and a decent swimmer, she's young (maybe a freshman?) and fairly unseasoned.

Daniel is a happy-go-lucky boy from Colorado, with dark, wavy hair and grey-blue eyes. He immediately gets along great with Bryan and Levi, like their long lost third amigo. Tall and lanky, he's much stronger than he looks. I think he's got a good chance at staying.

Sunday afternoon we meet the last two new arrivals, both boys.

Jepp is a huge blonde boy from Texas, whose family owns a large cattle ranch. Built like a football lineman, he's more sink than swim.

Finally there's Gary, Atlanta old money, which immediately clashes against Joseph's trashy new money. It doesn't really matter. Neither of them is cut out to be here.

I smile, wave or shake hands with everyone as I meet them, coming a week early putting me in a better position than I ever imagined when sulking about coming to Canada.

Everything would be wonderful except for one, not so minor thing. *No Pete.* Nearly all of the time I'm not at the pool, I'm hanging around the park, alone. There's been no sign of him.

He's my friend. I mean, I think he's my friend. I know I've been unconscionably rude. Then, of course, I dumped my life story on him. He listened to me anyway, and…well, called me on my drama. In a weird kind of way, I imagine him to be my own personal cricket conscience. Okay, a cricket conscience with an incalculably hot body and a hypnotic, shiver-producing voice. And he's *been there* when I needed him. So where is he now? Is he coming back? After how I acted, he probably thinks I need to be medicated.

After the first lonely hour spent waiting at the park, I bring my favorite book to while away the time, the original version of the Little Mermaid. The mermaid is supposed to kill her beloved prince (who marries another girl) in order to save her own life, opting to sacrifice herself instead, and finding redemption in her sacrifice. I don't know why I like this version. It just seems more realistic to me, somehow, than the newer, more kid-friendly versions. Unfortunately, as much as I try, no amount of reading can erase one nagging thought—*I miss Pete.*

I must be mental.

There's loads of room to dwell on my competing, too. What holds me back? I need to be honest with myself, maybe for the first time ever. I *know* I can win. No bragging, I just know how I feel in the water and what I can do there. What I'm not sure of are the ramifications of winning.

Possibility #1: I could get a whole lot of general attention, both locally and nationally.

I'm starting to get some attention here. Admittedly, I am starting to like the feel of it. Heady stuff. Could I cope with athletic fame? Keep myself in check, and not get a big ego about it? I've been exposed to enough talented, yet overall awful people, to know I don't want to be one of them.

Possibility #2: I could get more attention from boys.

While this has a very nice ring to it, I know how very inexperienced I am. Okay seriously, inexperienced is a major *understatement*. Knowing how to get, and keep, a boyfriend is woefully beyond my current skill set. How does someone decide which boy they want? Is there a formula? There may be a lot of fish in the sea, but I could be stuck in the desert for all I know how to catch them. Everyone learns sometime, I suppose.

Possibility #3: The other girls on the team, and at school, would be quite peeved with my sudden success, opening me up to a lot of unwanted hostility.

I'm thinking I might be able to handle that now…maybe. I can practice with Crystal, I guess. Otherwise, I'll just be nice to those who deserve it and ignore those who don't. Easier to say than do, but worth a try.

All of these thoughts make sense. Live up to my potential. Yes! How exactly to implement this plan? Well, I haven't quite worked it out yet.

I can keep it close in races – no sense in getting too good, too fast, causing people to wonder – but I will *not* be the first loser any more. Second wouldn't be bad if it didn't symbolize the old me, the classic underachiever – moderate schoolwork, nonexistent fashion sense and a total lack of social skills. No more! Say it enough times and it becomes reality, so here I go, into uncharted territory.

As far as the interpersonal stuff, winging it is working with the guys and Crystal pretty well so far. As the old saying goes, "If it ain't broke, don't fix it".

What I can't fix is Pete's absence.

***

I'm still full of my new "bring it on" attitude when I arrive at the pool Monday morning. This is the first day of real training with Coach Tim, and I'm much more enthusiastic about it now.

I arrive early for some extra warm up time – training technically starts at 8am – and I'm not the only one. Both Bryan and Levi stroll in at seven, looking ready for business with less horsing around than I've ever seen before.

Following right behind them, amazingly enough, is Crystal. The only local in the group, her training the past week has been pretty sporadic. Her coming in early is indicative of how Coach Tim likes to run his team. Note to self.

Some of the other new arrivals also hit the pool early, respectively Kari Ann, Daniel and Kym, all of whom I get along well with.

Local adults work out before work in the first three lanes, leaving us kids two. Kari Ann, Kym and I share one, while the boys share the other. Facing the option of swimming with three boys or three girls, Crystal brushes past us, giving me a triumphant sneer before pushing off the wall behind Bryan.

Noticing this, Kari Ann makes a highly expressive face at the older girl's departing back. Crystal missed it entirely. I'm warmed by the show of solidarity anyway. I offer her a smile and she gives me a high five, actually jumping to do it.

"Don't worry about Miss Cranky Pants. There's always one Prima donna and I happen to live with mine. My older sister."

Ah. No wonder she's so little affected by snobbish behavior.

Around a quarter to eight, blowing his whistle to signal the end of the open swim, the lifeguard rouses from his usual stupor. Taking the opportunity to get out and stretch, we wait for our coach-to-be on the cement block stadium seating.

Just as we settle in, Reg comes hurrying out of the locker room, looking disappointed he missed getting into the water a bit early. Taking it in stride, he greets everyone jovially.

At ten minutes 'til, Gary arrives, decked out with designer goggles and the most expensive swimwear he could possibly find. Total overkill.

Five minutes later, Joseph strolls out of the locker room with Jepp following, his mammoth shadow.

At eight am on the dot, Coach Tim steps out of the office onto the pool deck. Standing there for a moment, surveying the now empty pool, he directs his attention to the group of us, spread among the hard bleachers. His appearance, while somewhat cleaner than when I saw him last week, is no less scruffy.

Joseph and Jepp are antagonizing Gary, who doesn't appreciate this form of attention. None of them pay any attention to the flannel and jean-sporting greybeard coming towards them.

Finally Joseph looks up, assessing the new arrival before giving Tim his most leering sneer. "Hey man, I don't know what you're maintenance schedule is or anything, but we're here to meet our coach. No janitors allowed." As almost an afterthought he adds, spitting something on the floor at Tim's feet for emphasis, "You're doing a lousy job by the way. Step it up for the summer or I'll report you. I don't plan on catching some form of the plague while I'm here."

Ho-ly chowder! Who acts like that?

Jepp grins while Gary looks bored. Bryan, Levi and Crystal smile, ever so slightly, sharing knowing looks. The rest of us newbies probably wear identical looks of shock and mortification.

Tim stands stock still for a moment. Then, clasping his hands together, bowing slightly forward, he replies in a comically subservient manner. "Yessir, yessir, anythin' you wan' sir. Does you's like yur show'r soap a smellin' like dem fleurs out yonder, or soma dat pine freshes? Wha'ever ye like, sir, I's gets it. Yessir."

Josephs' mouth falls open, while somehow maintaining the smirk. Jepp is just about rolling off of the bench, he's giggling so hard (such large boys should *never* succumb to fits of the giggles). Gary looks like he might actually *respond* to the question.

Then "Janitor" Tim straightens up, transforming into nationally-acclaimed-and-the–man-in-charge-of-your-life-for-the-forseeable-future *Coach* Tim, looming in over the sitting Joseph.

Oh boy, here it comes, I think nervously, waiting for the sure-to-be-spectacular explosion. I didn't wait long.

"NOW THA'S ABOUT ENOUGH! If yer done messin' around, pretty boy, how bout you get yer butt in tha' water an' show me why yer here, *before* I fly ye home withou' need'n t'call ahead t' the airport!"

Picking precisely this moment to make his fashionably late entrance, here comes California Duane. Talk about bad timing. He saunters on in like he owns the place, his overconfident smile painted on.

Without missing a beat, Coach Tim whips his arm around and points right at him, never releasing Joseph from his locked glare.

"You! Out! Show up on time, or don' show up at all! Las' chance tomorra'!"

Placing his hands on his hips he drags his gaze around to the rest of us.

"As fer the rest of ye, if yer still dry ye can waste more o' my time by warmin' up in lanes one an' two. If yer already wet an' warmed up like ye oughtta be, ye can start out in lanes five an' four. I'll be pickin' individuals fer some tes' runs in lane three."

Most of us remain seated (or standing in Duane's case), stuck in place by shock, mouths universally agape. Bryan, Levi and Crystal the only exceptions, of course, are laughing quietly as they get up and out of range.

"Well? MOVE!"

We quite literally jump into action, leaping off benches and hurrying to our assigned lanes. Crystal again manages to wrangle Levi, Bryan and Daniel into sharing lane four with her, while Kari Ann, Kym and I splash into lane five. Kym seems unaware of the older girl's machinations, also missing Kari Ann's rolled eyes and the face she makes behind Crystal's back. I smother a giggle with my hand.

No one notices Cali-Duane turning an interesting shade of red and storming back to the locker room. He never came back.

The following three hours consist of lap swimming, punctuated with a break here and there, and a turn each demonstrating our different strokes and abilities for Coach Tim. It's us against the stopwatch, not against each other...yet. He also doesn't want us to tell him which events we compete in, preferring to make his own judgments.

I have a hard time deciding how fast to go, with no one to place behind, or ahead of. I've never really paid attention to my times before, or bothered to keep mine consistent. Whatever else happens, I now want to stay for the summer. My stomach churns with anxious indecision. I finally decided to go at about the same pace I swam with Levi on the first day. Comfortable for me, and Levi seems to think it's pretty strong. The frown on Coach Tim's face as I finish my turn, unhappily aimed at me, makes me wonder if I should rethink this strategy.

We break at eleven for a three-hour lunch and break period. The pool still has its other patrons to cater to, so they schedule most of the aqua aerobics and other classes during this window of time. We'll meet in the small weight room, located at the back of the building, before hitting the water again.

Dressed and almost ready to leave, I'm planning to haunt the playground again, a bubbly little voice stops me.

"Hey Lee! Where's a good place to eat around here?"

Kari Ann's asking me? "Um, no idea. I've been eating at the rental house." Everyone knows I'm here with my parents by now.

"It's okay! How about we go explore and see what we can find?"

My mind automatically jumps across town to the lonely park. If I spend my break with Kari Ann I won't be able to continue my vigil, which feels like a much bigger deal than it should be. Kari Ann takes my brief pause of indecision as assent, because the next thing I know she's calling out again.

"Hey Kym! You wanna come to lunch with Lee and I?" She blatantly ignores Crystal, who's changing right next to Kym. I'm really starting to like this girl.

Kym nods enthusiastically while I come to grips with not seeing Pete today. I don't get much chance to obsess though, not while Kari Ann and Kym are around.

Kari Ann's string of chatter seems unending, but she's so fun and has such interesting takes on everything, I really don't mind at all. The only thing I learn to watch out for are some of her wilder gestures, especially when she almost takes out my eye during a reenactment of one of her more dramatic tales.

While Kym is just as outgoing and friendly, she's more of a quiet type. Granted, anyone can appear quiet next to Kari Ann's bubbling enthusiasm. I must look like a giant mute.

We find a little café not too far from the community center, where we share a two-hour lunch. It consists of a little bit of food and an awful lot of conversation. We each take turns talking about our hometowns, the teams we usually swim on (I skip that part), things we like to do outside of swimming (short list for me), boyfriends (Kari Ann has a "brilliant" and "so handsome" one, Kym's currently single), what brought us here (I edit that story), etc.

It's easy and pleasant hanging out with these girls, and I'm thoroughly enjoying myself. Thoughts of Pete are mentally shelved for the time being.

We make our way back to the pool slowly, talking and laughing all the way, enjoying some sunshine. When we get to the locker room Crystal is already there, looking a bit sullen and otherwise not condescending to acknowledge us. The afternoon is spent with weight training, followed by a straightforward conditioning swim and no individual testing.

My mom meets me out front to take me to dinner ("*Surprise, honey!*"), effectively eliminating any plans involving the park again.

That evening, I dream of swimming. I'm not in a pool, there's just water all around me, and I'm following something. A sound maybe? By the end of the dream, I have no luck in finding…whatever it is. I awake, covered in a sheen of sweat and distraught. I don't usually remember my dreams, even little bits, and I feel like I missed something vitally important.

***

Tuesday proceeds exactly like Monday, except everyone shows up early for warm up. A bit grudgingly, perhaps, but they're there. Coach Tim arrives at eight on the dot again, splitting the morning into general training and individual sessions. I surreptitiously watch the others, not that it's any of my business. I'm not hiding out with the schedule here.

I spend lunch with Kari Ann and Kym again, mentally

throwing Pete an apology. Crystal left before she could be snubbed. I know I should feel bad, not condone this sort of behavior. Childishly, I can't help thinking *she* started it!

Daniel, Levi and Bryan meet us in the lobby as we're heading out—more like ambushed. As we make our way towards the café, Kari Ann, Daniel and Kym lead off. Thoughts of missing Pete get shouldered to the back of my brain as Levi and Bryan take up posts on either side of me. This is the first time we've gotten together outside the pool, and I'm literally way outside my comfort zone. Will I be able to keep up my confident girl façade? Despite escalating nerves, I wryly wonder if the three of us look like some sort of giant, walking wall.

The café isn't busy, and we easily manage a table for the six of us. Food ordering is promptly followed by another round of Who, Where and Why. I sit quietly, still sandwiched between the guys, not contributing much to the conversation unless asked directly. My thoughts are a mess, so I end up playing distractedly with my napkin. Occasionally Levi or Bryan will nudge or wink at me, like we have an inside joke or something, kick starting my pulse as my mind speeds through possible responses. Acutely aware of the heat radiating from the bodies on either side of me, I'm desperate to keep my cool. The paper rectangle in my hands is practically shredded well before the food arrives.

Kari Ann is, of course, completely comfortable. Even Kym is quite socially adept, despite my impression of her youth. Gah! I can't believe, after all of my self-reflection and decision making, I'm acting like such a loser! Old habits die hard I suppose. Giving myself a mental shake, I covertly dispose of my mangled security blanket under the table, focusing on trying to copy their more seasoned social skills.

Upon discovery Daniel has a girlfriend back home,

whom he absolutely adores, heart and soul, he and Kari Ann quickly bond over their long distance relationships. I keep to more neutral topics with the others. The camaraderie with Levi and Bryan is flattering, fun in a theatrical sort of way, but not nearly as naturally comfortable as the time I've spent with Pete. I haven't embarrassed myself too badly by the time the check comes, even managing to choke down a sandwich, though I'm entirely too happy to be headed back to training.

Another round in the weight room (different set of muscles this time) and a straightforward round of swimming finish off the day.

Waving at my new group of friends as I pedal away towards home, I consider stopping to see if Pete's at the park. It isn't too late. Unfortunately, it's my dad's turn to waylay me for parent-child-bonding.

My parents are incredibly busy. Their schedules are only going to be getting worse in the coming weeks, so they're making an extra effort to spend as much time with me as possible. Initially grateful for the guilt currency, right now I just wish they'd butt out for a while. My parents are way too perceptive for my comfort, and I have a lot on my mind.

I'm determined to try and talk to Pete again. I don't know why I'm so drawn to him and I just have to see if he, and the connection we made, is still there.

***

Wednesday morning is same old, same old... until the break. I'd prepared an evasive speech for my usual lunch partners, trying to make a fast getaway as soon as session's end is announced. Coach Tim halts me mid bolt.

"Hey'a Lee, d'ye mind comin' and talkin' t' me fer a moment?"

Like I'll say no.

"Don't wait for me! I'll see you later!" I call to Kym

and Kari Ann as they shuffle away at a snail's pace, eyeing me questioningly.

Kym smiles, tentatively waving in response, while Kari Ann's penetrating gaze makes me wonder if I should be taking notes for a pop quiz. The guys, not noticing a thing, have already pushed and shoved each other into the men's locker room. Shaking my head at their behavior, the smile falls off my face as I turn to face Coach Tim.

He's giving me the same appraising stare as the first day, his face a humorless mask. *Why* can't I read him as well as other people? Grinding my teeth, I straighten my posture and stare directly back. If he's going to boot me out of the group, I refuse to make it easy. If I'm not the best swimmer in the group (at least as far as I he's seen), I sure come close. I'm pretty sure I didn't fail anything. Mainly I'm stressed because I am *not* ready to leave. I mentally prepare to argue my case.

No one says a thing for a full two minutes. As the silence echoes in the deserted hall, I'm starting to sweat a little, holding my ground taking its toll on my nerves. The can of soda I quickly grabbed from the machine is shaking in my hands. Maybe he'll think the wet sheen on my brow is leftover moisture from the pool.

Coach Tim finally clears his throat to speak. "So, I wanna know what ye think o' the other swimmers in the group."

I blink, twice, before stupidly looking around to see whom he's talking to.

"You...um, I mean...what?"

My top-notch communication skills at least get a laugh out of him.

"I talked t' yer coach down there in Oregon," he pronounces it Or-ee-gone. "He tells me ye got some skills I cud use. Bein' hard o' hearin' isn' mentioned among the things we gotta work on though," he adds, with a wink. The rock hard façade softens a fraction and he's smiling. I'm not sure what to think.

"Yeah, um, sure. So…what did you want from me again?" my voice cracks pathetically. I crack open the can, taking a sip to coat my suddenly dry throat.

"Who're we cuttin' today?"

His question catches me completely off guard, and I nearly spray-paint him orange through my nostrils. As it is, the carbonation makes my nose burn and my eyes tear.

"Ex-*cuse* me?"

"Who're we cuttin'?" He repeats, patiently, like he speaking to a slow child. "Pool ain't big enough fer this group, and I only got a couple more days t' use the whole thing. Yer coach is right. You seem t' got a purty good idear of what this group can do, so *you* tell *me* who's gotta go."

My jaw drops, and I'm hard pressed to get it closed again. He's nuts! Abso-freaking cu-koo-ka-chu. Helping my regular coach schedule swim meets is one thing. *This*? Gee, whom do I get to make irreparably mad at me? Hmmm, decisions, decisions.

Despite the hour on the clock, I'm no longer hungry. Actually, I haven't picked my stomach up off the floor yet, where it dropped when Coach Tim asked me whom to cut.

He lets out an explosive sigh. "Look, I gotta feelin' about ye, ever since yer coach called me. Ye got a gift, kid. I c'n tell. On top o' tha', you gotta feel for others' gifts too. We just gotta git ye used t' *usin* yer gifts. Ye see?"

I nod mutely, mainly because it seems like the appropriate place to do so.

"So here's what we're gonna do. I'm gonna read th' names off th' list, and ye're gonna tell me In or Out, an' th' short version of why. I may or may not agree with ye, bu' tha's my decision. An' whoever is cut, is *my* decision. Nobody's gonna know a thing abou' wha' ye've told me unless you tell 'em. Got it?"

His meaning makes it through the drawl, like oxygen to someone drowning. I nod, in relief this time. *I can do this. It's just like helping Coach John.*

"All righ' then," he says, giving me a smile and a wink. "Let's git started so we can git ye somthin' t' eat.

"Bryan!" He barks, making me jump a little.

"Um, In…of course. He was here with you last year, right?"

"Don' got nothin' t' do with nothin'. It's what they can do *now* I gotta look at, so you do too. Why 'In'?"

"Well…" I falter. Closing my eyes, I take a deep breath, diving in. "He's a strong sprinter and he's got a competitive nature, enough to do him some good on the Nationals circuit. He's versatile, likes the 200 I.M. His rough edges can be polished to help him really reach his potential." My runaway mouth abruptly trips over itself as I remember whom I'm talking to. "S-so, he should be here…with you," I finish lamely, peeking over at Coach Tim to gauge his response. He just nods curtly before belting out the next name.

"Crystal!"

I sigh. While very tempted to say something unflattering, I feel compelled to call it as I see it. "In. She's a great freestyler, and has skills in other areas as well. She could use some work on her fly if she's going to be really competitive in the I.M. though." I can't help throwing in a mumbled "Not to mention her attitude."

No comment from Coach, but I think he may have cracked a smile.

"Daniel!"

The list continues, as I do my best to classify each person.

My "in" group consists of last year's swimmers plus Daniel (amazing long distance swimmer, needs help on race strategy) and Kari Ann (strong sprinter despite her tiny size, needs some stroke evening and to improve her flip turns). Everyone else is "out." I alleviate my guilt by suggesting Kym be invited back next year.

Coach Tim only nods slightly while jotting down more notes.

"Okay, so am I done now?" Practically begging to leave, my voice whines.

"No. Wha' abou' Lee?"

I'm taken aback. "What about L…me?"

"Wha's yer assessmen' o' *you*?" The gleam is back in his eye, not entirely friendly.

Yikes! What should I say? Do I tell him I can beat every person here? Do I tell him I've finally decided to start winning and would appreciate some practice with the whole thing before I go home? What about my real reasons for wanting to stay? The nothing-to-do-with-swimming ones? And my parents can't leave now…

"Well? How 'bout turnin' tha' talent on yerself? What's it tellin' ye?"

"Um…Nothing?" I squeak, coherent thoughts spinning off into space. "I plead the fifth? I have the right to remain silent?"

"No, in Canada you don'. Try agi'n."

Shoot. I rack my brain again. *Nope, still got nothin.*

"I…I guess it doesn't, um…work on me?"

Will he buy it? Not likely.

"Hmmph. Well, I guess tha's tha' then," but his eyes are saying *you don't fool* me kid. "Go on an' git yerself some lunch. Don' come back 'til after th' weight room session either. You need time t' digest."

I don't need to be told twice.

Roslyn McFarland

7

Winning?

I CAN'T GET the lock off of my bike quickly enough.

"Pete? Pete? PETE?" I call, a few minutes later, skidding to a stop in the park. I'll get a sandwich later.

No response. My breathing slowly regulates back to normal as I wait, willing him into existence, if at all possible.

"Doralis?"

I whirl and there he is! Standing by the tennis courts like he's been there the whole time, wearing the same t-shirt and shorts. My eyes drink in the sight of him. It feels like more than just days have passed since we last spoke. More like years. A surge of warmth and happiness floods my system. An unacknowledged missing piece.

"Oh Pete! I'm so glad you're here!" I blurt out, taking an involuntary step closer. "Where have you *been*?! I've been waiting for you every day!" Well, I *wanted* to wait every day. Whoops. I hope he didn't note my own absence.

"I'm very sorry. I tried! I really did try to come, every day. I—I missed you."

Now I really feel bad...and elated. *He* missed *me*.

"My family...," His face hardens for a fraction of a moment. "I couldn't get away to come see you."

"What about your family?" I'm curious about them. I already told him about my parents so it seems only fair to hear more about his.

"Well...we needed to discuss my future, I guess you

could say."

I wait for him to explain further. He doesn't. So exasperating! I cross my arms in frustration before replying.

"Sure, Mr. Vague, I could say that, if I knew what the heck you're talking about. What *about* your future? What's there to discuss? School or something?" I prompt.

Another long pause. I grind my teeth, waiting him out.

"Um, basically they're wondering if I plan on going into the family business. Or at least, what I'm going to do in it. There's not generally a choice."

Huh? No choice? I remember him mentioning the family business before, and his desire to avoid it. Is he from some sort of religious enclave or something? A closed community? The idea is just plain bizarre. "So, what exactly does your family do?"

"They're...artisans."

"All the build-up, for *that*? It doesn't seem so bad to me." Not exactly earth shattering. Then I remember the beautiful jar he gave me. Maybe he feels like he isn't good enough. I can relate. "Aren't you artistic or something?"

"Not really. At least, not the way they are."

Aha!...sort of. He really isn't giving me much to work with here.

"Ooookay." Now where do I go. "So what do you want to do? With your life, I mean?" Seems like a safe enough question. Apparently not.

"I'd really rather not talk about it." He's guarded, his voice almost...menacing. His eyes warn me not to pursue the topic.

I scowl back at him. Patience, as previously demonstrated, has never been a strong point of mine. After today, mine's about worn through

He must understand my frustrated expression because he quickly backtracks. "I don't mind talking to you. It's just sort of…complicated," he finishes lamely.

"Right. Complicated." I bite my lip, also biting off any accusation that he thinks I'm too dense to understand, taking a deep breath instead. "Okay then." Think, think, think. "So why are you even having this conversation with them now? You're about my age. Are you even old enough to make this sort of decision? I know I'm not." I pause to take a breath, suddenly rethinking my last statement. "And if you make a smart comment about my age, I *will* smack you."

"No comments then, promise!" He holds up his hands in surrender, laughing. "I'm sixteen. And yes, this is the traditional time to talk about this stuff, where I'm from anyway. I'm really sorry I can't tell you much more. There are…rules."

Weirder and weirder.

His voice is too distracting when he apologizes, and the revelation he's only a year older than me sends giddy waves sweeping through me. I really want to hear more about where he's from, also afraid to push too far into *that* mystery. I change subjects instead, to the other persistent thought residing in the back of my mind.

"I'm really glad you're here, Pete, and…talking to me like this." I look at him closer, wanting to see his expression – almost afraid to – when I say what's on my mind. "You told me, the last time we spoke, you didn't think you could talk to me. I couldn't be your friend. I'm…well, I'm glad you came. I really hoped you could…would, or…whatever."

Not the most eloquent speech ever made. I laugh nervously, feeling my cheeks get hot, refusing to look away in spite of the urge to hide my face in my hair. *Glad is* an understatement, a large one.

He sighs. Even his sigh is musical. "Something about you makes me feel like I *can* talk you. I really don't know why, Doralis. I can't explain it...even if it could be allowed. I just know this feels right...and important somehow. Like you can understand me better than my family does. Pretty ridiculous, huh?"

"You sort of lost me a little bit, but thanks...I think. I'm not sure if the word ridiculous belongs in a compliment. I'll take it though, if it makes your life easier." I smile before becoming more serious. "And just so you know, something about you makes me feel right too."

"I'm glad," a small smile finally surfacing on his full lips. "And I meant 'ridiculous' because my family has known me my whole life, and yet I remain a mystery to them. After only a few days I can talk to you like no one else in the world. How can I *not* be your friend? It's unavoidable, for me anyway. Again, I'm glad for it."

A lot more explanation than I expect, and his silver eyes are intense, filled with an emotion I can't quite place. Instead of freaking me out, like it really should, I'm comforted. He's right. Our...friendship feels unavoidable, and good. The only way I can imagine feeling better about my newly found friend, would be if I could actually understand what the heck he meant half the time.

We're silent for a while, a companionable silence this time. Glancing at my watch, reflexively, I'm shocked to see how late it's become.

"Oh ----!"

"What?" He asks, looking up quickly, obviously picking up on my agitation.

"I can't believe I've been sitting here for so long! I need to get back to the pool before Coach Tim decides he won't let me in anymore!"

I jump up and run to my bike where it lay sprawled in the dirt. I'm mounted and ready to ride before I stop myself, the bike tilting precariously.

"I'm so sorry I have to go. Are...Are you going to be

here tomorrow? Like, around lunchtime?"

"I don't think I can be." He's both remorseful and frustrated. "I'm going to be spending more time at home, a *family* decision, byproduct of our little…conversation. I can probably make it back in a couple of days though. Will you meet me again?"

Stupid question.

"Of *course* I'll meet you! Saturday, right? I can probably be here most of the day then, too." The idea sends a wave of warmth washing over me. "See you then?"

"Yes. See you then, my Doralis."

As if I didn't already love the way he said my name, the added "my" makes it almost incomprehensibly perfect. Involuntary shivers run down my spine as my lips smile.

"See you then…Pete." No way I can get away with either the "my" or his full name. He'll just need to settle for my lame version of his parting words.

I take one last look, his hulking form so oddly vulnerable, knowing it'll be a couple of days. I'm out of time, though, so I turn away, applying as much force as I safely can to the pedals of my bike. I'm already late to the afternoon session. Crashing and maiming myself won't help my cause much. And while I sincerely hope Coach Tim won't be too mad, I can't bring myself to regret the reason for my delay.

Pete.

I remember I haven't even told him about what happened. *Oh well, there's always Saturday*, I think to myself, with a little surge of pleasure.

The clouds come in, threatening rain and making the bleak landscape even more gray and washed out than usual. I don't care. To me the world's full of sunshine and warmth.

***

"Oregon!"

99

I made it back to the pool in record time, flying past the blur manning the desk and into the locker room.

Levi's familiar voice echoes loudly as I step out onto the pool deck. He sounds relieved. I don't figure out why until I take in the full scene in front of me. There are only *five* people in the pool. Every single person I labeled as "Out" is no longer here. No time to dwell though.

"Lee!" Coach Tim barks at me. "Nice o' ye t' finally join us! I know I told ye to take a late lunch, but don' ye think ye might be pushin' it jus' a bit?" He's not pleased.

I mumble a quick "Sorry!" as I hurry to the nearest lane, slipping into the water and beginning my warm up before he can expand on the subject.

The rest of practice moves along without a hitch. Coach Tim is a lot more vocal now, correcting every flaw. Thankfully, it's Kari Ann's lane I picked to get into. Unfortunately, I don't get a chance to ask her about what happened while I've been gone, not until after we finish for the day and make it back into the locker room.

"I am SO glad to see you!" She gushes, leaping at me for an enthusiastic hug as soon as the door closes, Coach Tim safely behind us. "I thought for sure I'd be stuck with miss high-and-mighty as the only other girl for the rest of the summer! Ugh!" She rolls her eyes dramatically before looking at me with curiosity. "Where did you go, anyway?"

"I, uh, talked to Coach Tim about some things for a while... stuff my coach at home told him about." Technically true...sort of. "It got late, so he told me I could skip weight training. I guess I lost track of time." I end weakly.

She doesn't seem to mind (or notice) the imperfection of my story, already launching into a play-by-play account of what happened in my absence. I listen gratefully.

"Okay, so we're all doing our circuits on the weights, right? Then Coach Tim comes in and starts calling us out one by one, alphabetically. The thing is, NO ONE is coming back in! It's, like, a *total* one-way door! I'm starting to get seriously nervous when he calls me. Freaking out almost. Then, he asks me why I'm here and what I think I need to learn. I have no idea what I said. Really! It's a complete blank. Anyway, it must be good enough because the next thing I know he's telling me to head back to the pool. Everyone else but Levi and you are there already. Can you believe it! I'm TOTALLY flipping out now, thinking he'd already told you to go home. I can't even tell you how relieved I was when you came in late. Kym's the only one who stayed to say bye, to you and I mainly. She was disappointed you weren't there, and upset she has to go home, but at least Coach Tim told her he expects her back next year, and to stay. So that's nice, but it did make her feel better..."

She continues talking about her suppositions of what happened with the other swimmers, injecting happy thoughts about my continued presence here and there, for the rest of the time it takes us to get showered and changed. I let her talk, mumbling agreement in all the right places. While incredibly grateful for Kari Ann's honest happiness in my remaining on the team with her, a feeling I reciprocate, I'm eager to avoid any further discussion about my conversation with Coach Tim.

As we part ways at the door, I appreciate the now falling rain as it obscures my retreating back.

***

By beating me to the pool, something entirely unexpected, the Minnesota boys are able to take me by complete surprise as I step out onto the pool deck the following morning.

One minute I'm twirling my goggles around my finger, still debating whether to use them today, the next thing I know enormous arms wrap around me and I'm being crushed in a massive bear hug by Bryan, who's bellowing "Oregon!" in my ear.

Not to be outdone by his statesman, Levi simply puts his arms around both of us with me in the middle, and gives a giant squeeze, laughing loudly in my other ear.

After a few seconds of learning what the inside of an Oreo feels like, the affection wears off as my need for oxygen increases. I start to try and wriggle free, somehow, some way, upsetting our precarious balance. The next thing I know we're all smacking into the water. Thankfully it's not a repeat performance of the day I met these big guys, as there's no one in the lane below.

They release their boa like holds and we splash our way ungracefully to the surface, all of us grinning like idiots. Them because they're so pleased with their little performance, me because I can finally draw an unhampered breath. It's also impossible not to grin at their overgrown, childish antics.

"I KNEW you'd make it!" Bryan exclaims at the top of his lungs. "I KNEW IT!"

"Yeah, yeah. If you're so smart, how come you looked so worried yesterday? You thought she was cut, admit it!" Levi retorts before turning to me. "Now *I* knew you'd make it."

"WHAT-EVER! You are so full of --!"

"Hey guys, what's the fuss?"

Crystal's ooey-gooey voice interrupts Bryans tirade before he really gets going. Standing on the pool deck, she strikes some sort of sultry pose, batting her lashes at the boys. I don't remember seeing her in the locker room. Now though, she's plenty close enough to have overheard all the bellowing.

"Oh, hey Crystal!" Bryan greets hr warmly. "We're just giving Lee here a proper welcome, since we didn't get the chance yesterday. Glad you were wrong about Tim cutting her!" He smiles good-naturedly. The look she's giving me is anything but glad.

Levi notices, more perceptive than usual, grabbing my hand and pulling me towards another lane. "Come on Lee, let's warm up," he says jovially as he continues to haul me away. "I want a rematch!"

I'm so stunned by his casual touch I let him drag me along. I can't tell what affects me more, Crystal's glare or this handsome boy holding my hand.

Fortunately, there's no time to dwell on either for the next few hours. The rigorous workout Coach Tim puts us through is enough to occupy anyone, tangled thoughts or not. When Kari Ann suggests we make a break for lunch without the others I agree whole-heartedly.

I'm able to enjoy our very girlie lunch even more without the preoccupation of Pete on my mind. Okay, not totally true. I am thinking of Pete, in a nice comfortable place in my brain instead of the anxiety-riddled place he's been before, when I didn't know when I'd see him next. Now I know the when, and that he likes me too…as a friend at least.

The afternoon flies by. Before I know it we we're done, time to head home, one more day gone.

My dreams are full of water and musical voices again…and happiness.

***

Friday starts out with the normal routine. Bike to pool, warm up, get barked at by Coach Tim, break for lunch.

All of us end up going to lunch together this time. *All* of us.

I planned on lunch with just Kari Ann. Kari Ann wanted to invite Daniel, to commiserate on missing her boyfriend. Daniel planned lunch with Levi and Bryan. Bryan immediately invites Crystal.

Ah, nuts.

Our usual café seats us at a round table this time. I basically have no choice but to sit and face everyone. After we order our meal, Kari Ann and Daniel immediately starting talking significant others, tuning the rest of us out.

Crystal proceeds to place her hand through the crook of Bryans arm, like he's escorting her somewhere, and oozing charm. He seems perfectly content to be shackled by her. As if this level of fakeness isn't bad enough, she glares at me while sweetly interrupting Levi and I every chance she gets. It's downright obnoxious.

I'm starting to get irritated. No, I *am* irritated by the end of lunch. Her assumption of claiming *both* guys as hers is ridiculous, selfish, nasty and…well, just plain not right!

I'm not exactly claiming either of them myself, so there's nothing to justify her rudeness and cutting me out, for sure. It's not fair. I don't deserve this. I've never done a thing to her! Enough is enough.

"So Crystal," I open, seeing her surprise at my temerity to address her highness directly. "Coach Tim says we're going to start timed matches soon."

He'd mentioned this little tidbit to me sometime during our awful afternoon chat. I'm not trying to relive it or anything, it's just great ammo to get under her skin. The coach told *me* something and not her.

"Of course, everyone knows that Ore-*gone*," she lies, neatly deflecting my ploy and inserting her own desire for my absence at the same time. Unfortunately for her the others *didn't* know. Additionally, they don't feel the need to be quiet about it.

"We are? Cool! I can't wait to race against something other than a stopwatch!" Bryan enthuses. I see Crystal's grip tighten on his arm, her nails digging into his skin. He's oblivious.

Ha!

"No kidding!" Levi joins in. "After all, we're not

training this hard just to beat our own times. Nice intel, Oregon." He grins at me, leaning in. My heart sort of stutters. I pull it together in time to catch Crystal's eyes throwing daggers. Not intimidated, I give her the sweetest smile I can manage. When she looks away I get an under-the-table-low-five from Kari Ann.

My coup of information is presented just in time. Coach Tim announces a mock swim meet, taking place that very afternoon.

"Now I know you folks don' all specialize in th' same events, so know I don' expect ye t' win every leg. I *do* expect ye t' give it yer best though, as if each *is* yer best event." He eyes each of us in turn. "I'll know th' difference," he warns.

Inwardly, I wince.

We're all sitting in the spectator area, waiting. One more appraising stare and he turns to his list, calling out the first event.

"Men's 100 free. Swimmers, take yer mark!"

The guys leap off their seats heading for the starting blocks. They take their marks and Coach Tim's sharp whistle blow signals the start. Flying off their blocks, they cut into the water within a moment of each other, swimming strongly. Down and back twice (in this pool), the 100 is one of the shortest events. It's over quickly, with Bryan the predictable winner, Levi right behind him and Daniel trailing a bit.

"Women's 100 free. Swimmers, take yer mark!"

I jump up, practically running to the blocks in my eagerness, adrenaline sprinting through my veins like in a real race. I enjoy the sensation. Revel in it. Usually I'm too busy trying to be inconspicuous.

Kari Ann is right behind me. On the blocks, we wait for Crystal to saunter over. My irritation flares at her casual arrogance.

Why are some people like that? Those people who, for some stupid reason, feel the need to either control or break others down, piece by piece. As if it makes them a better person. I'm suddenly sick of it. Sick of being the brunt of jokes, shoved aside by girls just like Crystal. Girls who think they're better than me, simply because I let them.

I'm done. *So* done. Resolved. It stops here and now, this place and time. This pool, this race. No more. From here on out, I stand up straight and stick up for myself.

And there is no way, no *freakin'* way, I'm going to let her beat me.

We take our marks as soon as Crystal deigns to join us. My leg muscles are taunt, ready, like a crossbow primed to release. I don't look at either Crystal or Kari Ann, keeping my focus on the water. The whistle blows and we're off, sailing through the air before knifing into the water.

I feel my limbs cut through the pliant liquid, easily powering me along, my legs kicking hard to propel me faster than I've ever gone – in anything resembling a race. I keep my senses extended, knowing without looking, purely by feel, where both Crystal and Kari Ann are in relation to me.

First flip turn. Kari Ann has the lead and I'm fully content to let her keep it. *Her* I like. I keep my pace steady and even, right next to her, a little behind.

Second flip turn. Crystal's gaining on Kari Ann, making her move to pass. Will she be able to, with just over thirty meters to go?

Third and final turn. Crystal passes Kari Ann off the wall. Well now that just won't do. I stayed close, just in case, and now put on a burst of speed I don't think anyone saw coming. I rocket by Crystal, slapping my hand against the cement wall first, signaling the end of the race…and my win.

The crowd is going wild. Levi, Bryan and Daniel are

anyway. Coach Tim just looks at me speculatively again. I hold his gaze until he looks away, ostensibly to jot something down in his notes. Then I grin at the guys, enjoying the celebration and their congratulations on such an exciting race.

Coach Tim calls them up for the next event. I smile at Kari Ann who enthusiastically congratulates me. We both sit back down on the benches, openly ignoring Crystal, who appears to be in some state of shock.

We cycle through 4 more events. The 200 I.M., the 100 backstroke, the 200 freestyle and the 100 fly. I let Kari Ann win the backstroke, she's really amazing in it, and I take the title in all of the rest. Crystal came in second or third in every race. The queen has been dethroned.

Crystal used to look at me with a combination of arrogance and disdain. Now it's pure, unadulterated malice. Without witnesses she'd probably try to drown me right then and there. I'm not about to let her get to me though, still riding the high of my wins. Kari Ann gives me a jumping high five and performs a cute little happy dance to celebrate my victory.

The guys' races end predictably, with Bryan taking first in all but the 200 Free, and Daniel taking third in all. We haven't gotten to the longer distance races yet, though, and I'm quite sure he'll dominate there. Levi's still grinning as well. We haven't done his best races tonight either.

All in all, it's been one of my best afternoons ever. As Kari Ann and I exit the locker room to go home, we're both still bouncing on adrenaline, chattering away like chipmunks with a new stash of nuts. Levi is waiting in the hall.

"Hey Lee! Great job today, lady! Really impressive!" Already flushed, my face grows warmer at this direct praise. He isn't finished. "Hey, you got a minute?" He gives Kari Ann a significant look of dismissal.

"Uh, sure…I guess." My euphoria is transforming into something decidedly more unsure, and I nervously look at Kari Ann, hoping for some guidance from my extremely confident new friend. I only receive a wide grin as she winks and waves goodbye. Traitor.

"So today's showdown has got to be some kind of record! I mean honestly, where's the movie!"

And…there he loses me.

"I, uh…what?"

"Seriously! I don't think *anyone* has ever beaten Crystal in *all three* of her best events before! That was *awesome!*"

Oh boy. I'd no idea today's races included all three of Crystal's top events. Okay, I had a *pretty good* idea. Not that it would have made a difference…

"It's a good thing they can't take back her scholarship. If they saw you today they might hold out for the real deal! You should have seen Crystal when she left!"

Nope, I consciously avoided it, despite my winning high.

"Her face? Pure classic! I think she's going to steam dry her hair by the time she reaches the intersection!" He's laughing at his own imagery.

I manage to weakly laugh with him, somewhat disappointed…and relieved. I totally misinterpreted his request to speak with me. It's not *me* he wants, just an opportunity to rag on Crystal. Obvious in hindsight. She did turn him down flat last year.

So now I'm looking for a way to make a break for it. I liked beating Crystal, no question, I just don't need to join Levi in his malicious reenactment.

"I, um, gotta go Levi." My brain races furiously while I think of something plausible. "My parents are expecting me tonight." Lame, but plausible.

"Yeah, okay. So I'll see you tomorrow night at 7 then. There's a great flick playing at the theater and we are celebrating!" He walks away from me as he finishes his sentence. A cocky smile and a wave and he's gone.

I stand there for a full minute, stunned. The power of speech, and motion, temporarily evading me as I try to make sense of what just happened here. One minute I'm deflecting a Crystal smear fest, the next minute I have a...*gulp*, date? My mind flashes to Pete and I push the thought away as unnecessary.

No. No, no, no. *Don't blow things out of proportion Lee*, I tell myself sternly. Bryan, Daniel and Kari Ann are probably coming too. With my ridiculous "Parents expecting me" line, he probably didn't take the time to tell me the "we" translates to "everyone" part.

Finding my motor skills, I walk towards the exit, shaking my head and smiling ruefully at my already overblown opinion of myself. I win a few races and already I think the world wants to date me.

Whatever!

***

Saturday morning dawns clear(ish), sunshine lighting up the grey-blue sky through the curtain-less window of my rental bedroom.

Coach Tim insists we take weekends off, explaining he'll be pushing us plenty hard enough during the week and our bodies will thank us for the break, so I'm lazily still in bed at seven.

Abruptly sit up. "Pete!" I get to see Pete today! Suddenly the grey-blue sky looks a little more blue and a little less grey.

I jump in the shower, rinsing all traces of chlorine out of my hair and skin. Dressing more carefully than usual too, I pull on a new pair of shorts and a blouse. Jerking a brush through my long hair, I perform a quick once over in the mirror behind the door, looking for errant store tags more than at myself. Either way, I pass my own inspection and head downstairs to the kitchen to grab some breakfast.

After a bowl of microwave spiced apple oatmeal, and jotting a quick note for my parents, I grab my book and leave for the park. Arriving just before eight, there's no idea how long I'll be waiting.

"Pete?"

No response. He doesn't pop out of thin air, either.

Sigh.

I settle down on the end of the slide, to read my book and wait. I make it through almost a chapter before I hear the sound I've been waiting for.

"Doralis? You're here!"

"Hey, that's my line!"

Moving towards me with slow, careful steps, he looks almost as excited to see me as I am to see him. I set my book aside immediately, unable to stop myself from appreciating the way his muscles ripple as he moves. My stomach makes little flips in response. He's my *friend*, I remind myself. This is no time to get greedy.

"How are things going with your family?" I ask, opening the conversation. "Better than before?"

"Yeah, I guess so." He stops, his usual safe distance away from me. "They've been...hovering a bit, I suppose. I've been keeping busy in the design shop, which is what they wanted, so they can't really say much."

"The design shop? Like, where they create all their art and stuff?" This is new information! I lean forward, eager to hear more about his mysterious life.

"Yes. It's more of a...building, with multiple rooms and spaces. Each...person has their own workspace, to do whatever they specialize in."

"Do you?"

"Yes." He smiles depreciatively. "One of the smallest

rooms in the shop. It's...adequate, for my needs. I'm getting used to it."

Ugh. "You're going to make me ask, aren't you?" I finally cave. "Okay, I'll bite. What exactly *are* your needs? What do you do in there? I thought you told me you aren't artistic enough to do the same type of stuff your family does?"

"I am and I'm not." He ducks his head in embarrassment. "I'm sort of doing my own thing, doing the stuff I can do."

"Well, as long as we're being clear." More intellectual than saying, *excus-uh-whats-it?*. "I don't suppose you're planning on actually telling me what it is you do?" I ask, after another longish pause.

"Nope."

"Of course not." What am I thinking?

"I can't. I can't even really tell my family about it, not yet anyway."

"Why? I mean, so you can't tell me. Fine. I'm your friend but an outsider, someone you hardly know. I get it. So why can't you tell your family?" A really ugly thought occurs to me then. Impossible, somehow the question came out anyway. "You aren't doing something...illegal, are you?"

"No!" His response is vehement. "Well, not precisely anyway." Backpedaling. Again.

Huh? I can only imagine how overwhelmed by his physical wow-ness I'd be if he didn't keep confusing the heck out of me.

"It's just, what I'm...doing, well it usually requires some training at a...a special school. My family is sort of well known for the work they do, so no one gave me the option to try out for the...program. I decided to work on some of the...things they do there on my own, that's all."

He's having a difficult time trying to explain, and I

don't think it's intelligence related. I like to believe I get where he's coming from. Trying to fit in with others expectations can be just plain hard.

"And I'd really, really like to tell you. You're not an outsider to me."

I smile, additional color infusing my cheeks. I hardly know this boy. How can it feel so inexplicably *good* to hear he doesn't think of me as an outsider? It's a shiny-happy-feel-good moment.

"Well, I wish you could tell me too. I'm not going to bug you about it though, okay?" I quickly jump to another subject, not waiting for his response. "So how big is your family anyway?"

"Ah, well, in the immediate family there are my...parents of course. And then I claim two sisters, one older, one younger. There are a number of aunts, uncles and cousins...around, as well."

"Sounds nice." I say, sort of wistfully. "I'm an only child. Both of my parents are only children too, so I guess they figured I didn't need any siblings. Of course that means no aunts, uncles or cousins either."

"I'm sorry," he replies sincerely. "Though I almost envy you in a way. My family always seems to be into everything I do. I suppose I'd miss them terribly if anything were...different."

I shrug. "It's never really bothered me. Holidays are pretty uneventful." I smile. Boring is more like it. Just the three of us, same old, same old. I'd rather know more about him.

"What are your sisters' names? Can you tell me about them?"

He chuckles, relaxing. "Turamiel is my older sister. She's married and doing really well professionally. She's the one who made the container I gave you, with the salve for the...mos-kit-toe bites." Boy, he *really* doesn't know what mosquitoes are, does he? "She makes all sorts of boxes and containers. Simple, basic ones, like the one I gave you, all the way through the spectrum to some really complex designs. One full line produces incredible music. Her creations are becoming quite sought after."

The one he gave me is *basic*? Wow. I can only imagine her complex designs. And music too? What does she do, make recordings of her brother's voice? Works for me. No wonder they're sought after.

"And your other sister?"

"My younger sister is Kelpsie. She's not old enough to choose her...field, yet. She is quite good with sculpture though, athletic enough for it."

"*Athletic* enough? For *sculpture*?" By now I almost expected the weird twist. "Not the most obvious extreme sport."

He chuckles again. I can't get over how much I love the sound. The world is right when he laughs. And his silver eyes glow. It's obvious how much he cares for his family.

"Yes, well, let's just say the way she does it could qualify for the Olympics."

"Uh-huh."

What's most odd is how I'm caring less and less about the weird factor. I love hearing about this wacky family with mysterious talents. It sparks my imagination. Everything seems magical and wondrous when Pete says it...unless he's calling me out on my bad behavior.

"So what's new in the pool world?" He asks, effectively changing the subject.

"A mock swim meet yesterday." I dangle the information teasingly, like he does to me all the time.

"And...how did you do?" Intense, his eyes narrow in speculation.

I pause, just a little, to drag out the drama before

finally relenting. I'm such a softie.

"I won. Four out of five matches. And the one I lost, I lost on purpose."

"Well done! Congratulations!" He proclaimed loudly. "I *knew* you could do it!" His smile stretches across his face with genuine pleasure. Unfortunately, he doesn't move any closer to me.

I can't begin to describe how good it feels, having his genuine approval—so much better than anyone else's. I sit there blushing and grinning like an idiot, my spirits as light as a butterfly.

"So, may I ask why the one loss? Or maybe I should be asking what inspired you to win?" He winks at me knowingly, my heart spasms in response.

"Besides you calling me a coward you mean?" I force a laugh, giving myself time to organize my thoughts. I know what happened, I'm just not sure how to articulate it, especially when being distracted by too-perfect-to-be-possible muscles and shimmering silver pools.

"Well, there's this girl on the team. I told you about her, remember? Crystal? This is her fourth and last year here and she's always been sort of the coach's favorite. Queen B complex, you know? Anyway, she thinks this gives her the right to be as nasty to the other girls on the team as she wants, with no repercussions. So…I got sick of it. She ticked me off, so I decided she wasn't going to win. I *like* the other girl, Kari Ann, so I didn't mind letting her win at *her* best event."

Said out loud, the whole thing sounds kind of petty to my ears. I'm suddenly anxious about what he might think of me. "Does that make me a…well, not a bad person. Maybe not as good a person as you thought?" I lock my eyes on his ridiculously handsome face, waiting for a reaction.

"Of *course* it doesn't make you a bad person! You, my

SEE NO SEA

Doralis, are a wonder."

Whew!...and, yikes?

"I'd think worse if you backed down. There is nothing wrong with you. Except, perhaps, for a ridiculously flawed self image."

Wait, what? Before I can decide whether or not to take offense, he continues.

"Sounds like the girl needed to be taken down a notch or two anyway. Wish I could have seen it!"

"Or three, or four notches," I happily agree, not wanting to dwell on his prior comment.

"So how did the rest of the team react to the dethroning?" He's still relaxed and smiling. Life is good.

"Really well. Surprisingly. I mean, I knew I could count on Kari Ann to be excited. She's the other new girl I mentioned, and *so* not impressed by Crystal. I wasn't so sure of the boys. They really surprised me, all three guys going wild right along with Kari Ann. It felt...amazing!" I feel my face flush with remembered excitement. "Something I could get used to."

"Yes, I'm sure," Pete responds in a happy-for-me yet smug voice. His body language is yelling *I told you so!*

I pause for a moment. I've neglected to mention something. Not that it should matter to Pete, my friend-at-a-neutral-distance. It still feels kind of weird talking to one guy about another.

"Yeah. Um, Levi even invited me out to celebrate."

The silence following my statement feels heavier than Mount Hood. Pete sits still as stone, a Greek statue, frozen in place and time.

"Pete?" I nervously prompt. His reaction is starting to freak me out.

"He...he asked you out? Like a date?" Thawing out, Pete looks like he's just tried to swallow a cow. I'm not sure if I should be concerned or offended. For the briefest

115

moment my temper flares and offense wins.

"Well yeah he asked me! What's the big surprise? I'm not *totally* hideous or anything!" I take a deep breath, trying to lower my blood pressure. His response throws me off and I come back with hostility. Not cool.

"Anyway, it's not a date or anything. I'm pretty sure the whole group is going. Everyone but Crystal I hope." I finish with a pathetic, lopsided attempt at a grin.

Silence again. Like a lead box dropped on the park, sealing out all sound. My grin slowly fades as I watch him struggle to simply breathe.

"Pete?" Have I somehow offended him? What did I say? "Seriously, it's no big deal. I'm just another swimmer to these guys."

Pete is turning an interesting shade, somewhere between purple and green. I'm about to go over and try the Heimlich maneuver when he visibly pulls himself together.

"I doubt that," he says finally. While his expression is controlled, there's a slight crease between his brows, and something different in his voice. As if someone turned the music down.

My breath huffs out, knocked from my body by equal parts hurt and confusion. Why is this so difficult? When did we get off track and catch the train to Nonsense Junction? I open my mouth to argue when my stomach betrays me with a massive rumbling sound.

"It's getting late," Pete grumps.

How late is it? I scan the horizon, locating the fuzzy orb of light they call the sun here. It's a good distance further across the sky than I'm expecting, still fairly early in the day though.

"I guess you'd better go eat before your *celebration*," he continues acidly, hunching his huge shoulders. Definitely not a happy Pete.

I'm at a loss for what to say. I feel really bad he's

upset, I just don't understand why.

"See you tomorrow I guess."

I blink and he's gone—again—before I can say a word. Vanished. And I've somehow hurt him.

I'm so confused. *I* hurt because I can tell *he's* hurting. But I'm a bit angry too. How dare he get all worked up because I'm going out to celebrate with my team? So what if one of the guys asked me. I thought he wanted me to have fun, be more involved. Hypocrisy at its best, or something else?

My traitorous stomach rumbles again, louder this time. I frown down at it. It's really been a long time since the oatmeal, and I'm not getting any of my questions answered today. Grudgingly I get up, dusting off my shorts as I trudge out of the park.

8

Firsts

MY PLANNED DAY at the park dramatically shortened, with hours to kill before the movie and my usual release of swimming unavailable, I decide to try distracting myself with some of my mom's magazines. Flipping disinterestedly through summer handbags and accessory trends doesn't take my mind off of anything, so I toss the magazine aside in disgust. Leaning back and closing my eyes, my fingers try to massage away the unpleasant thoughts of pain-filled silver eyes through my temples. The next thing I know, the stomping entrance of my dad at the front door abruptly awakens me.

"Hey kiddo!" He enthuses, as I blink rapidly, trying to clear the sleep fog from my brain and eyes simultaneously. I don't typically nap midday. It's a bit disorienting. "What's the scoops?"

I smile. My dad's Americanisms are so cute. He hardly ever gets them right – like he works out to get "buffed," or his favorite classic rock band "Blind Cheetah".

Oh yeah, he asked me a question.

"Yeah, hi Dad. Well, I did pretty well at our mock meet yesterday and I sort of, um, got invited out to celebrate tonight." No need to tell him by whom. I'm not lying. It's an understatement plus an omission, a quality teenager-esque response.

"Hey, that's wonderful!" He's unmistakably thrilled his reclusive daughter is exhibiting signs of a social life.

"What time are you supposed to go?"

"The movie starts at seven." I look for the wall. What time is it now? "Oh! Dang it!" Six o'clock! No way I'll be able to get changed and bike across town in time.

My dad, who's been decoding my mom's emotional behavior for years, catches on straight away. "Don't worry honey. How about you go get ready and I'll drive you over. I know where the cinemas are. We'll make it. Okay?"

"Thanks!" I make a break for the stairs, not stopping to question his generosity after a long day's work. My budding popularity is a big deal for him. I know he's never understood his quiet, understated daughter. Love and accept, yes. Understand, no.

It's okay Dad. Back at ya.

Once in my room I tear off my clothes and jump into the shower, out in record time. Yanking a brush through my hair, I realize there's not enough time to dry it. Oh well. I grab my new jeans, ripping off the tags before attempting to hop into them, almost toppling over in the process. I also yank on one of my new shirts, green with a square cut neckline and three quarter length sleeves (full length on anyone more petite).

A brief look at myself in the bathroom mirror is satisfying, tousled mane and all. The new outfit accentuates my athletic build, the simple combination of jeans and shirt easily the most flattering outfit I own. Opting against full make-up, I slap on some tinted lip-gloss and call it good. Shoes on and light jacket in hand, my money in the pocket, I dash out of my room and down the stairs to my waiting dad.

"Nice work honey. You look beautiful."

"Thanks," I mumble, eager to be out the door and in the car…like now.

Dad grins knowingly, in that really irritating way parents do, but at least he moves his feet and picks up his keys off the entry hall table. I jump into the passenger seat of his flashy car as soon as he remotely releases the door locks, impatiently waiting for him to lock up the house, stroll over to the car, get in and casually start it up. I smile at him through grinding teeth. The bike may have been faster.

My dad pulls out laughing. I stick my tongue out at him before turning my attention out the window. Big mistake. We're passing the park, making me automatically think of Pete.

He left with a combination of hurt, anger and indifference I can't yet wrap my mind around. I hope I see him tomorrow. By then I'll be able to tell him about what a mundane evening I've enjoyed and he can just relax. The thought makes me smile.

Still smiling, we pull up to the front of the movie theater, right on time. The smile fades with a kick of nerves when I notice Levi standing by the entrance, waiting. Alone.

"Is that the guy you're meeting?" My dad asks, not visibly bothered, even though my little celebration is more date sized than I'd eluded.

"Yeah, one of them. The rest of the group must already be inside. The movie starts in about a minute after all." I don't know whom I'm trying to convince. Nearly hyperventilating, my body isn't fooled.

"Sure, honey. Do you need me to pick you up later?"

Huh. It never came up. "I'm not sure Dad. I think Kari Ann has a car here." I'm BSing for all I'm worth now. "Can I call you after the movie's over, and let you know?"

"No problem hon. Have fun and I'll talk to you then!" His casual and sincere manner belies the fact he probably knows something's up. Unfortunately, even I'm not sure what that is.

Levi spots me then and heads in our direction. I jump

out of the car and wave goodbye before he gets to us, protecting my weak storyline.

"Hey Oregon, lookin' good!" His eyes run over me from head to toe.

I blush at Levi's hearty welcome and appraisal, unsure how to respond. It's his usual camaraderie…yet not. Most boys my age don't just hand out compliments, unless there are ulterior motives involved. Then again, what do I know?

"Hey Levi. Um, you look good too." An understatement.

Wearing jeans as well, his look designed just for him – loose here, tight there, accenting his muscular legs and…other attributes, perfectly – topped with a fitted rust colored silk tee, showing off all of his hard earned muscles in just the right way and a perfect complement to his hazel eyes. His sporty shoes are brand new, the latest fashion, and don't detract from his evening look in the least. He's simply gorgeous. The sparkle in his eyes and the confident crooked smile on his face tells me he knows it too.

He reaches my side as I take all this in. Casually and confidently, as usual, he places one hand on the small of my back, showing me the two tickets in his other hand.

"Shall we?"

I nod, mutely. There's no question now. It's going to be just us *and* he bought my ticket for me. I'd mentally prepared for a big group outing. The possibility this could be my first date never crossed my mind…once I'd stomped it out.

My stomach is already churning as I attempt to swallow down my nerves. It doesn't work. I'm hyperaware of his warm hand on the small of my back, steering me into the theater. He stops us at the refreshments counter by the simple expedient of removing his hand. The smell of over-buttered popcorn wafts towards us like a steamroller, making my nervy stomach convulse more.

"Hey, do you want anything?"

I shake my head no, temporarily removed of the power of speech. At least I hope it's temporary. At this point anything's possible.

"Okay. We can get something after the show. Work for you?"

I nod, still all I can manage. He smiles at me before replacing his hand on my back to steer my otherwise motionless form to the appropriate theater. He either doesn't notice the sudden change in me, or doesn't care.

A second smirk, just before we enter the darkened theater, and I rethink my conclusion. He *knows* how nervous I am, and he's *amused* by it!

My temper sparks – directed at Levi or at myself, I don't know – allowing me to unfreeze enough to regain some control of my body, if not the situation. I make myself step away from his unnervingly warm hand.

"I really don't care where we sit. Why don't you go first and pick something?" I smile, regaining confidence. Unfortunately, my master move sort of backfired on me.

"Sure." His eyes and teeth gleam in the dark, reflecting the light from the opening credits, as he leads me up the stadium seating stairs to the back row...the dark and deserted back row, at least 4 rows behind any other movie goers.

I sit in the seat Levi directs me to, hyperaware of the well built boy seating himself next to me while trying to focus on the movie screen.

What's playing? It never occurred to me to check. Within the first fifteen minutes I'm relieved to find we're watching some sort of action comedy, and not anything romantic whatsoever.

I'm incredibly tense— my deal (fight) or bolt (flight) response barely contained—sitting rigidly straight, hands folded in my lap, my eyes straight ahead. Is he going to try anything? An arm over my shoulder? Hold my hand? Or maybe even try for a kiss? What do I *want* him to do? No easy answer there.

After the first half an hour or so, I take the chance of peeking sideways through my lashes at Levi. Of course he's totally relaxed, lounging in his seat like the recliner at home, his legs casually crossed and elbows on each armrest, enjoying the film, completely without my self-conscious anxiety. His total ease, compared to my total lack of it, makes me mad…at myself.

Get a grip Lee! I berate myself. *Exactly how pathetic are you? Confidence! Remember??*

Taking a deep breath, I close my eyes and perform a meditation exercise. As I breathe out, I imagine all of the stress and bad energy flowing out of my body, loosening one muscle at a time. Within a few minutes my posture relaxes notably, and I feel a lot better. I firm my resolve.

Go with the flow.

Opening my eyes, I feel more like my old self again, until I glance over at Levi. His face in the shadows, his profile is turned towards mine. He's laughing. I can feel his shoulder moving with his mirth where it's pressed against mine. I freeze again. Busted meditating on a date? My first date? OMG. I remind myself to breathe.

"Too scary for you?" he chuckles.

"No, just trying not to nod off. Not one of this actor's better films," I shoot back, hoping I can hide my prior panic with some of my own acting.

He lets me off the hook with another light laugh before turning to face the screen again. I do my best to actually concentrate on the picture. My big mouth will get me in trouble later if Levi wants to critique what we've just seen. It's really not a bad flick.

The film ends and people start exiting while the credits rolls. Located at the top back of the theater, we're the last to make our way out. Just like at the pool, Levi grabs my hand as he leads me down the stairs. I tell my firing emotions to take it as a brotherly gesture, not remotely romantic. He's being gentlemanly. Right?

At the bottom of the stairs, as we're rounding the corner to the exit, he uses the hold he has on my hand to expertly spin me, like we're in a ballroom. I'm taken by complete surprise, but it's a fun, silly sort of move, and I laugh as I whirl around the corner. My back lands gently against the wall of the dark hallway as his other hand lands on my waist. Chuckling again, he takes another step closer, pulling me in.

Eyes widening in shock, my laugh sticks in my throat, choking me. Realization strikes and his lips come in for a landing on mine. Suddenly I'm kissing Levi. Or, more accurately, he's kissing me. My brain wildly tries to sort out all the thoughts and feelings careening through my system.

Holey Moley! This is it! My first kiss! Part of me is thrilled. My hormones certainly kick in. I can't help enjoying the sensation as my lips automatically try to respond, kiss back. Definitely no beginner at this, Levi's mouth moves softly yet firmly on mine. With one hand on my waist he raises the other to stroke my cheek, pressing his body closer.

Another part of me, the logical thinking part not ruled by hormones, isn't sure if I want this or not. I like Levi, sure. I'd be crazy not to. He's handsome, taller than me, older, smart, an accomplished swimmer, easy to hang around and obviously extremely confident. Everything I could ever want or ask for in a guy, right? Most girls would be over the moon right now. So why am I closer to a panic attack than on cloud nine?

What do I do? My mouth sort of moving, my arms trapped within the circle of Levi's arms in front of me with my hands frozen on his muscular chest, my body is rigid with indecision.

He breaks away from me before I can move or process anything else, looking at me in his oh-so-cocky, sure of himself way.

"First kiss, huh?"

My already flushed face practically combusts as the blood rising to my face keeps pace with my stomachs descent towards my feet. *Obvious first kiss? How humiliating!*

"Don't worry about it, I'd be happy to help you practice." He's grinning more to himself than at me. He leans over to give me another quick peck on my immobile lips before slinging one of his muscular arms casually over my shoulders and directing me towards the exit.

Just as we're about to leave the building, I remember my promise to my dad.

"Wait!" That came out a bit louder than intended.

Levi jumps a bit, startled, giving me a curious, tolerant look, eyebrows raised and mouth smiling. A couple other strangers look over at me too, wondering what's up with the tall crazy girl I'm sure.

Embarrassed I continue, "I told my dad I'd give him a call after the movie to let him know when and where to pick me up." I omit the part where getting picked up is optional. I don't know if Levi even has a car, but after the surprise kiss in the darkened theater, I'm not feeling confident about being alone in a vehicle with him, my emotions still a tangled mess.

"Sure, no problem. Do you want to borrow my cell phone? I think there are pay phones here too, if you prefer."

Dang! I forgot my cell. If I use his phone, my home phone's in his call log, problematical only because I'm a basket case who can't sort out logical thought from hormones. If I opt to use the pay phone, I look like a cowardly little girl. Not willing to risk further embarrassment after the *obvious* first kiss, I accept his phone, his hand brushing mine in a meaningful sort of way. I yank mine back a little too quickly, focusing on dialing. Before I connect the call, I remember I don't know what to tell my dad.

"By the way, where should I tell him to meet us...or, um, me at least?"

Levi seems pleased he's getting a say in the matter, not like he'd doubted it much.

"There's a café just a half block from here. Say an hour and a half. Enough time for us to eat and...talk some more." He smiles winningly, an undisguised gleam in his eyes.

"K." I gulp and hit the send button. Though happy to spend a bit longer getting to know Levi better, I'm more than a bit overwhelmed too. A time limit sounds just fine to me.

I convey the message to my dad, who thankfully doesn't ask a lot of questions, agreeing to see me soon. Hitting the end button, I hand the phone back to its owner. He flashes another smile, once again placing his hand on my lower back and steering me out the door.

The restaurant is very busy when we arrive. We're able to snag a small table in the center of the room. It gets us served, but no privacy. Bonus. Levi hasn't made any more moves, and I don't know if I want him too.

We drink our coffees—decaf for me, I'm wired enough already—and indulge in some artistic looking specialty desserts, all the while chit-chatting about nothing deeper than the local artwork papering the café walls.

It's comfortable, and I'm genuinely having a good time at this point. Levi is such a nice guy, and undeniably good looking. My dream come true in every way I thought counted. So why is it so hard for me to relax and enjoy the thought of kissing him?

The topic of my train of thought returns from paying the bill. "Your dad will be here in a few. Shall we wait outside for him?"

I instinctively know what he really means. With no valid excuse to say no, my drink finished and the bill paid, I nod dumbly instead, getting nervously to my feet.

Levi steers me out the door and into the cool night beyond—so gentlemanly. The next thing I know he's pulled me off to the side of the building. My back is to the rough brick wall and he's kissing me again before I can even think to stop him.

My body responds without permission, or tries to, while my mind fights for coherent thought. One of his hands is braced next to my head while he places the other on my lower back, pulling me into him. My heart goes wild, my blood pressure skyrocketing, while my pesky brain wonders if these are symptoms of pleasure or terror.

Before I can decide, Levi abruptly pulls away from me, turning to lean on the building next to me, entirely nonchalant.

My confusion clears in the glare of a pair of headlights turning into the café's parking lot. Levi must know cars a lot better than I do—not exactly hard—to spot my dad's car from so far away.

Exhibiting even more dating savvy, he walks me into the light nearest the door just as my dad pulls up. It looks like we were just exiting the building. I don't think he factored in my inability to look calm and collected.

"Um, thanks for the movie and coffee and...stuff, Levi." I stammer while reaching for the car door. What else can I say?

"No sweat, it was fun," he replies warmly. Turning towards my dad respectfully, he offers his hand to shake through the now open door, across the passenger seat.

"Good evening sir, thank you for loaning me your daughter this evening. I know she expected a larger group but the others plans changed at the last moment. I'm terribly sorry for the lack of communication."

"Thank you for taking her out. I'm sure she had a nice time." My dad is obviously impressed by Levi's manners, shaking the proffered hand without hesitation.

Wow! This guy has all the lines! I think, awestruck. *What a load of bull!*

And my dad, king of the word sling, doesn't even blink.

Levi smoothly turns back to me. "I look forward to *practice*, Lee," he says quietly, as he hands me down into the car like royalty, emphasizing his parting words with a wink.

Blushing furiously now, bordering on heatstroke, I know the "practice" Levi refers to isn't swimming. I give him a tight smile and keep my mouth shut, not knowing what else to say, sticking to waving as we pull away.

"Have a good time honey?" my dad asks pleasantly.

"Yeah Dad. Um, we saw a good action flick." *What else...* "The place we ate is kinda cool. Lots of local art."

"Sounds great, honey. Levi seems like a nice boy too. I'm glad you got out tonight."

I mumble something incoherent in response before turning to look out the window, a lot to think about.

Later, after bidding my dad goodnight, I take sanctuary in the space they call mine for now. Lying back on my bed, I try to put into order all of my crazy thoughts and feelings by making a mental list.

Levi is, in many ways, perfect for me.

- He's taller than me. Not a huge high school demographic, and a major bonus.

- He's undeniably gorgeous. He could easily be dating the head cheerleader at my school, giving the football quarterback a run for his money.
- He's a swimmer, and a talented one. I could actually spend time with him doing the one thing I love most in the world.
- He has great manners. At least my dad thinks so. He sure knows when to turn on the charm.
- He's a good guy. I get along well with him, when I'm not stressing out over stuff. He's easy to talk and pal around with.
- He's a good kisser. Not that I have any basis for comparison, but he sure seemed to know what he's doing.
- He likes me.

It's the last one, while good, which strikes me as sort of confusing. I know it's true, I can tell. My problem is all the mixed signals he's sending. Exactly *how much* does Levi like me? He's confident, for sure, saying and doing all the right things. So why does it feel like something's missing?

One questions remains. The biggest question. How much do *I* like *him*. I know how much I *should* like him. So why I don't feel the way I think I should be? He's great as a buddy, sure. I just never fantasized about making out with a "buddy".

This makes two very red flags on my mental list.

As I lay there mulling things over, wishing I could talk to someone, my thoughts turn towards Pete of their own volition.

Now Pete is someone I can talk to, about things that matter. Unfortunately, considering how he reacted this afternoon, it's probably not the best idea. I'm still not sure why he'd locked up on me this afternoon. I think I can still tell him anything. Hopefully. My central core warms with the idea, remembering his voice and the way he looks at me.

Climbing under my sheets, I feel marginally less confused, and happier than the rest of the evening combined. I let sleep wash over me, looking forward to my vague dreams, knowing they'll be filled with water and music.

***

The next morning I wake up slowly, trying to make sense of the distorted thoughts and sensations my dreams left me with. Then I remember the evening before and come fully awake at once...blushing hotly. Thank goodness no one's here to see. No vampire stalkers in my mundane life.

The daylight streaming through my window doesn't offer any clarity. My list and its problems are unchanged from last night. I finally give up thinking about it, getting out of bed to get myself ready for the day.

Hopefully I can find Pete sooner rather than later. Talking to him will set me straight. He's nothing if not honest. No games there.

Dressed in shorts and a tee shirt, I make my way downstairs towards the kitchen. As I turn the corner I almost run into my dad, who makes a brilliant save, keeping the contents of his coffee cup from sloshing all over himself, or the floor.

"What are you doing up?" Shock and surprise color my voice. My parents are *never* up this early on a Sunday!

"Good morning to you too, sweetie." He gives me an amusement filled peck on the cheek. "Your mom and I have a breakfast meeting. They should be banned on Sundays, I know, but there's no other time we could meet." He rolls his eyes in exasperation, taking a swig of his still slightly rocking coffee. A piercing look and I'm on my guard. "So tell me more about your evening honey. Or more to the point, about this Levi character."

There it is. Nothing much gets past my dad. As smooth and charming as Levi performed, he isn't fooling anyone, especially not my dad. I should know better. Edging past him into the kitchen, I get some orange juice out of the fridge and take a drink straight from the carton, stalling.

"Well…he's from Minnesota. He's here with one of his friends, they both made the team. Um…he swims mid distance, and he's going to be a senior this year." I pause, not sure what else to say. My dad has no such qualms.

"Okay. So last night was a date? That's not what you told me, honey. Would you care to elucidate?"

Busted.

"I told you the truth Dad, honestly!" I hasten to explain. "Levi asked me to go celebrate after I did well in our mock races on Friday. I *assumed* everyone was going, because we've all been going to lunch together most of the week. I'm not trying to be evasive Dad, I swear."

I refrain from pointing out he hadn't bothered to ask me much about it either. I don't think it'll help my cause.

"Ça va. I believe you Lee. I know about that type of boy though." He grins rakishly at me. "I *was* that type of boy. And yet, your mother married me anyway, despite the obvious flaws." He chuckles at the memory before sharply turning his attention back to me. "So when are you seeing him again?"

No question of if, just when. "I'll see him at practice tomorrow."

"Not today? No more plans I should be aware of?"

"No…"

Nothing with him. *Nothing you should be aware of anyway.*

"…It's not like that Dad. It's not like he's my boyfriend or anything. Last night's the first time we've hung out without the rest of the group…"

Oughta do it, but I'll tack on a bit more for good

measure.

"...And no one's mentioned getting together outside of the pool again, either."

So there.

He doesn't look like he's totally buying my story, despite the fact it's entirely true. I'm saved from additional verbal sparring by the entrance of my mother.

She always makes an entrance, even if it's only into her own kitchen with an audience of two. She's impeccably dressed and made up of course, believing it's never too early to look fabulous.

"Good morning sweetheart!" She addresses me perkily, adding a kiss on my cheek for good measure. When she turns to kiss my dad I hastily look away.

"Ready to go, love?" He asks, as if the answer isn't obvious.

"As ready as I'll ever be when not in my proper place in bed on a Sunday morning." She laughs her tinkling laugh as I mentally block thoughts of what else she's probably alluding too. TMI for any kid.

Dad chuckles too, as he takes her arm to escort her to the car. "Have a nice day Lee!" he calls back over his shoulder. My mom gives me a parting wave, the garage door closes and they're gone.

I breathe a sigh of relief.

Still early, I don't know when I'll be able to connect with Pete, so I busy myself with eating breakfast and making myself a picnic-type lunch. Finished, I grab my old towel to lie on, my battered book and head out the door.

The gray overcast morning matches my mood, with the potential of burning off and turning into a decent day. I hope, I hope. Upon reaching the clearing in the middle of all the equipment, I dump my things on the ground unceremoniously.

"Pete?"

Nothing.

"PETE?"

More nothing. Total silence.

I stand there for a moment, not really in the mood to settle down and read yet. Looking towards the tennis court area, where Pete usually materializes from, I decide to try exploring a bit. Pete obviously isn't here to catch me. What better time is there?

My mind made up, I pick my way to the back, skirting the ever-present large puddles, and face the tangle of leaves and branches. Scanning the trail to the right, behind the tennis courts, and then to the left where it wraps back behind the play structures, it seems totally secure. Probably the reason they built the park here in the first place. Well, Pete's coming from *somewhere*.

Thinking of him brings up a clear memory of his voice, its music and texture. I shiver a bit with pleasure before determinedly shoving the thoughts aside. I'm here to talk to Pete about *Levi*. First things first, I need to *find* him.

After hacking my way through the dense greenery for a while, praying there aren't any nests of mosquitoes or other things I want no part of, I make my way back to my original position, glaring into the dense wall of green. I found no hidden paths, receiving only a myriad of scratches for my trouble.

Really frustrated now, I sit down abruptly on the not quite muddy dirt. Pulling my knees up, I rest my chin on them as I mentally curse my total lack of progress.

"Good morning Doralis."

Caught completely by surprise, my head whips around with my torso twisting to follow. I catch my balance just before tumbling headlong into a puddle.

What the...!

Pete's there, on the other side of the puddle, *behind* me!

"Looking for me?" he adds before I can close my gaping mouth.

"Well, yeah! Where'd you come from?" Obvious question. The rattling of my heart in my chest prompts the follow up. "You scared the bejubies out of me! I practically brown shorted it here!"

He ignores my crass comment. "Where'd I come from? An interesting question." He sounds hesitant, his eyes almost afraid. "After thinking about it all last night, I've decided to answer it for you." He dramatically pauses. "You should know I am breaking a *lot* of rules by doing this."

My breath stalls, tight in my chest, but I'm too excited to learn more about this amazing mystery to question him. *Rules schmules!*

"I'd like to explain myself further, however I think it may be easier if…well, if I show you something first." His expression is completely serious as he continues. "I beg you to please keep in mind, things are not always as they appear to be."

Oooookay.

I wait, the thrill of excitement running up my spine, watching him. Waiting for whatever it is he wants to show me

Pete takes a deep breath, the rise and fall of his broad chest threatening to distract me. Locking my gaze with his, he gives me a crooked smile, takes a single step forward and…disappears!

"Pete!" My hair flies wildly as my head whips back and forth, looking for the behemoth of a boy, who vanished before my eyes. "PETE!"

"I'm here." His disembodied voice floats around me.

"Okay." My eyes flicker around the park at warp speed, confirming there's no one and nothing there to see. I can't take the suspense any more. "What's with the invisible man trick? Where's '*here*'?"

"Look in the big puddle."

The big puddle?

I'm practically sitting next to the dirt pool in question, so I scoot my body around until I'm right at its edge. I feel ridiculous, holding my breath as I lean over to peer into the water, no idea what to expect. Seriously, I'm obviously losing my mind here. The puddle water appears both murky and clear at the same time. Strange. As I gaze longer, still questioning my sanity, an object moves forward, resolving itself into a more solid form.

It sort of looks like…it's…

…a *fish*?!

Roslyn McFarland

9

Angelfish

BEFORE ME, IN the depths of what should be a shallow puddle, is one of the biggest, prettiest fish I've ever seen.

Predominantly silver, black stripes run vertically down its body and through its fins. And the fins! So long and beautiful, floating through the water like magnificent silk scarves. It's an angelfish, the freshwater kind you see floating their way through doctor's office aquariums. It's luminous silver eyes shine with emotion and intelligence.

An angelfish...the size of a large dolphin...in a park puddle...with *Pete's* eyes!

I close my eyes, shaking my head vigorously. Turning away, I peer sideways at the puddle through my lashes. Nope, he's still there, in all his aquatic glory. No matter what kind or how pretty, I'm still looking at a fish.

Pete's a fish?

My brain is having a hard time grasping this concept. Hard time nothing. I'm beginning to wonder where I might find the nearest straightjacket and anti-hallucinogen. I know the air here stinks, but seriously? Is this some kind of a sick joke?! I continue to stare, my mouth hanging open.

"Are you going to say something?" The giant fishes lips sort of move. The sound of Pete's voice feels like it's being placed directly into my head, versus being spoken aloud.

I attempt to reply. "Uuhhh..." Nope, brain still malfunctioning. Might as well admit to it. "Sorry, I got nothin."

His voice chuckles, the fish eyes looking amused (don't ask me how). "Well you're still here. That's saying something I guess."

My mouth starts moving then, of its own volition…and doesn't stop. "Saying something? Like I must be losing my freakin' mind?! I'm talking to an angelfish the size of Flipper! And oh yeah, by the way, he happens to live in a puddle behind a children's play park because that's where giant fish live! Or maybe I'm being affected by some crazy new drug created for theme parks, released into the über-pollution here as a trial run? I'm still sitting here because I'm probably not sitting here! I'm probably in some corner of a padded room, banging my head on a wall while having conversations with my friend the imaginary fish! Or maybe…"

"I'm not imaginary." He cuts me off abruptly.

"Oh great, my hallucination is reassuring me I'm not hallucinating. I feel so much better." And just a teensy bit hysterical.

"I'm not exactly a fish either."

Stopped cold, I glare at my finned invention. "Are you saying I'm *not* seeing and talking to a giant Angelfish?" I demanded shrilly.

"No," he replies, speaking gently, pacifying the crazy girl. "That's exactly what you're seeing and doing. And things don't always appear to be what they seem, remember?"

"No kidding!" What's that noise? Oh, it's me hyperventilating.

"It's me, Doralis," He continues, softly, warmly. "I'm Petoile d'Angelus from the water city of Goroannocee. Please, Doralis. Whatever else I am, or you think I am, I will always be your Pete."

I'm stunned. It's him. It *has* to be. No one else could know, or pronounce, his full name. And *no one* else could produce shivers running down my spine like an electrical current with the simple act of saying they're *mine*.

"It *is* you." It comes out as little more than a whisper. They say admitting the problem is the first step. "H-how?"

"I honestly don't know."

I frown at him. "Please, you *have* to know more than I do about this! At least you knew you existed!" *Acting normal, acting normal, acting normal...*

"Well, you got me there," he admits sheepishly...fishily...whatever.

"I'm pretty sure you still win in the surprise category today," I reply dryly. It's getting nominally easier to talk to him like a normal person...as long as I don't think too much about the whole gills and fins thing.

He laughs. The sound I love. His eyes sparkle with happiness as well, and my heart gives a little lurch. Whatever form the rest of him is in, his eyes reveal his soul.

"Okay then," I continue, strengthening my resolve to act, and breath, normally, "how about telling me what you *do* know about all this. As I said, I'm still waiting to wake up in a padded cell."

"Sounds fair." His fishy head dips in a nod. "First, thank you."

I start and blink, taken off guard. "For what?"

"For still being here. For still being willing to be...my friend."

He looks and sounds so sincere...like he's caught somewhere between happiness and a pit of despair.

"I thought you'd be running away the second you saw me. No one does this, reveals themselves to humans in their fish form. Or talks to them outside of the Douxgraine for that matter."

"Wait, wait, back up the truck. Fish form? Aren't you human? What other form is there? And what the heck is a

Dou-whatsit?" This is not going well for me. Three sentences in and I'm totally confused.

"I will explain all. I just wanted to thank you first. If you...didn't mean a lot to me, I'd never think to try this in the first place. You impress me even more by staying."

Blood floods my face. Fish or no fish, my crazy connection with Pete remains, and I really like hearing how much he likes me too.

"So, where to begin." His voice sounds strained now, unsure. "Well, first of all, I told you I come from a place called Goroannocee." It sounds like *Go-Row-No-Sea*. "It is in every ocean, yet in none, in every lake and pool, yet in none. We survive because the Nocee" (pronounced *No-Sea*, ironically*)* "We live apart from the human population. And yet, our community and culture is still inextricably tied to yours."

"Wow, okay. Thanks for clearing *everything* up." Adding a heavy helping of sarcasm, I stop him with a gesture, topped with a huff of frustration. "If you're actually meaning to be totally obscure and confusing, you are succeeding beautifully. I don't have a clue what you're talking about."

"Sorry." He pauses, gathering his thoughts. "Where I come from is not on any of your human maps. We, however, have mapped and can access most of your human world. You see there are windows to the human world from mine. Some may be used merely to observe. Some are true portals, where objects and people can actually pass from one place to the other."

"Okay," I said slowly. "making more sense now. You're saying you know about us because your...people have been *visiting* us for...I don't know, forever?"

"Close enough," he chuckles. "History is not a subject I ever paid close attention to, so I truly don't know how far back the...relationship goes."

"All right." My brain is still clicking though all this new information, trying to put the pieces together. "So this...puddle is actually one of your portals? It's not just a window, because you came through, right?"

"That's the really strange thing," he replies, urgency in his tone now. " This *isn't* a portal, or at least it shouldn't be. It's not even technically in Nocee territory."

He must notice my eyes glazing over with confusion again, because he pauses before trying to clarify.

"Most working windows and portals are within our territory, mapped out and monitored very closely, requiring special permissions for the very smallest purpose. I found *this* portal by complete chance. While exploring outside of territory bounds I came across this cave system, where I found a window. A window, which has somehow made the transition into a portal."

I'm incredulous. "So you're telling me this...portal is in an underwater cave?"

"Exactly." He waits for me to process. Nice of him. I'm trying to picture this fantastic place, and failing miserably.

"What are you thinking?"

I exhale loudly, pulling together my thoughts. "I'm thinking I should be checking myself into the loony-bin for even sitting here this long." I smile at him hesitantly. "Honestly though, this is a lot more fun than a straightjacket. Not to mention, if this is some massive hallucination, I'm whole lot more creative that I ever thought I could be."

The fish gives me a deep look, kind of cocking its...head(?).

"I don't think you're crazy."

"Well thank you sir. Having a giant fish confirm my sanity makes me feel so much better." I'm cracking up laughing at the whole ludicrous situation.

"I like your laugh," he tells me quietly.

I abruptly quiet my chuckle, embarrassed. "Um, thanks." My face flaming like a brushfire, I can't look at him. Time to change back the subject. "So, mystery portal?"

"Yes, well, it happened shortly after I came of age. My family immediately started in on me about what kind of artisan I'm going to be. It's not what I want so I began to avoid them, going off on my own, and found this place. It's peaceful. I've never seen any of my people around this cave system and hardly anyone ever comes to the park. When they do come, I've always stayed undetected—until you."

"Okay wait. I'm torn between a few questions here." I hold up a hand to pause him for a moment. It's all so fantastic, where do I start? "You're sixteen. How did you 'come of age' already?"

"Well, in your world you are considered an adult at eighteen, correct?"

In *my* world. It's so bizarre to be taking such a statement in stride.

"Yeah, so?"

"It's sort of an arbitrary number, if you think of it. I've met individuals older than eighteen who are little more than children, mentally, and then there are those physically younger who are much more mature than most. You for example."

"Whoa there big fella! If you consider me a mature example of the human population, I don't think I want to know who you'd consider immature!"

"A lack of experience does not necessarily dictate an individual's maturity level." He retorts, sounding like my English teacher.

With nothing to argue his line of reasoning, I evade it, trying to go back to the original subject. "So your...culture, has different rules for who is considered an adult?"

"Yes. My people grow and mature a bit faster than those of humans. Our community considers children fully mature by the age of 13 for girls and 14 for boys. Technically I've been an adult for two years."

"Hey, me too!" I joke, trying to make light of the unbelievable.

"Yes, you'd most definitely be considered fully mature," he replies, a whole lot more serious than me.

"Ooooookay then." My heart rate increases at the implications of what being *'fully mature'* could entail. "Change of topic please. Average, all-American, underage teen getting weirded out here."

He chuckles.

"So, I found this cave," He lazily waves one of his long flowing fins at me. "and this window. A window, because no one ever heard me. I also couldn't reach through."

I'm confused again. Not a stretch under the circumstances.

"How can that be?" I asked. "I mean, you've been meeting me for weeks."

"I can't explain it." I think I see him make a fishy shrug.

"Well how did you know even to try?" I persist. "If it didn't work before, what made you think anything changed?"

"Honestly, I didn't know. I guessed. First, you heard me. And when you kicked the rock into the puddle, it came through – narrowly missing me by the way. I realized something changed. Somehow the window made the transition into a portal. Don't ask me how. Portal...technology is *not* my area of expertise."

Past lunchtime, my traitorous stomach makes a horrendous noise, interrupting us and embarrassing me.

Flushed, I mumble something unintelligible as I pick up my pile of forgotten items, bringing it all back to the edge of the puddle and setting myself up a little picnic on my towel. As I pull my food out of the brown paper bag it occurs to me he might be hungry as well. Should I share? My sarcastic brain notes I didn't bring any super sized fish food with me. What exactly does he eat anyway?

"Um, do you want anything?"

"No, thank you," he demurs. "I prefer to eat in my natural form."

My attention peaked, mouth full of sandwich or not, "Whadyamean?" I mumble.

He laughs. Because of my question or lack of manners, I don't know.

"What I mean is I prefer to eat with my hands. Dining as a fish is awkward."

I finish chewing, swallowing my own lump of PB&J with difficulty. No kidding. "So come out and join me."

"Human is not my natural form either."

When he doesn't continue, I roll my eyes in exasperation. "You do realize your cryptic responses are infuriating, don't you? Not to mention, hands," I wiggle my fingers at him as I make my point, "are sort of a human thing too."

"Sorry," he replies, chuckling. "I don't mean to be unclear, I'm just not sure what or how much to say. I've never done this before. Even without breaking about a dozen laws, I'd still be awkward at this."

Sigh. "Okay, ignoring the obvious questions about what laws you say you're breaking right now, let's go back to an earlier piece of crazy. You can change shapes?"

"Yes, most Nocee people can. Right now I am officially considered a Deusame, because I can change from my natural form into a fish form and back again. A Troisame has three shapes. I'm technically not supposed to take human form, not without significant training and then clearance."

Questions, questions…though it explains why he looked so awkward sometimes on his two, extremely nicely shaped but otherwise new-to-him, legs. I'm burning to ask one question in particular. Ah…Nope, can't do it. Let's go with something a little less personal. "Okay. So do all…Nocee…turn into angelfish?"

"No, I am unique in my form," his voice smiles. I can't read fish faces very well. "Most families are genetically drawn to a certain type of fish. My family *are* an angelfish family, saltwater angelfish, commonly found in and around ocean reefs. I am…different."

"Well I for one am glad. I think you're beautiful." Wait, what did I just say? My head practically pops off of my body with the rush of blood to my cheeks. Forward much?

"Thank you," he replies, not reacting to my embarrassment…until he decides to add to it. "I think you also are quite beautiful."

"Um…thanks…" My face cannot physically get any redder.

I take another bite of my lunch, chewing slowly, not knowing how else to respond to boy's flattery…fish or not. Mercifully he changes the subject.

"Please tell me more about you. You are still in school, right? Tell me about it."

I swallow. "What do you want to know?"

"Everything! Where is it? What is the building like? What kinds of things do they teach you? How is it structured? How do you learn? Anything!"

How anyone could be so excited about high school is beyond me. I can sum it up in two syllables, *bo-ring*! But his eyes are bright with interest, so I do my best to explain anyway.

The afternoon passes with me doing most of the talking, even though I much prefer to hear him. We haven't even scratched the surface as far as my questions. I'm just starting to think I may need to head back to the house, when Pete brings up a topic I'd completely forgotten about.

"So how did the celebration go last night? The whole team there?"

Oh...frud! I vividly remember Pete's reaction yesterday. With the whole otherworld fish revelation, my unexpected date mattered less than my sandwich.

Pete is looking directly at me—sort of, for a fish—waiting, and radiating impatience.

I look away, sighing with resignation, with nothing to say but the truth. My creativity caves under pressure. "You were right, okay? It did turn out to be just me and Levi." I internally wince. "My dad dropped me off at the theater, we went to a movie. Afterwards we drank coffee and ate dessert at a café close by, and my dad picked me up. No big deal." My cheeks warm as I think about the part I'm omitting.

Unfortunately, Pete noticed.

"So a date then." His voice is expressionless. "Did he kiss you?"

While it doesn't sound like he really wants to know, I still feel like I need to be honest. I originally showed up prepared to discuss this stuff with him, my empathetic friend. Now I fervently wish I possessed a way avoid it.

I can't look at him as I answer, focusing instead on a random design I trace in the dirt with my finger. "Well, yeah...he did... kiss me."

Pete makes a noise like a strangled grunt.

I cautiously look over at him. While not totally clear on the whole fish body language thing yet, his eyes speak volumes. He's hurting. This whole date and kissing revelation hit him a lot harder than I ever dreamed possible.

I feel a stab of something go through my own body, as I look deep into his tortured eyes. Shared pain? Guilt maybe?

"So do you like him?" Pete asks, managing to sound almost normal despite the pain I can read.

Okay, not the direction I wanted the conversation to go.

"Well,...I guess." I'm not very convincing, even to myself.

He takes a deep breath, bubbles swirling around him. "What I mean is, how *much* do you like him?"

I think before responding, my mind spinning. There's only one possible answer. "I don't know."

His countenance and posture changes, hardens. Like he's resolved himself to a specific plan of action or something. "Can you do me a favor?" he asks, nervous and hopeful at the same time.

"If I can, sure," I want to do something for this...individual, who's become my friend (it's so hard to think of him as a fish, despite what my eyes are telling me), yet I'm wary enough to leave myself an out.

"Well, I won't be able to see you again until next weekend. You know, the whole family business thing."

"Yeah." This part I understand.

"So I'm wondering if...if you could try not to get any...closer, to this other guy until then?"

His voice is so poignant, a mixture of hope and despair, my heart immediately goes out to him. How can I possibly refuse?

"Um, okay. Sure." This I can do...right?

Not the most eloquent of responses, it seems to do the job. His bearing gains confidence almost immediately, more forward, his fins less droopy.

I'm reading fish body language now. This is so totally bizarre.

"Thank you."

Looking away, I notice the position of the sun in the sky for the first time in a long time. It's later than I thought. I really need to start wearing my watch more regularly. "I'm sorry Pete, I gotta go. My parents are waiting for me." Looking down at the impossibility of the beautiful fish form in the puddle, I don't know how I can leave. I may not hallucinate him again.

"Sure, okay," he quickly replies, more confident and determined than ever. "I'll see you next weekend then, same time, in the morning."

His obvious desire to see me again sends a thrill through my body, despite what's in my line of sight. I quickly gather the remainder of my picnic lunch and awkwardly stand.

"See ya, Pete."

"Goodbye, my Doralis. Until next week."

And with a flick of fins and tail, he's gone.

I stand still for a moment longer, staring at the now empty, rather standard looking large puddle.

"I really do need a straight jacket," I mumble. Despite my sarcasm, I really do want to believe. Believe in Pete and the magical world he belongs to.

I turn and trudge back to the rental house.

To say I have a dilemma is a quantifiable understatement.

On the one hand, there's this totally hot guy who sort of tricked me into a date—while totally pathetic I needed tricking, not the current point—and kissed me in a couple of shadowy corners. While my heart rate unconsciously speeds up at the thought of those kisses, my analytical mind says something about the situation still isn't right. I'm not wag-my-tail happy. Why? Levi is the total package—hot, nice, a swimmer, tall—so what in the world is stopping me?

Pete, of course.

The connection I want to feel with Levi is the one I feel with Pete. Pete, who's…unreal. Literally!

I sigh in frustration.

Other than checking myself into the nearest sanitarium, the only thing I can do about Pete is wait for next weekend. I can wait another week to decide if I'm truly crazy or not.

As for Levi, Pete asked me not to get any closer to him.

Sure, why not. I mean, considering I never realized we'd gotten close in the first place, not until we're making out in a movie theater. No problem! With almost no control over the situation, keeping my distance should be a piece of cake.

What it comes down to is I don't feel strongly enough about Levi to make a decision either way. Fantasy or not, I'm more emotionally drawn to Pete, and just plain intrigued by him. Enough to let things lie for the next week…as much as I can, anyway.

My decision to remain undecided made, I let myself into the house, ready for a fun-filled parental evening, bonding over board games.

That night I dream of water again, and this time there's a beautiful Angelfish with me.

10

Invitation

I GET UP the next morning, following my routine as if
nothing's changed. Throw some clothes on without paying
a lot of attention, brush my hair and teeth, grab my ready-
to-go swim bag and I'm out the door.

Pedaling through suburbia, I'm getting more and more
nervous. How will Levi act? What will he say? Will he try
to...gulp... kiss me again? What should I do if he *does*?
What about my promise to Pete? My thoughts spin like the
pedals on my bike.

The first to arrive, I slip into the water and give myself
over to the sensation of swimming. Nothing calms me more
than the rhythm of my body and the feel of the cool water
as it washes over my skin, clearing my mind, comforting
my soul.

About fifteen minutes later, Levi and Bryan show up.
As soon as the men's locker room door opens, my calm
pulse skyrockets. I'm forced to stop mid lane, getting my
breathing back under control before I inhale when I'm
supposed to exhale.

The guys each throw me a big grin, waving good-
naturedly. They jostle each other a bit, confident and cocky
as ever, before each choose a lane and get in to start their
workouts. Just like always. No lingering looks, no attempts
at further conversation from Levi. And, though I'm sure
Levi told his buddy everything, there are no knowing looks
or mocking grins from Bryan either. Nothing out of the
ordinary whatsoever.

Huh?

I know I'm a total rookie to the whole dating thing, but shouldn't there be *some* sort of change? This works for me...I guess. It'll sure make it easier to keep my promise to Pete, but I'm still really confused. Letting it go for now, I get back to something I understand, my workout.

At the lunch break we all walk over to our usual café. The guys walk with me, as usual, joking and being playful along the way, like they normally do. They're my teammates, my buddies. More like big brothers than a potential boyfriend and his best friend. I'm relieved at the normalcy of the camaraderie...I'm also still totally confused by the utter lack of acknowledgement of Saturdays date.

Kari Ann looks at me with undisguised curiosity during practice. Noticing how completely normal the guys are acting, she shrugs off her questions as either unimportant or invalid, never mentioning a thing either.

The only change is Crystal, who glares at me almost non-stop now. It's not just because I beat her on Friday. While the guys are nice enough to her still, their attention is a little less focused. Less of a reigning queen and more like the rest of us rabble now, she doesn't like it one bit. Of course she's totally blaming me.

I'm not going to cower. I'm not a gloater either. I try my best to ignore her.

Afternoon practice progresses the same as always, everyone waving goodbye to me as I pedal my way back towards the rental home. All in all, today's been both reassuring...and strangely unsettling.

Making my way past the park I wish I could talk to Pete, also grateful I can't. I need to figure out how I feel about this mess myself before I can talk to him about it.

My mom's there when I get back to the house, puttering around in the kitchen. It looks like we're taking a break from take out.

"Hey Mom," I call out to her, as I set my swim bag down in the foyer.

"Hi sweetheart! How was practice?" She calls back brightly, over the banging of pots and pans.

"Fine," I reply, the canned response kids give to parents when they don't want to discuss their day.

Unfortunately my mom is more insightful than most.

"What happened with Levi?" She asks innocently.

Of course. I mentally groan. Not only does she remember the name of the guy she's never met, she obviously knows about my first date Saturday.

"Nothing."

Put the superbrain away, Mom. I mentally plead.

Wandering into the kitchen, I'm hoping to distract her from the topic by sounding indifferent and rummaging around in the fridge for something to drink.

"Nice try honey." My thoughts exactly. "How did Levi act around you today? Is he being nicer to you? More indifferent?"

Aw geez. Mom's trying to psychologically profile the situation now. Not a big deal, except she has the college degrees to actually do it.

"Neither Mom, everyone acted exactly the same as always."

"Ah, I see."

I drink my milk (*yuck, skim*), waiting impatiently for her to go on. The only thing she continues is the preparation for our dinner. *Grrrr!* "Okay fine, I'll bite. See what?"

"He's one of those boys."

"Huh? You know Dad said the same thing. What exactly is 'one of *those* boys'? Is there some sort of manual I didn't get?" I add, feeling surly.

She laughs, her perfectly pitched laugh, finding the

situation amusing. "What I mean honey," she ignores my sarcasm, "is he sounds like the type of boy who usually gets his way with girls. Therefore, he doesn't take dating very seriously."

"Oh." I'm not sure how I feel about this particular revelation.

"Your dad says he's a good looking kid, well spoken with parents." (I'm sure it's not all he said.) "I trust his assessment. I'd like to know what *you* think of him."

This is *not* a conversation I planned to share with my mom. Then again, who else is there? I really need to talk to someone…about most of it anyway. I can leave out the part likely to get me medicated. My mom is here, willing and well…qualified, I guess.

"Honestly, I don't really know how I feel about him." I study my toes. "It's sort of a weird situation. I like him, for sure. He's tall, good looking, really nice and he pays more attention to me than the guys at home ever have." I pause, collecting my thoughts. "I should be crazy excited, right? I mean, I am. Except, I'm not." I look up at her nervously. "Am I making sense?"

She sets the stirring spoon down, turning to give me her full attention. As usual, she sees way more than I want her to. "So who's the other guy?"

I gape at her, my eyes wide and my mouth hanging open. How does she *do* that?

"Um, just a friend. Not part of the team. I met him at the park around the corner." I mumble, studying my feet again and blushing scarlet.

"I see. A local boy, huh?"

"Uh, I guess." Could anyone call Pete 'local'?

"And just a friend," statement, not question. "How long have you been seeing him?"

"Not long." *As a fish or human?* "We just talk," I hastily add, looking up at her again.

"Okay, love, I believe you." She regards me thoughtfully again. "So is it safe to say you feel more of a...let's call it a connection, with this other boy, than you do with Levi?"

Somewhat startled by the question, I answer without thinking. "Well, yeah, of course! Pete's like no one I've ever known." A more true statement I've never uttered. "But he's just a friend. It's not like, *romantic* with him."

"Ah, I see."

Here we go again! It's so irritating to be clueless sometimes. Giving her my most exasperated look, I wait her out.

"Okay, I'll explain," she finally relents, her voice morphing into professor lecture mode. "On the one hand, there's Levi. He's good looking and fun, and it feels good to be wanted by someone so sure of himself, and I'm guessing popular. However, his affection is primarily superficial, which you can feel. This makes the mixed signals he's sending all the more confusing and explains why you aren't sure of him."

I open my mouth to say something...protest maybe? Nothing comes out.

"On the other hand there's this Pete fellow," she continues, not missing a beat. "Whatever he looks like, he is something of a mystery. Your relationship is also based on a deeper level of communication and understanding. I'd also be willing to bet this Pete character likes you more than you're saying."

If my eyes were wide before, they must be popping out of my head by now.

"You're very intuitive, love, you always have been. You probably see for yourself the way these boys feel about you. Knowing my little girl, I don't see you becoming attached to someone based on the superficial stuff."

I stare at her for another couple of heartbeats before I finally remembered to pull myself together. "Thanks mom," I finally choke out. "You've given me a lot to think about."

Seriously.

"Anytime, love." She smiles warmly. "Dinner will be ready in a little bit. There's some time to settle your thoughts before Dad gets home." Then she winks at me before picking up her spoon to resume her stirring.

Geez Mom, is this a gift I can inherit? I think. *Please?!*

For once I'm grateful for her perceptiveness. I wander out to the living room and sit on the neutral colored couch, not bothering to turn on the television. Pulling a pillow into my lap, I'm comforted by having something squishy to hold on to. Then I just stare at the faded pattern of the chair across from me, not really seeing it.

My mind kicks into high gear, crunching through bits and pieces of information, putting them in order, getting my ideas more composed...clear. My mom's right...about everything.

Dang it!

I like Levi—of course I do, he's plain likeable – I just don't like him in *that* way. I can't. And I already knew it. Our relationship is about as deep as...well, not a 'puddle', the simple analogy isn't exactly appropriate anymore. No, Levi is more like a babbling brook you can cross in two strides. It feels nice and cool running over your toes and may be fun to splash in, nothing more.

Now Pete, he's a different story. More like the deepest reaches of the ocean...unfathomable. There's way, way more to him than I know now, or may ever know. I feel like I could talk to him forever and still not get it all. Of course I know next to nothing about Pete. He is, *literally,* from another world! A particular tidbit I'm pretty sure my mom didn't take into consideration. The fact he's also fish—at least some of the time—probably isn't a part of her reasoning either.

So now let me see if I've got this straight. One guy has proven he sort of wants me—the boy with the same interests as me, who'd be totally out of my league in any normal world—and all I want is friendship. The guy I like instead—who intrigues me and I'd like to get to know better, scales or not—is totally beyond me...in the most literal, physical sense of the word.

I am so hosed.

* * *

The rest of the week passes in a strange sort of blur, with everything around me going either too fast or too slow.

Once I decided I'm not interested in Levi, as anything more than a friend, I relax completely around him. He seems to sense it, and instead of being offended he's totally fine with it. More than fine actually. He seems to almost like me *more*.

Boys are so odd.

Over my emotional hurdle, practices fly by. I enjoy everything about them – the swimming, the camaraderie, the continued winning in our mock meets.

The only one *not* happy with the situation is Crystal. She looks even more pissed at me. Oh well. I'm not losing any sleep over it.

Conversely my evenings drag. My parents work late most nights, and they're always distracted.

I can sense a pattern in the making, so I stop by a small bookshop on my way home on Wednesday. There's only so many times one can reread The Little Mermaid. With a tiny selection, it's a good thing I'm not feeling picky. Only needing a distraction, I pick up a couple used copies of books filled with inspirational short stories. Feel good reading without the long commitment, exactly what I'm looking for.

Levi asks me out again on Friday. It's surprisingly easy to turn him down. He takes the rejection well, as if he expected it, not like I could possibly be serious. He even tells me he's not giving up, not done helping me "practice'" yet. I laugh it off, my shrill tone giving away my embarrassment.

Kari Ann, in hearing distance the entire conversation, looks ready to explode with curiosity. I wave her off, joking about the wacky sense of humor of Minnesota boys. Temporarily mollified, I don't know how long it'll last. She's one sharp cookie.

By the time practice concludes Friday afternoon, I can't stand the wait anymore, and I'm too hyped up to even consider going home. I know we aren't supposed to meet until tomorrow, but will Pete be at the park...or in his puddle?

Riding into the ever-deserted playground, I dismount and lean my bike less than carefully against the tennis court's chain link wall. My aim is off, and it clatters to the ground with more noise than I think should be possible. I wince before quickly spinning around as a new sound reaches me—a musical chuckle. There's no one in sight, which doesn't mean a thing.

"Pete!"

"I'm here, Doralis," he chuckles again. "I'm wondering what that bicycle ever did to you? You're never very nice to it, always dropping it on the ground."

I rush over to the puddle and there he is, my dolphin sized angelfish, flowing fins and all. I *knew* my imagination couldn't possibly be so good.

"I'm not much of a bike person." I smile down at him as I take a seat in the dirt.

"Yeah, me either," he jokes.

Happy contentment settles itself into my core. Whatever I have with Pete, it may not be romantic—how can it be?—but it's good enough...for now. *Sigh.*

"I'm so glad you're here Pete. I know we said we'd see each other tomorrow. I just couldn't wait."

"Couldn't wait to verify you're crazy?"

"Who's crazy? Are you telling me I'm hallucinating? Are you really a talking bear or something?"

"Frog actually. How'd you guess?"

We laugh together this time, my utterly normal voice sounding oddly harmonious with his.

"No, seriously now. I'm glad you came tonight as well. I've been wanting to ask you something." He still sounds happy, though maybe a little more hesitant.

"What's up?"

"Well...I'm wondering..."

"Yes?"

"Um...I'm wondering if you'd like to see...where I live. Tomorrow morning?"

My mouth drops open in shock, which I'm doing a lot lately. Maybe I'm the frog.

"Are you serious?"

"Yes...very," he answers, sounding serious...and sort of scared.

"Um, I don't know..."

Pete's entire body language changed. If a fish can pull off a look of absolute dejection, this one definitely did.

"No! No! I *want* to go!" I quickly inject. "Of course! Hello? Who wouldn't? What I mean is I don't know if I *can*, as in actually make it through the portal. It's just ...do I need to bring scuba gear or something? To be honest, I'm not sure where I might find some around here."

Pete is the picture of aquatic relief. "Nope, I've got it all worked out." He's confident, though oddly embarrassed. "Don't worry about what to tell your parents either. I've got it covered too."

I never even thought about my parents, or telling them

anything. While they don't usually require long-winded explanations, a little something is generally expected. Feeling a bit guilty, my curiosity totally overrides my guilt.

"How?"

"You'll need to wait for tomorrow to see," he smugly replies.

"Oooookay. I suppose if I'm going to trust a giant talking Angelfish, and go to his...world for a visit tomorrow, I can buy he somehow has the whole parent permission thing covered too."

"Great! As long as you're open," he jokes, lips turning up in a warm fishy smile.

I smile back.

"I've actually got no go now, Doralis," He sounds almost as disappointed as I suddenly feel.

"Why? Did I come too late? Is your family expecting you for dinner or something?" A nice thought. I know mine are out tonight.

"No, it's nothing like that. There are a few things to take care of before I can meet you tomorrow. It's either now, or in the morning."

"Now!" At least I already received my fish fix this evening. Waiting any longer in the morning to go on this adventure? Excruciating.

He laughs again, his beautiful fins rippling in the water, the combination mesmerizing. "Okay then. I'll see you in the morning," his voice all the more musical with leftover laughter.

"Bright and early," I assure him, or maybe warn. Either way, I know I'll be up with the sun...possibly before.

"Sleep well, my Doralis."

One large silver eye gives me a slow wink. Then he's gone.

Turning to retrieve by bike from the ground, my heart

both heavy and light, I give it a cursory once over. It's fine. Maybe an extra scratch or two, nothing bent.

Back at the house, I latch-key my way in, trudging through to see what I can scrounge out of the refrigerator. I'm sitting at the kitchen table, crunching on a big bowl of cereal, when the reality...or more to the point *unreality* of what I plan to do tomorrow sinks in.

The spoon falls from my nerveless fingers, plopping into the bowl and spraying me with milk. I don't notice, too busy trying to grasp what I've gotten myself into.

Holy chowder! I'm planning to visit another world!

Tossing what's left of my cereal, I rinse out my bowl and place it in the dishwasher, heading for my room and one of my feel good books.

I must be more tired than I thought. About a minute after my head hits the pillow, I'm out, sleeping a dreamless sleep.

***

The following morning I wake with a start, my room oddly bright because of the lights I never turned off. My eyes snap open and I'm instantly awake. This is it. I'm going...somewhere!

Smiling at my own ridiculous thought, I get ready at lightning speed, while still trying to be thorough. After strapping on my bikini and tossing on some sweats and my windbreaker, I jog my way over to the park, not bothering with the bike today.

I've gotta be outta my freakin mind!

What in the world am I doing in a semi-dark park, at oh-my-gosh-it's-early, getting ready to take a swim with a fantasy character? My heart races like an out-of-control-stock-car on a mountain path, without guardrails.

"Doralis! You made it!"

Pete's voice is probably the only thing in the world capable of penetrating my almost-a-panic-attack right then.

He sounds so happy to see me, his joy unconsciously soothing and slowing my ping-ponging nerves. The whole trip doesn't seem so crazy with him here.

Sitting down with my legs crossed, I peer down at him. "So what do we do now, Oh Knowledgeable One?"

"Well, assuming there's a swimming suit under those clothes, you strip while I take care of your alibi."

I stop, windbreaker half pulled over my head. "Oh no! I forgot to leave my parents a note!"

"Don't worry about it. That's what this is for."

In one front fin he's balancing a small stone. It glows dully with some sort of blue phosphorescence.

"What do you mean? What is it?" I finish removing my jacket, trying to look closer without falling in.

He answers my question with a question. "Do you believe in…magic?"

"You're serious? Considering I'm sitting here talking to an oversized fancy aquarium fish, it's not much of a stretch to believe magic could be involved."

"Yeah," he said, sheepishly now. "I suppose at this point it's sort of stating the obvious, isn't it. Well, in my culture, the use of what you call magic is a known and sought after skill, though we don't call it magic. It's an ability to manipulate the energies inherent in the world. Natural, in a magical sort of way."

I giggle again—I can't help it. I don't know if Pete's really being funny or if I'm slightly hysterical.

"Okay, okay. So anyway, the part you don't know, I happen to possess some of this talent."

"Besides turning into a giant fish?" I finally gasp, reigning in the giggles.

"An inheritance any Nocee can do," he answers seriously. "Additional talents are far rarer and sought after. I may be strong enough for the High Council's Enforcers or the Portal Keepers…if I were allowed to train."

"The who?"

"Remember when I told you they won't let me test for training? Well the testing is a big deal, public, and the majority of Nocee fail. My family is prominent, no one will risk upsetting them, so no test for me. The problem is, I *really* need training. I know I posses a gift. I can…modify memories, among a few other little tricks."

If I weren't sitting down, I'd be falling down. Maybe I've taken in a little more than my already overloaded brain could handle.

"You can…what?"

"Yeah, I can modify memories. I'm not skilled enough to create new ones from scratch yet, or do anything else, but I can slightly modify what's already there."

Deep breaths—inhale, exhale and repeat. "Okay, so how does all…this, relate to the funky rock? Can't you just wave your arms and say abracadabra or something?"

"Nothing so trite," he chuckles. "Energy manipulation requires using an object as a focus, to house the project. Spell. Whatever you'd like to call it. I'm using this stone as my focus." He holds it up for me. "Pretty, isn't it? It doesn't naturally glow you know. The iridescence will fade as the energy in it fades."

I squint at it, trying to see more than meets the eye. It's pretty, yes, and pretty regular for a rock…aside from the glow.

"So what does this one do then?"

"It masks your absence."

My heart lurches. "Oooookay. Not sounding so great here Pete…"

"It's not overt," He adds hastily. "Anyone who has a tie to you will automatically assume you're doing whatever it is they are most likely to believe true. It only kicks in when they actively think about where you are today."

"Oh. That sounds better, I guess." Handy, even.

"So are you ready to come in?" he asks, flipping the stone out of the puddle and into a patch of gravel near the tennis court, where it blends perfectly.

Grimacing, I square my shoulders and ball my hands into fists with determination. *I'm okay, I'm okay, I'm okay*, I tell myself. I am *not* going to freak out. Quickly, I finish stripping off my sweats and shoes.

"Yeah. Um, ready."

I look past him through the water. Not much to see.

"So what do I do once I'm in?" My voice trembles a little.

"I've set aside some things to help you breathe while you're here. They're in an air pocket I found, deeper in the cave system. I estimate it will take us about a minute and a half to get there. Are you okay with holding your breath that long?"

A minute and a half? Piece of cake! I do more all the time, messing around when swimming by myself. Granted, I'm relaxed then, not totally wired.

I keep it simple, nodding my agreement.

"Great! Once you're in, just follow me through the passages to the cave with the air pocket. The water is pure enough to see clearly. I'll keep it slow and wait for you. We can talk more once you're through. All right?"

"Yup, got it." My voice sounds strangled. I close my eyes, trying to ignore the sheer impossibility of what I'm about to do. Taking deep breaths, I slow my heart rate. When I finally feel calm and focused, I reopen my eyes.

"Come on in, the water's fine."

"Ha. Ha." I'm not about to let him get through my self-imposed tranquility.

I dip a foot in the puddle, experimentally. It feels weird, neither hot nor cold, just sort of…comfortable. Stranger still, its texture is unlike anything I've ever felt. It's water, no doubt, and somehow…different, smoother, softer. Indescribable.

I sit down at the edge, both feet in the water now, like sitting on the ledge of a swimming pool. My legs, near the top of the water, are tingling. Something to do with the portal?

"Once you're all the way in, just hold your breath and follow me. Don't worry," Pete repeats, trying to reassure me.

"Worry? I'm following a fish through a magic portal, into an unknown world where no one will ever be able to find me. What's there to worry about?"

Pete thinks my sarcasm is hilarious. His laughter surrounds me.

Taking a final glance around, I see no one. Inhaling deeply, I close my eyes and push off the ledge, letting gravity pull me straight down.

As I plunge through the portal, I feel the tingle travel along my whole body. Then I'm through the opening...into the unknown.

11

Goroannocee

AS THE TINGLE ceases and my free-fall slows to a stop, the first thing to register is the feel of the water. Completely encased in its warm embrace, it's unlike anything I've ever felt before. So pure, yet the texture is closer to the abrasion of the salty ocean as it caresses my skin.

I can't take more than a moment to revel in the feeling though. Another part of my brain reminds me I'm supposed to be following Pete. Cautiously, I open my eyes to look for him.

Incredible. I'm definitely in a cave, the textures of the rock practically leap out at me. Reaching out a hand to touch the wondrous uneven surface, something else catches my attention. A small light is subtly glowing on the rock wall ahead of me. Just beyond it, I see the flash of Pete's tail as he swims away from me.

"Come on!" I hear, his voice receding.

What am I doing!!! I glance up desperately, at the hole with the piece of Canadian sky in it. *I could go back...*

No, I can't. The thought is almost repulsive, surrounded as I am by such fantastic sensations. I'm here now and I am going to see this through. My heart rate starts to slow towards normal as I push off, swimming away from the portal.

When I reach the little light on the wall, I find a small pebble, not unlike the one Pete showed me earlier. Looking ahead, there's another faint glimmer. I can't see Pete at all now, so I propel myself towards the next lit pebble...and the next one…and the next.

I'm following a winding tube. No straight lines. Dark spaces, I assume to be other tunnels, branch off from mine. I can't see more than a few inches into them before the light is swallowed by absolute darkness. Some of these are to the left or right, some above me…or even below. It's very disconcerting to swim over a bottomless black hole and I'm suddenly extremely grateful for the trail of luminous breadcrumbs. I swim faster.

Coming around a corner I finally see Pete, the most beautiful, impossibly huge angelfish, waiting for me. More importantly, he can get me out of this labyrinth. If not so necessary to keep holding my breath, I'd breathe a sigh of relief.

Pete, with no such restrictions, sighs for me. "Finally! I started to get concerned when you weren't right behind me."

I nod and shrug. What else am I supposed do under water?

"Up there," he continues, waving his fin in the general direction of a space ahead of and above him. "There's an air pocket where I stashed the items you'll need."

I nod at him again, kicking my feet and surging forward. I feel fine. How long have I been holding my breath? Expecting oxygen deprivation kick in at any time, I want to get another breath ASAP. I can see the shimmer now of what must be the top of the water in the air pocket, dimly lit by more of Pete's pebbles I guess.

Two more kicks and I'm there, expelling stale air and inhaling deeply almost before my head breaks the surface. My lungs expand with some measure of relief.

Blinking the excess water out of my eyes, I take in my new surroundings. A shelf to the right of me, I'm otherwise in a spherical bubble of rock, flowing unbroken into the water all around me. The way I came in is also the only way out. The bubble only spans about ten feet across, maybe four feet clearing the water. The small shelf covers about a three-foot section of wall. I can probably pull myself up to sit on it.

"Yee-ipe!!" I practically shoot out of the water as something unexpected and foreign touches my leg. My stupidity registers as soon as I've safely landed on the small perch. It's Pete of course.

Drifting up beside me, one of his trailing fins barely brushes my calf again. His low, musical chuckle bounces through the chamber, echoing around me. I feel both foolish and a little angry.

"It's not nice to sneak up on people you know!"

"What am I supposed to do, bang on the walls?" He's definitely amused.

His sarcasm makes me briefly wish for a spear gun, however unreasonable. *No one* sneaks up on me in the water. I always feel them coming.

Unsure of what to say, I try a diversionary tactic. "So where does the air come from?" The walls around me are seamless. It's a valid question.

"I honestly don't know." His amusement still there, he's at least taking my question seriously. "Every time I've come here it's always fresh."

Pulling my eyes away from the marvelous walls of the stone bubble, I notice for the first time the other objects on the shelf with me.

Curious, I reach out and pick one up. Some kind of slipper or shoe, it's surrounded by an opaque membrane with colored veins of some sort throughout the material. From a distance, it could look like a fishless fin. There's a second matching one, and a few other pairs in different colors and patterns. They're flippers.

I look over at Pete, questioningly.

"They're for your feet, to help you swim a little

faster…easier."

"Thank you Captain Obvious. Did you happen to overlook the fact I only own two feet? Or is this a fashion statement I'm unaware of?" Hooking a pair onto my hands, I flap them, splashing him.

"Hey now!" he laughs, flapping his own fins back at me. "Look, I guessed you're foot size. Other than large, there's still a range of sizes."

"Oooo, ouch, the big feet thing again. Like I never heard *that* one before." I'm still smiling when another thought comes to mind. "You know, the very first time I heard your voice you made fun of my feet. Who knew, right?"

"Who knew what?"

I roll my eyes. Sometimes he seems so much smarter than me. This is not one of those times.

"I meant, who knew me and my big feet may one day be down here, seeing all of this…with you." I don't look at him, concentrating on stuffing my feet into different sizes of the funky flippers, trying to find the best fit.

"Not I, certainly." He makes an odd snorting sound, weird considering his current form. "This is a little…outside of how things are normally done around here. I wasn't exactly looking for anyone, let alone you in particular. Once I did meet you, it felt completely right to bring you here. Do I make sense?"

"Not really. Then again, I'm still not convinced I won't wake up in a few minutes."

"Nope, sorry. While it may not be reality as you've known it, this is no dream."

He turns away, muttering something sounding like "You may *wish* you could wake up…" He's so quiet, I'm not entirely sure I heard him correctly. Before I can ask, he changes the subject.

"Found the right fit yet?"

"Sure thing," I reply, sticking out my legs and wiggling the fins on my feet to illustrate. "They fit like they were made for me."

"Hmmm," he replies thoughtfully. "Maybe so. They match your eyes."

I look back down at my feet, startled by both his observation and his tone. My pulse performs a high speed skitter in reaction. Oh yeah, my feet. Focusing my eyes again, I realize he's right. The filaments splicing through the fin-like membrane are green and gold, with dashes of copper here and there. I'd never noticed, highly surprised he did.

Turning back to the contents of the ledge, I pull out a rectangular piece of fabric. It's decorated solidly across the top with a pattern of stones, pearls and shells. On two corners there are loops.

"What's this?" other than fantastically pretty.

"A masciel. Humans use them to breathe under the water. The loops hook over your ears and, if the mask is a proper fit, it will conform to your face. It creates an almost imperceptible air pocket, allowing you to breathe and speak under the water."

"I take it, then, I'm not the first human to visit your world?" I'm relieved to hear it. Without knowing what to expect, the fact other humans visit here makes me feel a little better.

"Ah, no...not exactly."

I start trying on the masciels, the hesitation in his answer flying right over my head. The first is a deep salmon color, almost red, with very little in the way of decoration. I hook the loops over my ears and wait. It practically falls off, drooping and sliding down to the end of my nose.

"Yeah...no. Definitely not a fit."

The second is a light yellow color with black coral

beading. I can't even get it hooked over my second ear. Way too small.

"Strike two."

My third choice is pale green, with freshwater pearls woven in a band over the top, and what looks like gold water drops along the outside edges and along the bottom. Not plain, and not nearly as much bling as the last couple of options. I like it, hoping like crazy it fits as I hook the loops over my ears.

Both loops cooperate, a good start, and the band feels snug, not too tight, over the bridge of my nose. A moment later there's an odd sensation, as the mask sort of flows a little closer to my skin. It also feels like a second layer is emerging under the first, gluing itself to the edges of my jaw line and under my chin.

The next thing I notice is a change in the air I'm breathing. The cave air's not bad, far from it—it's actually a few steps up from Prince George. The air I'm breathing now is unbelievably pure and clear. Like being on the tip-top of the glacier of Mt.Hood, back home. I close my eyes, inhaling deeply. *Wow!*

Pete's chuckling. "I'm glad you got one to fit. Now, are you going to sit there breathing all day, or are we going for a swim?"

He spoke the magic words. My eyes fly open and I grin at him. Not sure how well he sees my mouth through the thin looking fabric, I'm sure he can see the excitement in my eyes.

"Let's go!" I slide back into the water next to him, reflexively holding my breath as my head submerges. The lower half of my face feels just as dry and protected as above. Whew! Realizing I'll need to breath sometime, I inhale experimentally. The air is just as sweet and pure as before. Relieved, I turn towards Pete expectantly.

"No leaks?"

I shake my head no. The mask feels odd as it flows against my skin, the silky material pressing down on my abnormally dry face, not hindering my breathing at all.

"Okay then, follow me!" And he's off, swimming much more quickly than I think an Angelfish should be able to.

I kick my newly finned feet, taking a moment to get the feel of them, zooming after Pete before he turns the first corner. The glowing pebbles line the passageway, as before, but this time I don't need them to find my way. I easily keep up.

We follow a twisting, turning route, and I'm completely lost within the first couple of minutes. How on earth does he find his way through here?

After what feels like hours, probably only a number of minutes, I start to notice some subtle changes. The darkness is slowly fading, from black to gray. Small plants spring up here and there, bringing additional dimension and texture to the previously lifeless rock.

The opening of the cave system appears after an abrupt turn. I'm concentrating so hard on keeping up, while keeping clear of the rock walls, I almost smack right into the near solid wall of green springing up directly in front of me.

"Whoa!" I backpedal furiously, using both hands and feet.

"Are you all right?" Pete stops to the side, away from my furious thrashing.

"Yeah," I confirm, a little breathless. "I didn't expect a plant blockade. A little notice might be nice." I shoot him a quick accusatory glare, totally unsettled and trying to cover it. It feels odd talking behind the mask too. "Where are we?"

"This is the kelp forest. It borders part of our territory. This cave is on the outside edge of it, hidden by the kelp fronds. I don't know if anyone else knows it's here. Even I found it by accident." He gives me a wry look, still very weird to see on a fish.

"So where do we go from here?"

"Just follow me. Once we're about halfway across, we'll officially be in my territory again…and I can change my form."

"Really?" I'm stunned. After hoping for days to see what he refers to as his 'natural form', nearly obsessing over it, everything else neatly drove the thought completely out of my mind – until now.

"Yes." He sounds unsure. "Are you positive you want to see?"

I can almost hear his thoughts. I accepted him as a guy, and then as a fish. Can I accept his true form? Since there aren't any clues to what he may be, I go with my gut instincts on this one.

"Of course I do! You're still *you* Pete. I liked you as a regular guy (if regular guys can be mind numbingly hot) and I didn't run when I saw Fishzilla. I followed you into a hole, for crying out loud! Why wouldn't I trust you now?"

"All right then." Sheepishly and still unconvinced. "I guess I shouldn't be nervous…but I am."

"I don't see why. I'm the one taking a trip to Oz here." I laugh. His attack of nerves is contagious and I clear my throat to cover the quavering in my voice.

"Oz?"

I sigh, rolling my eyes. "Never mind."

"Okay. Well, stay close then. The kelp in this forest is very dense, and it moves. There is no way to accurately mark a trail, so you need to stick with me or I'll lose you. Don't let it happen. All right? Ready?"

If I my nerves weren't ramped up before, they sure are now. I try to hide it with bravado. "Yup. Let's do this!" I wince, sounding ridiculous, even to my own ears.

Pete nods at me, a small smile on his fish face now—I think. He parts the huge lengths of leaves with his front fins, making his own pathway into the thick greenery, before swimming through. The kelp starts coming back together almost immediately. I hurry to follow him, pushing against the thick, waxy feeling stalks in an attempt to keep my way clear.

Moving through the tall seaweed, I follow Pete's tail fins, the only part of him I can consistently keep in my line of sight, my curiosity peaked, and my mind on fire with anticipation. I swim as quickly as possible, fighting with the ungainly plants while trying to keep the unfamiliar facemask from getting knocked off, beyond eager to finally see Pete's true form.

We twist and turn through the underwater jungle. Then, with a sharp flick of his fins, Pete disappears from my view. My heart rate accelerates as I start to panic, and I shove harder, clawing my way through the plant life in desperation.

I can't lose him! Not here!

When I reach the place where his tail fins disappeared, I find a break in the vivid greenery. There's some sort of clearing.

Roughly, I push the last couple of stalks out of my way, making a less than graceful entrance. Across the clearing in a shadowy corner I spot Pete's tail fins again. As my eyes traveled upwards I get a shocking realization. Those are Pete's tail fins, I'm sure of it. The rest of what they attach to has altered into something else entirely.

Whoah!

I don't realize I'm holding my breath until the shadowy form moves slowly into the marginally better light of the clearing. My hands fly to my face, my eyes wide. I can't remember how to breathe, let alone speak. Only one word springs to mind.

"*Pete?!?*"

Pete's silver eyes stare cautiously at me from what is now a very human, yet inhuman, looking face. Already crazy handsome as a human, this form is a much more refined version. If Levi is gorgeous, then Pete is almost god-like. Okay, demigod-like maybe. However you want to put it, he's simply unreal!

His black hair and black brows frame his quicksilver eyes. His mouth is perfectly formed, yet very masculine, leading my train of thought down an impure track, making me blush. His skin is smooth, with a slight silver sheen to it, shimmering and emphasizing his muscled form with even the smallest of movements. The muscles themselves look like they've been hand carved by a master sculptor, with unsurpassable definition and proportion, and no shirt to hide them.

My eyes travel over his perfect stomach to where it blends into the most unique and beautiful thing about him. While he's not a fish anymore, not even close, Pete still has...a tail.

And his tail is unquestionably beautiful as well. Mostly black with some silver in his fins, just like his fish form tail. Its length is muscular and strong, while the fins are long, graceful, almost delicate looking. Here in this clearing, I feel like I'm seeing those fins for the first time.

The weirdest thing of all is this doesn't weird me out. Pete looks...right, somehow. The whole situation seems right to me, like the world finally makes sense.

"You're a *merman*," I breathe.

Pete ducks his head, unsure of either himself or me. He's crazier than I am if he thinks I won't like him *this* way.

"Um, actually we call ourselves Nocee." Oh yeah, the No-Sea thing, in every body of water and in none. Irony at its best. "The whole mermaid, merman thing, you humans came up with on your own."

"Oh, um, sorry?"

What I really want to say is *'Who cares what you want to call yourself! You're the most amazingly perfect...being I've ever seen in my life!'* My breathing is ragged, nothing to do with the masciel.

"Will you come with me?" he asks, holding out one perfectly formed hand to me.

Well duh!

All I say, though, is a quiet "Yes," as I reach out my own hand to take his.

His skin is smooth, not scaled, and not exactly the same texture as human skin either. It's almost the satiny soft, not quite slimy feel of a fish, if you stroke one with the grain of its scales, versus against. Almost, yet much, much nicer.

Our hands fit almost perfectly together, making me absurdly and inexplicably happy.

Before I can think about it any further, he's pulling me along after him. I thought I'd been doing pretty well, with my mask and fake fins on my feet. My efforts aren't comparable to the way Pete moves through the foliage. He's quite literally in his element.

Pulling me along carefully, gently, he helps me to keep pace with him. I don't care if he yanks my arm out of the socket, as long as he continues holding onto my hand.

The clearing must be right on the edge of the kelp forest, because we come to the end of it very quickly. Pete pulls me up beside him, winding one magnificently strong arm around my waist.

I can't decide which is more distracting, the pulse altering sensation of his touch or the panoramic view stretching out in front of me. My head is in sensory overload, regardless.

"Welcome to Goroannocee," he breathes quietly into

my ear.

12

Colors

I'M SHOCKED, STUNNED, dumbfounded,...!

The scene before me is fantastic, something out an Avatar movie. It makes Seaworld look like a cheesy pizza parlor, or the Undersea Gardens look like a twenty-gallon fish tank.

And the *colors!*

It's as if I've been watching a junky old t.v. my whole life, barely one step above black and white, and someone just introduced me to the finest 3-D plasma screen ever made. I feel like I'm finally...*seeing!*

"Oh!" The involuntary gasp breaks my trance.

Pete pulls me tighter to him in a gentle hug. "What do you think?" he murmurs.

"It's...amazing!" Incredible, wonderful, beyond description!

The physicality of his presence breaks through my visual shock and I become hyper aware of his bare torso against the mostly bare skin of my back. It feels good, *he* feels good, good enough to override what my eyes are trying to process. His body as silky soft as his hand, I can feel the strength and hardness of perfectly formed muscles as they flex with his movements. And we fit together so perfectly, like I'm made to be there in his arms.

I think I may very easily pass out with the overwhelming feel of *him*. My skin is on fire, so utterly sensitive and aware of his touch. It's a good thing he has a secure grip on me. Then again, we're in the water. I won't fall. At worst I might float around aimlessly while unconscious.

A near hysterical giggle escapes me at this ridiculous thought. He loosens his hold, just enough to turn and look down at me, his eyes questioning. As I look back I'm made aware of something else. Pete is *huge*! I've never felt petite before. This must be pretty close to it.

"Amazing," I repeat, staring back into his silver eyes.

"My sentiments exactly." He smiles at me.

My heart thumps audibly. His smile is just so wondrously beautiful.

While keeping one arm around my waist, he reaches for a lock of my floating hair, winding it around his finger.

The movement allows me to break my gaze away from his face for a moment, so I can compose myself. I'm distracted by the hair in his hand and by the other pieces I can see in my peripheral vision. My mousy, not quite blonde or brown hair is the exact shade of pure 24 carat gold, polished and shining.

"Oh my…!" It's one thing to see such vividness in a magical world like this, quite another to see it reflected in yourself.

As I reach for some of my floating hair, my skin grabs my attention next. There's a pearl-escent quality to it here, a muted shimmer, depths of color lying dormant under the tan-less pale surface.

Dang! Where's a full-length mirror when you need one! I look up at Pete again, my eyes wide in awe and wonder. He chuckles, a warm caress for my ears.

All I need is to smell and eat something strange and every one of my senses can be completely overloaded. A small part of my confused brain idly wonders how much shock a person can take before their entire system shuts down. More than this, apparently.

"You are so beautiful." The look in his eyes conveys how strongly he means it.

"I...I don't know what to say," I blurt out honestly. "It's all so much!"

"Don't say anything." He smiles warmly, pleased by my reaction. "Let's go explore!"

Explore. Yeah, okay.

Then he releases my waist, taking only my hand again.

No! I'm not done feeling that yet!

He tows me towards a large patch of color I noticed when we first emerged from the murk of the kelp. As we move closer, the hues start to materialize into distinct individual forms.

Anemones, thousands of them! And the colors! My new appreciation for pigments is definitely getting overloaded here. It feels like I'm drowning in them...in a good way.

"What *is* this place," I whisper.

"It's one of the outer anemone gardens. There are a few of them in Goroannocee. This one is the furthest from the main city, so it doesn't get a lot of visitors. It's also really quite boring compared to the Imperial Gardens."

"How is that even possible?" I wonder aloud.

As we drift closer, I notice more, discerning different shapes and sizes. The area is filled primarily with anemones—red, yellow, white, pink, burgundy, green, and all combinations—mixed with a few pieces of coral accent pieces. There are also a number of taller species I don't recognize – not being an oceanographer—with flowing fronds, full of design and pigment as well.

"Those are some of the sea worms," Pete explains in his musical voice as I lean closer to examine the softly waving forms. "Feather dusters, peacocks, fans and a few Christmas tree worms over there." He continues, gesturing to the side where I see a group of hot pink fronds spiraling up to a point. They looked like mini neon-colored Christmas trees from some wacked out tree farm.

"Well, they're a lot nicer to look at than the earth worms I'm used to," I laugh, delighted.

Pete laughs with me, enjoying my undisguised pleasure.

He continues to hold my hand as we explore. His touch is warm and strong, while at the same time gentle and caring. Maybe I'm reading too much into the contact, but I'm far too happy to care about much right now. I can't imagine ever having a more perfect day in my life.

The anemones range in size, from smaller than a dime to bigger than our reclining chair back home. However, the lovely chair sized, soft pink anemone with thousands of flowing and stinging tentacles, does not tempt me to take a seat. Some are squat and dark green, orange or maroon, like the ones I'm used to seeing in the tide pools on the Oregon coast. Others are tall and elegant, almost white in color. Then there are some tiny crystalline specimens. In such bright shades of pink, red and purple, they almost hurt my eyes. Almost. I'm enjoying these new vivid pigments so much I can hardly tear my eyes away from them.

Among the waving tentacles and other various animals—I have to remember they aren't plants—is an array of even more brightly colored fish. They zoom around, going about their business, not noticeably bothered by our presence. I reach out a cautious hand. A tiny bright blue fish and some of his rainbow colored buddies come to investigate, probably expecting food or something.

I've been unconsciously moving about the area, going wherever my whims take me, pulling an indulgent Pete along. Enjoying his descriptive monologue—he knows practically everything about the plants and animals we're seeing—I don't notice its cessation until a sudden tug on my hand brings me up short.

"Doralis, stop!" His voice is quietly urgent, almost near panic.

I look up at him, wondering what the problem is. He isn't looking at me but over my shoulder at something. I turn, fearful at what can frighten him, more afraid not to look. Nothing prepares me for what I see.

It's enthralling. Bulbous, bobbing, crystalline forms— many shapes and colors, and every size imaginable—fill the area behind me.

Jellyfish. Thousands of them…less than ten feet away from us.

"Oh! They're exquisite!"

"And deadly," Pete replies, slowly wrapping his strong arm around my waist and pulling me back the way we came. He never takes his eyes off of the undulating tentacles closest to us.

"Okay, so what's the big deal? I know some varieties are pretty poisonous. We're plenty far enough away though. It's not like they're the speediest swimmers or something." I try to joke, lighten the mood.

Without answering, he continues pulling me away, slowly and steadily, and he hasn't relaxed at all yet.

Just then, one of the bright little fish following us around ventures out closer to the mass of jellyfish. His quick, jerky little movements are abruptly cut off when a tentacle comes out of nowhere. It snaps into the fish with blinding speed, stunning it, before wrapping around the now still form and pulling it out of sight.

!!!!!

I can't breathe. I can't even think right, so shocked by the deadly speed of what I just witnessed. *That could have been me!* A couple animals drift our way in deceptively slow pursuit, tentacles searching, drawn by the movement of possible prey. My heart feels locked in my ribcage, and I can't make my limbs respond. Pete pulls me faster.

When we reach the middle of the anemone field, he spins me around to face him, keeping his steadying hands on my shoulders. Looking deeply into my wild eyes, concern etches his features.

"Doralis, it's okay. We're a safe distance now." He cups my face in his palms, eager to calm the terror he sees there. "I'm sorry. I'm SO sorry. I should be paying closer attention. This particular Anemone garden serves two purposes. The first you know, it's just a pleasure garden to visit and pass the time. The second, however, is to act as a visual reminder, as it borders jellyfish territory."

A pleasure garden next to certain death…sure, makes total sense.

Fear stretched nerves snap and I finally react. "Exactly when were you going to share *that* little tidbit with me?" I screech. "Look at the pretty anemones, just don't mind the bloodthirsty jellyfish over there. They're for entertainment purposes only. Ugh!"

I pull away from him angrily, immediately missing the feel of his touch on my face, yet too keyed up to stay still. I kick my way back in the general direction of the kelp forest. At least I know this path is safe, since I've already crossed it. Moving my legs forcefully, I try to release some of the manic energy generated by my brush with blobby danger.

Pete catches up with me almost immediately. "Doralis, wait. Please?"

The "please" makes me waver. So sincere, he sounds so hurt. I slow for a moment before kicking out again, keeping my eyes focused straight ahead. I'm not done venting yet.

"Please?" He asks again, this time catching my hand and pulling me towards him. As soon as I look into his face I'm a goner, drowning in the liquid silver of his eyes.

"That is *so* unfair! Knock it off!" I try sounding angry.

With my thoughts turned to mush, it comes out more weak and pathetic than intimidating.

Misunderstanding me, he drops my hand immediately, his eyes reflecting his hurt and confusion.

Well now *I* feel horrible. "I'm sorry Pete, that's not what I meant." I reach for his hand this time. As I take it, I notice for the first time he has short fins on his forearms, running from wrist to elbow. Once again, something which should be weirding me out and doesn't. It only makes him more beautiful and special.

I clasp the hand I hold in both of mine, reveling in the feel of it. I stare at our twined fingers, needing a moment to collect myself.

"I *am* sorry Pete. I shouldn't overreact."

He uses his free hand to brush back some hair floating in front of my face, cupping the side of my head in one big hand. Bringing my gaze back to his face, his eyes are softer now, tender. I remind myself to breath.

"I know, my Doralis. I must remember you don't understand how different everything is down here. Things are not always what they seem to be."

"Like giant angelfish turning into Mermen?" I hesitantly tease.

He smiles down at me, his body drifting closer to mine. My heart staggers in reaction. "Something like that, yes."

I sigh, closing my eyes while trying to calm my pulse. "Well, what now?" *Get a grip Lee!* I open my eyes to look at him. "I've gotta be honest, I think I'm kind of through exploring for the day."

"I understand. Well, I'm *trying* to understand is probably more accurate. Let's go back through the kelp forest for now. We can stop in the clearing again, if you like." He ducks his head self-consciously. "Then we can talk for a while…before I must change my form."

"Sure, okay," I agree quickly. "Why do you need to change forms?"

He turns to tow me in the right direction before answering. "It's part of our laws here. The kelp forest and anemone territory are part of our borders. The law says anyone within our borders must be in their Nocee form, with very few exceptions. Conversely anyone who crosses the borders must use their fish form."

"So am I breaking the law, then? No fish form." I grin at him, trying to lighten the mood. It doesn't work. I think he mumbles something like "You have no idea," looking grimmer than ever.

Soon enough we're back to the safety of the kelp forest. I look up at the massive stalks. Seeing them from the outside (not paying much attention when we first came through) they're absolutely ginormous! They reach as high as I can see, a solid wall of lush verdigris.

How in the world does Pete find his way in all this? I wonder.

Keeping a firm grip on my hand, he plunges in without hesitation, shoving kelp stalks and leaves out of the way forcibly enough to stay moved until I pass. We reach the clearing moments later.

He releases my hand at once, the cold absence of his touch immediately felt. To distract myself from the loss, I take in my surroundings. I'd been a bit overwhelmed by my inhumanly gorgeous merman buddy the last time. Excuse me, Nocee buddy.

There's not much to it—a couple of rocks sticking up out of fine sand, surrounded by living walls. It's definitely private though.

"I apologize for my mistake, taking you there before explaining more about my land," Pete begins. "I put you in unnecessary danger and I am so very sorry. Therefore," he straightens his posture, an unusual twinkle in his eye, "I am obligated to answer all of your questions. Take your best shot, so to speak."

"Wow. Really? No evasion or double talk?" I float down to sit on a boulder. "I don't know where to start."

He settles down next to me, in the fine sand, curling his tail around. Geez he's beautiful! I can't get enough of him, now with nothing else new and otherworldly to distract me. My eyes run over his face, with the black hair, silver eyes, strong nose and jaw line, his muscled torso, his arms with their small black and silver fins, and down to his incredible black tail with the silver streaks. He interrupts in my visual caress.

"Well?"

Embarrassed, I try to reroute my scrambled brain. Where do I begin?

"Okay, I got it. You told me there are more portals to my, um...the human world, right?"

"Yes. All the working portals are located in the main Nocee city, where they can be guarded and monitored. Any portals found outside of the immediate area are destroyed as a matter of course. We take the privacy of our world very seriously."

Sudden intuition prompts my next question.

"I'm not supposed to be here, am I?"

He stares at me for a moment, guilt written across his face, before shaking his head. "No, you're not. I'm sorry." He gives me a pleading look before continuing. "Any passage by a *Nocee* is strictly monitored and documented. You need special permissions to bring a human through. It's a lengthy and difficult process, so most don't even bother."

I think about the three tries it took me just to get my driver's permit, a supposedly easy thing to do. "I guess I can understand...sort of." If it means being here with him, he can smuggle me in anytime. "Wait a minute. You'll get in trouble if they find me here, right?"

He nods, his body language defiant, not fearful.

"Why?"

"Excuse me? Didn't I just explain?"

"Not why you'd get in trouble, I'm not *totally* dense you know." I smile at him, with affection—okay, so I feel more than affection—and concern. "What I mean is, why take the risk?"

He looks at me for a while, not answering, his expression shifting into something I've never seen – directed at me anyway.

"You're worth it, of course."

My head feels totally hollow, nothing to say coming to mind. It's not just his simple words, it's the feelings behind them. I can't break my gaze away from his eyes, so filled with honest emotion…filled with…?

Fortunately for me, he breaks eye contact first, swiftly glancing at the clearing around us. "It's getting late. I need to get you back to the portal."

I look down at my waterproof watch, remembering for the first time I put it on this morning. Four o'clock already! How?

Looking around me, disoriented, I don't have the slightest clue which way to go. My eyes land back on Pete. Waiting for him to take the lead is probably the best option. Or, like, the only option.

"You'll need to follow me this time," he confirms, regretfully.

"Yeah, sure," Pushing myself off of the rock and kicking forward, I hope I won't lose sight of his already retreating form.

Once again, as soon as I'm in the confines of the kelp, all I can see of Pete are flashes of his tail fins. It takes all of my strength and maneuverability to keep up with him, and even then I just barely do it.

We arrived at the mouth of the cave, which is really small. Barely big enough for fish-Pete to fit through, it looks totally different on the way in than on the way out. It's also covered with kelp and miscellaneous greenery, camouflaged almost perfectly.

"How on earth did you find this Pete?"

"Well, technically it's not on earth," my angelfish replies teasingly. Somehow, he transformed while I followed him. He's still beautiful, though I prefer his natural form...for obvious reasons. At least his good humor returned.

"I came across this cave totally by accident, and left myself a marker, so I could find it again. I've been coming back regularly ever since."

Preceding me into the cave, he avoids further questions. I follow as close as I can, terrified of getting lost. I shouldn't worry. It's dark as we enter, but as soon as the low light from the entrance disappears behind me I can see the faint glimmer of Pete's glowing marker stones. The way back seems much shorter than the way in. Before I know it we're back in the air bubble.

I pull myself up onto the ledge without being told, knowing I can't take my mask or funky flippers back with me. The air without the mask, while still good, is stale. I wrinkle my nose in distaste, *not* looking forward to breathing back in Prince George. Ugh!

Pete swims closer to the ledge. Before he can speak I jump in...figuratively.

"Let me guess, I hold my breath and follow you back to the portal, pulling myself back through as quickly as possible so I don't drown. Am I right?"

"Yes, correct." He nods.

"One problem. What if someone's there?"

"Not a problem. One of my stones keeps people away from the park. I placed it right after the first time I discovered you could hear me. Not another human since. Granted, it didn't exactly work with you, did it? You still came back."

"No, I guess it didn't work on me. Odd. I'm grateful though." I add quietly, looking down at the mask still in my hands. "You know, I've never experienced a better day in my life, even with the whole jellyfish thing. And not just because this is the most amazing place I could ever dream of, it's…it's because I'm with you." Now I look up at him, his eyes the same in any form. "Thank you Pete."

He doesn't say anything for a long time. I become uncomfortable, unable to read fish nearly as well as I can merman.

"So…can I come back tomorrow?" I ask, both to break the silence and because I really do want to come back. I haven't had enough, of Goro-whatever, or of Pete. I'm not sure if I ever could. This is my version of heaven…minus the homicidal jellyfish of course.

"Do you want to?" He sounds strangely hopeful.

"Of course! If you think I'm going to let you off with just the few questions I got answered today, you are sorely mistaken. You're still on the hook buddy…so to speak," I add, giggling. He either didn't get the pun or didn't mind, probably the latter.

"I will be waiting with baited breath then," winking at me. He got it.

I laugh, warmed by his humor, and his desire to spend more time with me. "Well let's go then! The sooner I leave, the sooner I get to come back!"

Holding my breath, I slip from the ledge, plunging down deep before pushing strongly off the wall, as if in a swim competition. Moving swiftly out of the cave, Pete's form flashes ahead of me. I follow him and his lights toward the portal.

Daylight filtering through my exit home starts

brightening the passage. Pete moves aside and I don't hesitate, shooting straight up and through, leveraging my weight with both hands to pull myself up. The tingle of the transition surrounds me the whole way through. I pull my feet out as soon as my body clears.

A quick look around verifies Pete's right. There aren't any witnesses to my miraculous reappearance. I turn back, leaning over the puddle. Pete's still there, fins fluttering in relief.

I take a breath of air, preparing to speak, and practically choke on the foul smelling stuff. Talk about a major buzz kill to my otherwise wondrous day. I'm tempted to simply jump back in. Common sense reminds me my parents are likely home and waiting for me. They might be a bit put out if I decided to stay in Pete's world, never coming home.

I finally get my lungs to stop their spasms, long enough to talk, if hoarsely. "Thank you Pete. I…well I just don't know how to describe how I'm feeling right now. Thank you," I repeat. A part of me wants to say more. How do I put into words all of the emotions I'm feeling?

"You're welcome. More than welcome really. And…and I'll see you tomorrow." He sounds like he's planning to say something else, too, staying silent instead. I don't know what, so I let it go and stick with the obvious.

"Yeah, see you tomorrow Pete. I can't wait!"

He gives me what passes as a fishy smile, flicking his fins and disappearing.

I sit back on my heels, my mind still full of amazing images from my day. Then I realize I'm still dripping wet, and it's colder than I'd like, sun or no sun. Grabbing my towel, thankfully still where I'd left it, I scrub my body down briskly before pulling on my clothes. There's no way to dry my hair. Maybe I can sneak in and jump into a hot shower before anyone notices. Still reluctant to leave, I turn and make my way back to the house.

My parents aren't there. Managing to dodge that particular bullet, I hurry up to my room for a shower.

More traditionally wet, I head for the kitchen. I am starving! I can't believe how much swimming all day with Pete took out of me. I don't know what he eats, but I'm going to have to seriously carbo load if I plan on spending much more time in Goroannocee.

Later, after scarfing down almost the entire contents of the refrigerator, when settling into bed, I select my old book instead of a newer one. It's still early and though I'm exhausted (*weird*) I'm also way too wound to even think of sleeping yet. Suddenly my ancient volume of 'The Little Mermaid' seems more interesting. I wonder how much of it could be true?

When I do finally drift off, my dreams are more vivid and colorful than ever before. Still in the water, this time Pete is with me...in his merman form. My relaxed mind lets my emotions flow and, lost in my dreams, I'm really and truly happy.

Roslyn McFarland

198

13

Surprises

AS THE LIGHT of dawn finds its way through my window, I'm out of bed and flying through the house as quickly humanly possible, excitement giving my feet wings. I'm hungry though, *really* hungry, so I force myself take time to eat something. I never realized we didn't stop to eat lunch yesterday, too busy exploring.

I'm stripping off my outer layer of clothes even before I reach the puddle, knowing there will be no witnesses. So eager to see Pete, and to go through the portal, the cool morning air doesn't even faze me.

He's there. My already high spirits lift immeasurably when I spot his softly glistening form and flowing fins. I'm flushed, buoyed by warmth and happiness just being near him again.

I don't pause to wish him a good morning, too keyed up to get out of Bad-Airsville and into watery bliss. Grinning at him I jump—feet together with my arms crossed in front, elbows tucked firmly at my sides—straight down into the puddle. Of course he's quick enough to get out of my way, though I hope I managed to surprise him for once…even a little.

"Nice move. You missed though." His chuckle follows me to the air bubble.

Thrilled as I am to be back in this land of wonder, the sarcasm reflex is still deeply ingrained into my teenage brain. Of course I can't make any comments back at the moment, which is really frustrating. Limited, I stick my tongue out at him as I continue kicking.

Reaching the cave bubble quickly, not wasting a moment, I pull myself up onto the ledge and reach for my swim fins. I'd set them and my mask off to the side yesterday, eliminating the need for another fitting session. The others I'd shoved into a far corner.

When I'm ready, I turn to see Pete waiting for me patiently. Can angelfish smirk?

"Someone might think you're in a hurry or something." His voice tinkles with repressed laughter as he winks at me. I grin through the mask and jump back in.

Breathing through the masciel is as good as I remember. I don't let it distract me this time though. "Where to?"

"Well, we saw the Anemone Gardens yesterday. How about a tour of the Coral Fields?"

"Sounds good!" More than good of course…as long as Pete's with me.

Once again I follow him to the mouth of the cave—we can't hold hands when all he has are fins. This time we barely hesitate at the wall of green blocking the cave entrance, plunging right into the shifting stalks. I'm more confident and keep up with Pete more easily. In no time at all we're at the clearing. Still managing to zip ahead of me at the last minute, he's already there and in his merman form when I push my way through.

My heart almost stops again, seeing him this way, my stomach suddenly rebelling against my larger-than-usual breakfast as it twists in nervous response. He's so impossibly gorgeous and amazing. I feel so very, very privileged to be here…and more than a little intimidated.

He reaches out to me. "Shall we?"

I don't hesitate, placing my smaller hand into his silky smooth one, feeling the heat generated by our combined warmth flare, running up my arms to warm my whole body. I look at him in awe. This is just like my dream…what I remember of it anyway. My new happy place.

We break through the kelp together, the view as breathtakingly stunning as before. I'm more inclined to look at Pete this time.

Taking in his profile and the way his muscles move under his skin as he swims next to me, my breath catches. Hearing my little gasp, he turns to look at me curiously, catching me staring. Blushing hot, I pretend my attention is able to focus on something other than him, not fooling him in the least. He simply gives my hand a light squeeze.

We make our way across the Anemone Garden again, more quickly this time, giving the jellyfish territory a wide berth.

Soon we arrive at the coral fields. I'm stunned. *Again.* It isn't just the color this time, though plenty of them assault my senses, it's the textures.

I'm overlooking a large valley filled with every type of coral I've ever seen, and many more I've never heard of or thought possible. From solitary branches and delicate leaf-like groupings, to massive boulder sized varieties. It's hard to take it all in.

Unlike the rock formations some coral resembles, or the already dead coral reefs frequented by avid snorkelers, these are living creatures. The corals polyps, brightly colored flower looking things, can retract back into their hard shell. They're all out now, making what could be a relatively barren landscape more magical than even the Anemone Garden.

"I thought coral only extend their polyps at night?" I comment, pulling the information from the dregs of remembered biology class.

"When will you learn things don't necessarily follow the same rules here?" He smiles down at me, unintentionally jump starting my heart in the process. "For example, this type of coral," he gestures to a spiky clump, the kind seen most often stained neon bright on the shelves of beach knick knack stores, "is most commonly found in the reefs surrounding a body of land in your world, while this one," referring to a large boulder looking variety nearby, "is never found anywhere but the very deepest seas."

He takes me on a guided tour, pointing out the differences between sea fans and gorgonians, the textures of brain coral and bubble gum coral, and even directing my attention to a tiny little porcelain crab as it moves along, keeping things clean.

As enchanting as everything is, I stay close to Pete this time. Any of the innocuous looking life around me may be more dangerous than I know, and no one needs a repeat of yesterday.

We're moving through a forest of large plate table and soft coral when I feel the water around me shift, the way it does when someone else enters a pool.

"Huh," I mention, not really thinking about it as I continue my lazy exploration. "It feels like someone's coming."

I'm admiring a tiny little blue and yellow fish, who's playing peek-a-boo with me, when a massive force hits me. Flying sideways, I don't realize its Pete until we land in a crevice—hard—completely surrounded by coral and plant life.

"Wha…" I start, when his weight finally lifts from me.

"Shhh!" Without even looking at me, he places a finger on my lips, effectively cutting me off. His eyes are locked on some point in the distance and he looks completely stressed out…and scared. I get the point.

What now? My anxiety escalating, my heart rate accelerates enough to give me a slight head rush. Mouth clamped shut, my only movement is a slight shift to stop a stray piece of coral from digging into my back. It hurt!

Peeking over Pete's shoulder, I'm barely able to see through the layers of intricate webbing. For the moment there's nothing in the dark empty water. No matter, I know what I feel. My heart continues to pound and my ragged breathing is too loud in my own ears.

I feel the water shift again, giving me something to pinpoint, and look towards its source. From the gloom emerge three very large forms. They're fish, predators all, and nowhere in the world can you find them hanging out together in a natural environment.

In the lead is a huge barracuda. It's long sinuous body small in comparison to the two figures following it. A misleading observation. Barracuda are known for their lightning speed, ferocious dispositions and of course, let's not forget about their razor sharp teeth.

Swimming just behind and to its right is a very ominous looking hammerhead shark. With its distinct t-shaped head, I know it has better vision and sensory skills than most everything else in the ocean. Already unmoving, I try to become as still as the stone I rest on, not even breathing.

My breath sticks in my throat anyway, as the final member of the group comes into view. The most massive shark I've ever seen, even in documentaries, with rows of sharp ivory points subtly glimmering despite the gloom. I wouldn't be much of a snack for a creature this size, but I guess it could use me as a toothpick. Even with my knowledge of marine species already severely taxed, this *must* be a great white.

The three loom closer. I haven't taken a breath in a while and my body is beginning to complain. I ignore it. My eyes are the only things I allow to move as they track the progress of this deadly trio. Beside me, Pete is as still as the shadows he masterfully blends into, not producing the slightest tremor in the water. If not so scared at this moment, I'd be impressed.

The predators appear to be searching for something, the barracuda the obvious leader. He holds the lead yet glances at the hammerhead regularly, as if checking the others senses.

For one horror filled, terrifying moment, I think we've been discovered. The hammerhead changes direction, moving unerringly towards our crevice. Squeezing my eyes closed, I will them to go away. *Nothing to see here.* The water pressure around me increases, weighing me down, suffocating me more that the lack of oxygen. It's like a small space closing in on someone who's claustrophobic. I'm sure this is the end, imagining myself ripped to shreds.

Miraculously, I feel another shift. I crack one eye open, just enough to see what's happening. Incredibly, the hammerhead is swimming away from us, regaining his position in the formation.

As soon as their leisurely pace takes them around a corner and out of sight, I let myself breath again. Slumping forward, I curl into a ball and put my head in my hands, trying to remember how not to hyperventilate.

I've always held a healthy respect for underwater predators, like sharks. However accomplished I may be a swimmer and as much as I love the water, it's *their* territory. I'm just a visitor, who might be on the menu.

Coming face to face with my theory, quite literally, well...I can't remember ever being so scared in my life. Such a level of fear never existed in my protected little world. Its discovery doesn't exactly make me happy. The only positive thing going for me right now is not soiling myself. Also, my heart's still beating, if erratically, which is another plus I guess.

Pete finally stirs. Immediately by my side, he rubs my

back soothingly.

"It's okay Doralis," he murmurs, "they're gone. They can't hurt you now."

So what he's saying is, hurting me had been on the agenda? This little tidbit of information does not help me relax. I shove the thought away, focusing on my breathing and how good his hand feels as it moves in circles over my back.

Wrangling myself into some semblance of control, I slowly straighten up. Dropping my hands from my face, I turn to Pete, intending to thank him for his support and concern.

I get out "Th—" before I'm stopped by the expression on his face. Pete's staring at me as if I've grown a second head.

"What?" I ask, alarmed again.

When he doesn't say anything, continuing to stare at me with his eyes wide and mouth dropped open in shock, I make my own conclusions.

"Are they coming back?!" I choke out. He doesn't respond, still frozen in place. *Why isn't he saying anything?!*

My darting eyes catch a brief glimpse of something, an unnaturally bright, lime green flutter. I peer at it more closely, my own eyes widening in horror as I realize what it is.

There, hanging off of a branch of coral and moving slightly with the motion of the water, is my masciel.

My hands fly to my jawline, then patting frantically at my nose, finding nothing but smooth skin. Turning to Pete, understanding and wonder reflected off my own face now, I ask the obvious question. "How am I breathing without my mask?!"

Because I *am* breathing. Been doing so for a while now—hyperventilating at the moment—never noticing my source of breathable oxygen has been ripped off. Right now I'm practically hyperventilating water.

"Pete?!"

And I'm talking!

"How is this possible? What is happening?"

He shakes his head in less-than-helpful negation, apparently still rendered speechless. He doesn't know either.

My wildly spinning brain can't focus. Ping-ponging thoughts of when and how my masciel was lost compete with, and are losing to, the soon-to-be overwhelming question of how I'm not *dead,* or at the very least *drowning.*

"PETE!!"

My panicked shriek finally cracked through Pete's shock induced daze.

"It must have happened when you knocked me in here, to hide from those…predators." I muse aloud.

"Sentries," he croaks, shaking his head as if trying to unlock his voice.

"What?"

"They're Sentries." He continues, regaining a piece of his composure. "Not a random grouping. You'd never see those three predators together here, let alone in your world, unless on patrol. They swim circuits, looking for anything out of the ordinary."

"So they're…like you? Like…Nocee police or something?" My lack of breathing apparatus is momentarily forgotten.

"Yes. Their traditional family forms are predators, making them natural choices for protective duty. They don't get along well outside of their work though. There's too much rivalry." He glances at me nervously. "I told you most of my people follow their families into their professions. Now you can see why. On duty, however, they're as ruthless as they are large, willing to enforce punishment for the smallest infractions."

"*Per*fect. You know, dealing with bullies was bad enough before they had hundreds of razor sharp teeth and a badge…sort of."

He ignores my comment, shaking his head as if to clear it. "Enough of them! *How are you breathing without your masciel?!?*"

"I asked you first!" I retort, my anxiety ratcheting up again.

We stare at each other for a moment, each waiting for other to say or do *something*. I'm waiting for him to explain what in the world could possibly be happening. He's probably waiting for my body to realize it isn't getting any oxygen. Neither of these things is happening. Finally another horrific thought occurs to me.

"Um, should we still be here? If those Sentries are doing a circuit, won't they circle back?"

Pete's eyes widen further – if possible – as he realizes the truth of what I'm asking. The next thing I know he's snatched up my masciel with one hand, grabbing my hand with his other, and we're flying back towards the relative safety of the kelp. I kick hard, not enjoying being dragged this time, wanting to get out of the open as badly as he does.

Even with the additional burden of having to tow me along, Pete is *fast*. We reach the clearing in no time at all. He releases my hand as soon as we're there, then starts doing the merman equivalent of pacing back and forth.

I settle down on a rock again, waiting for some revelation, trying to process my combination of terror, anxiety and…excitement. I mean seriously, breathing under water? How cool is that! Totally high on the freakazoid meter, but the most cool thing ever! Ever! While I revel in awe at my newfound ability, coupled with wonder at this amazing new world I've been immersed in to (quite literally), I wait for Pete to digest it all as well. I wait quite a while.

He's muttering to himself as he paces. "I just don't understand...she's not a Nocee...how can this *be*?...and she knew the Sentries were coming...it's simply *not possible*..."

Exasperated I finally speak up. "Um, hello? Sitting right here? I sure as heck don't get it either, and while I'm freaked out and amazed all at once about it, let me be the first to point out the obvious: apparently it *is* possible."

Startled, he looks at me as if he's forgotten the topic of his grumblings sits there in front of him. I fold my arms, raise my chin in defiance and glare at him. As the subject of this screwball situation, I'm *not* going to be ignored while he paces, trying to make sense of it all.

"Oh, yes of course, I'm sorry Doralis." His voice is shaking a little. "I guess I should be talking to you and not about you, huh?"

"Preferable for me."

"It's just...this is so unprecedented! I've *never* heard of a human being able to breathe without a masciel before and I have no idea what to do!"

His expression is anguished, mixed with a heavy helping of panic. It hurt to see him this way, so I go for the obvious question again. "Why do we need to *do* anything?"

He pulls up short. "Excuse me?"

I take a deep, unfiltered breath. "Well, I'm not really supposed to be here anyway. You didn't get a permit, or whatever, and I came in through an unmonitored portal, right?"

He flushes, a glittering shimmer on his skin traveling from his neck to his cheeks. It's really pretty. It takes effort not to get distracted by it.

"Well...yeah."

"So if I'm already not supposed to be here, what difference does it make if I need a masciel of not? I mean, okay yeah, it's totally insane, and I should be drowning right now. But I'm not. Amazingly, I'm just fine, breathing and talking with my friend the merman. I don't think it could get any stranger at the moment. So, do we need to figure it out this second?"

He ponders what I say, studying my face like I am purposefully leaving something out. I fidget under his scrutiny.

My miraculous ability to breathe without the mask makes me nervous, no question. It's an unknown factor. My whole summer defies the boundaries of weird, so I should be used to it by now, right? Unfortunately this masciel thing is making Pete wig out too, which is totally terrifying.

I always liked my scheduled life, avoiding drama and surprises, and look where I am now—in another world, literally, full of nothing but surprise and drama. I should be repelled. In reality, it physically hurt to imagine having to leave. I don't know how often, or if, I'll ever be able to come back. The thought brings with it the sensation of being stabbed in the chest, repeatedly. Suddenly my ability to breathe is questionable again too.

Then there's Pete—his inhumanly perfect face and chest combined with a strong muscular tail, and those silver eyes, almost glowing with warmth when he gazes at me. I blush, thinking about how those looks make me feel. Which would be harder, not being able to come back to Goroannocee…or not being able to see Pete again? My brain can't process it. They're too intertwined.

Pete's anxiety finally smoothes into something more calm and he gives me a small smile. "You're right. Worrying about something we can't do anything about, even if we needed to do something, is pointless. I should be treasuring my time with you, not wasting it."

Just what I've been thinking, if less eloquently.

Pete looks away from me, his skin shimmering in a blush again. "There's something I've been wanting to do, if it's okay with you. It's probably easier this way too." He won't look me in the eye while he's speaking.

"Um, o-kay," I hesitantly accede, not sure what I'm agreeing to.

When Pete looks up and into my eyes, the warmth, longing and intensity I see in them is overpowering. I gasp in shock, otherwise immobile. I know what's coming.

While anxious, I'm not panicky, like when Levi kissed me. Then, I wondered if I even wanted to kiss him. My body responded automatically, if mechanically, while my brain analyzed the situation remotely. Levi's a nice guy, he just doesn't do much for me.

This time is totally different.

Pete overwhelms me – his voice (of course), his knowledge of so many things (under water), his ignorance of others (charming), his beauty (including the tail), and most of all his friendship. All of my watery dreams lately, though the details remain fuzzy, are all about *him*. I *want* him to kiss me. More than that, *I* want to kiss *him*.

With his silver eyes still locked on mine, Pete slowly raises his hand to brush some stray strands of golden hair away from my face. Then he places his hand on my cheek, lightly caressing my face before curling a couple of fingers to cup my chin. His touch is so warm, so suddenly sensuous, it sends shockwaves through my whole body. Then he gently tilts my face up a little, bending his head to meet mine.

When our lips meet, I know *this* is what a kiss is supposed to feel like. His lips are warm satin, the heat of them shooting straight through me, electrifying my whole body. My emotions are a tsunami, wiping away any and all thoughts unrelated to the feeling of Pete's mouth on mine. My hands unconsciously reach for him, wrapping around his strong torso, pulling me closer to him. The water, so warm and natural, is almost a nuisance now. I want the heavier gravity of land to push us closer together.

The hand on my chin moves to the back of my head, where he twines his fingers through my hair, holding me gently, securely. His other arm comes into play too (finally) as he wraps it around my body, his hand at my waist. He's so smooth, so warm and soft, yet so very strong. Everywhere my skin touches his (a lot in a bikini), all I can feel is tight, corded muscle...and something between an electric shock and a burning fire blazes everywhere.

Our lips and bodies mold together perfectly. We float into the center of the clearing, lost in the bliss of discovering each other. I never want this first kiss to end.

Of course, end it does...eventually. Pete manages to pull himself away, his eyes locking on mine once more, a little breathless.

"Wow!"

My sentiments exactly.

What actually comes out of my mouth is something closer to a strangled "Mmm-hmm".

"We are meant to be. I *knew* it."

I can't disagree. I've never been so completely happy and content in my life.

We spend the remainder of the day exploring in and around the kelp forest, when we aren't exploring our newfound compatibility for kissing. He never fully releases me the entire time, always holding my hand or encircling my waist with his strong arms. It's heaven on earth...or, wherever.

Finally, it's time for me to leave. I can't put it off any longer. My parents are expecting me for Sunday dinner and game night. Bonding with my parents totally loses its lure when compared to spending time with Pete. I know I need to go though.

Pete escorts me back through the cave system, where we deposit my flippers and unnecessary masciel, never once letting go of me. He pulls me back to the portal, holding me close and kissing me all the way. So intent is my concentration on his lips, and the interesting things he's doing with them, it never occurs to me to notice that Pete doesn't bother resuming his fish form.

Finally I break the kiss, as much as I hate doing it.

"I have to go."

"I know," he says. "I just can't bear the thought of not seeing you again for a week." His eyes are intense as he pulls me in again, his mouth meeting mine before I can reply. His lips mold to mine, his tongue tracing, darting into my mouth, as my head practically explodes with pleasurable sensations.

Reluctantly breaking away again I gasp, "I've *really* got to go."

He looks so miserable I try to find some words to cheer him up. "Hey, it's like a long distance relationship, but better because we know how close the other is." I lay my hand on his cheek, resisting a strong impulse to stroke his smooth skin and pull myself back into his embrace. "I'll be thinking about you, every day."

He takes my hand from his cheek, bringing it around to kiss. "And I you, my beautiful Doralis. My love."

Stunned, I can't say a thing. Did Pete just tell me he loves me? What do I do? It could be a simple term of endearment, used all the time. I can't be sure. My feelings are an amped up jumble.

Fortunately he doesn't appear to notice my confusion, simply brushing my flowing locks away again, cupping my face in his large hands and kissing me tenderly, before giving me a boost out of the portal.

In the reality of crummy air, the dirt turning to mud on my wet feet, I still can't make my mouth form words. Instead I blow him a shaky kiss, which he mimes catching and holding to his heart. A moment later he's disappeared.

I trudge back to the house in a daze, eat my dinner mechanically, and lose at...whatever we played. I get ready for bed in the same hazy state.

Looking at myself in the bathroom mirror, I place my hand on my face where his fingers stroked my cheek, remembering the feel of his silky skin on mine. I flush and smile at the memory.

Getting into bed, I lay staring at the ceiling for what feels like hours.

Pete loves me?

I still don't know if what I feel for him is love. Overwhelmed by him? Yes, absolutely. Physically attracted? Well duh! Do I miss him when he isn't with me? Unquestionably. Does all this mean I love him, too? No idea.

I fall asleep, already dreaming of Pete.

14

The Gift

THE FOLLOWING WEEK absolutely drags by.

Monday morning finds me at the pool, as usual, trying to lose myself in the water. Unfortunately, what once felt so good now places a distant second compared to the water of Goroannocee. Everything is better there…with Pete.

So I go through the motions, mechanically socializing with the team at lunch, finishing the day and biking home.

Kari Ann, as observant as ever, is the first to notice a change in my behavior. On Monday she looks puzzled by my zombie impression. On Tuesday her eyes narrow in speculation. By Wednesday she's wearing this determined, don't-mess-with-me look.

I know I'm going to hear about it when at lunchtime she shoos the boys off, proclaiming today for girls only – excluding Crystal of course.

We arrive at a new café, less chance of seeing the others, where she steers me to a private little table in the corner. After pushing me into a chair, she places her hands on her hips, leaning forward and piercing me with her glare. The Spanish Inquisition starts before she bothers to sit.

"Okay, spit it out. Who is he?"

Uh oh! What do I say!? My mind flails. "I…I don't know what you mean." I stammer, unconvincingly.

She shifts, folding her arms over her chest, her posture radiating just how much she isn't buying it. Her crystal blue eyes blaze.

"Look, you're my friend. In fact you're the best friend I've got here in Grizzly Adams country. We may not have known each other very long, but I know you, and I *know* something's up. Levi's been flirting with you non-stop, and you aren't even giving him a second look. Despite the immaturity, the guy's definitely high up on the hottie charts. *That* means there's another guy. So *spill!*"

My mind is a tangle of conflicting thoughts.

First, I have a best friend? I can't remember the last time someone referred to me that way. Cute, smart, confident Kari Ann thinks of me her best friend? Wow. It feels really good.

Second, Levi's been flirting with me? All I've been aware of is his usual goofy behavior. He jokes, grabs and pushes me around, making all sorts of teasing remarks. There are no deep emotions attached. I can tell. He's being a buddy. If that's flirting, then I'm totally clueless. What's new there?

Kari Ann is waiting for me to say something…impatiently. Her toe's tapping out a beat to be envied by most professional drummers. Bringing me to the third item spinning through my brain. What can I say about *Pete*?

"Ummmm, yeah…okay. I did sort of meet a guy here."

"I KNEW IT!" She squeals, simultaneously jumping and clapping.

"SHHHHH!!!" I beg her, watching for the waitress.

Kari Ann finally takes her seat, still bouncing in elation. Mid bounce she leans towards me over the table conspiratorially, since it looks like I'm going to cooperate. "So dish! Where did you meet him? What's he like?"

Okay Lee, you can do this. Stick to the truth…just not all of it.

"I met him at a park near our rental house. I was bored and he was…in the neighborhood. We just…started talking." Man, I really get why Pete sounds so cryptic all the time. This is hard!

"When did this happen? Last weekend?"

"Um, no. Sort of the first week I got here."

"WHAT?!? You've been seeing this guy for a *month* and you didn't *tell* me!!!"

"No! It's not like that at all!" I jump in, trying to shush her again while figuring out how to explain myself. The other patrons don't appear t be paying any attention to us, but I'm still not in the mood to broadcast my tenuous love life.

"We've just been talking, and only on the weekends because he has to...work, during the week. I only just started...seeing him, I guess, this last weekend." My face is beet red, remembering Pete's kiss.

Ever alert, Kari Ann notices, firing at the bulls-eye. "So did he kiss you?"

I think my head might pop with all the blood rushing into it right now. I can't even choke out a response, so I try to hide my steaming face in my ice water. A tiny smile breaks through as I remember though.

"He DID! Woohoo! You *go* girl!" She performs some crazy hand gesture, her head bobbling.

"What is that? East-coast-pixie-ghetto?"

She ignores my sarcastic diversionary tactics. Before she can launch all of her questions, the waitress (bless her grouchy little heart) shows up to take our order. I use the break to finish downing the entire glass of ice water, attempting to cool my face from the inside out.

"So is he cute?" Break over. "What does he look like?"

This could be problematic. I take a deep breath, needing to wing this one a little.

"Well, he has black hair (*with silver streaks*), silver grey eyes (*minus the grey*), and he's taller than me (*in two out of three forms*)." What else can I say?

"Good body?" She smiles slyly at me.

"Um...yeah," I stammer, not able to look her in the eye. Talk about a major understatement. The expression "a great piece of tail" comes to mind as well.

"Oooooo! Nice! So when did he kiss you?"

"S-Sunday."

"Aha! No wonder you never answer any of my calls on the weekends. You've got Mr. Mysterious Hottie on the side!"

My blush ramps up again, darn it. Hottie, absolutely. Mysterious, she has no idea.

"Don't worry," she continues, "I don't mind. I know what it's like to want to spend all of your time with someone." She sighs, diverted by thoughts of her boyfriend.

I jump on my opportunity to get the subject off of me.

"So is Ted coming to visit? I thought you said something about it last week."

"Yes! He's coming at the beginning of August! For a *whole week*!"

Mission accomplished. She spends the rest of lunch telling me about when exactly Ted is coming, and all the things they plan on doing while he's here. I smile and make appropriate noises when necessary. Otherwise, I'm free to relax.

Back at practice, I study Levi's antics with the new awareness provided by Kari Ann. I must admit, there's probably something to what she said. Yet, I still don't feel any strong emotions coming from him, which is confusing. Why would he be pursuing me otherwise? At least it makes rejecting his advances a lot easier. I don't know what I'd do if I thought he was genuinely in to me.

Kari Ann takes it upon herself to be my own personal guardian angel, bless her heart, deflecting most of Levi's more aggressive tactics. She handles each situation with him way better than I know how to.

As we're leaving Friday evening, Levi makes one last attempt to corner me. Fortunately Kari Ann is exiting the locker room at the same time, and she stubbornly refuses to leave my side, despite the dirty looks from my wannabe date.

"Yeah, so uh, LEE, you want to catch a movie with me again on Saturday? You know, since we had such a great time before." He leers at me, throwing in an obvious wink.

O.M.E. as in Eee-ew! I actually feel sort of sick at the thought of him trying to kiss me again. His exaggerated confidence is getting annoying too. Nothing can compare to Pete, not for me, especially not an overbearing boy from Minnesota.

Before I can figure out a way to tactfully respond, despite Levi's total lack of tact, Kari Ann jumps to my rescue.

"What a great idea! Lee and I were just talking about what to do this weekend, right Lee?" She turns to look at me expectantly, bringing me into her little white lie.

"Um, yeah. Right."

"I think a movie night sounds fabulous! Ted told me about a great one he saw the other day. Daniel said his girlfriend recommended it too." She adds, almost as an afterthought. "And I'm sure Bryan will want to come, don't you think? He is your roommate after all." Flashing Levi a perky smile, she's the picture of friendly innocence.

Levi looks like he's developed a really bad taste in his mouth.

"Yeah, right. Bryan and Daniel should be available." He shoots Kari Ann a loaded look, not going down without scoring a point of his own. "I think I'll invite Crystal too."

Ouch. Touché.

Kari Ann doesn't flinch. It's amazing. "Great. I guess we'll see you tomorrow night. Late show."

"Yeah, right. See you then." Baring his teeth at us in a parody of a smile, Levi stalks off.

Still smiling cheerfully, Kari Ann turns back to me. Her smile falters. "I hope I didn't mess up any plans with your guy."

The concern in her eyes erases any dismay I feel about having my day with Pete cut short. Okay, the late show isn't exactly cutting it very short. It's still short*er*... a little. Anyway, my new best friend looks like she really needs an evening out. I'm feeling a glimmer of what she must be going through, being away from her boyfriend. Spending a little time with her is the least I can do for all of the moral support she's been giving me.

"It's no problem, really. I'd probably be home anyway." While obviously relieved by my reassurance, she looks at me curiously. I hurry to fabricate a plausible explanation. "He has a really early curfew." It could be true. "But he's an early riser like me, so it works okay."

"Great!" Her honest enthusiasm is back. "I totally want to hear more about him tomorrow. How about I pick you up?"

Her offer carries a double bonus. I won't need to ask my parents for a ride *or* be grilled by them. Trying to explain how this time it really *is* a group outing sits about as high on my priority list as getting athlete's foot.

"I'd love it!" Grabbing some scratch paper and a pencil from the front desk, I jot down my address for her. Remembering she has a pretty basic cell phone, I ask, "Do you have a computer you can use to get directions?" My computer rests comfortably on my desk at home.

"Oh yeah," she replies nonchalantly. "My parents made sure my room's totally stocked so I won't get bored being by myself. I can pull up pretty much any movie or game I want. It's really not the same as spending time with friends." She glances away, suddenly awkward. "Thanks."

"For what?"

"For letting me work myself into your weekend. I'm sure you'd rather be with your guy…whatever his name is." She won't look at me, feigning interest in the random postings as we pass the community board instead.

While she's right about my wanting to be with Pete, it doesn't make it okay for me to blow her off all the time either. Which, outside of our lunches, is exactly what I've been doing. Unintentional or not, I feel bad about it. Really bad. I always missed having a best friend, or even close friends, and here I am totally ignoring the one who's been handed to me on a silver platter…even if it's only for the summer.

I am a complete schmuck! I mentally kick myself.

"His name's Pete, which doesn't really matter right now." I take a deep, steadying breath. "I really should apologize to you. I haven't been a very good friend, while you've gone out of your way to back me up and be *my* friend. You shouldn't need to work yourself into my weekend. So I'm sorry." I give her a guilt filled smile. "I promise to try and not let it happen again."

Kari Ann hardly misses a beat, comically throwing one hand on her hip while shaking her finger at me with the other, frowning and doing a good impression of last year's cranky third period math teacher. "Just see that you don't, young lady!" Which is as far as she gets before the grumpy façade dissolves into a fit of the giggles.

The next thing I know she's managed to pull me down for a hug, freakishly strong for such an itty-bitty little thing.

"No worries, Lee. I know how it is. I got your back."

I hug her back, so grateful my total clueless-ness hadn't affected our budding friendship. "Thanks Kar. Back at ya!"

She releases me, a devious sparkle back in her eyes. "Speaking of having each other's backs, it looks like Miss

Funshine will be joining us for the movie tomorrow. Put on your thinking cap and let's see if we can come up with some good stuff for our dethroned Queen B." Kari Ann had picked up on my unintentional nickname for Crystal before the end of our first day. Instructions given, she heads for her car, waving goodbye with a last, "See you about eight!"

I wave back before turning to wrestle with my bike lock. My ride back to the house uneventful, I wonder if Pete will be in his puddle tonight?

I'm almost to the park, resolved to stop and (hopefully) see Pete, when a honking horn startles me so much I narrowly avoid swerving into traffic. As it is, I wobble all over the place until I can regain my sense of balance enough to stop.

Before I can turn and glare at the stupid driver, a perky voice makes me rethink the idea.

"Hi, Lee honey! Sorry if I scared you, love!"

"No problem, Mom," probably the last person I can get away with flipping attitude. She's been there, done that, and ran out of patience for such things years ago.

"I just wanted to let you know we're all going out to dinner tonight. You'd better hurry back to the house so you can change sweetie."

I'm not about to be fooled by her sugary smile, as she waves and precedes me home. This is not an optional invitation. *Ugh!* I push off, pedaling after her. This can mean only one thing, a work-related dinner.

Not only am I *not* going to get the chance to see Pete tonight, I get to smile and play perfect daughter for my parent's colleagues. Oh joy.

I make it home with barely enough time to change into the outfit my mom picked for me. How thoughtful of her.

The evening is pretty uneventful, the only positive thing about it, besides my medium rare steak (super yum!), is the time kill factor. By the time we make it home, I can legitimately get ready for bed without anyone checking my temperature.

I drift off quickly.

***

I wake up Saturday morning at the usual time, my body's internal clock working fine, instantly alert. As soon as my brain realizes I'm waking up, my body is out of bed and pulling

on my bikini with lightning speed, only one thought in my head now.

Pete.

Grabbing my towel, I rush out of the house like it's on fire.

Once I make it to the park, I slow down enough to stow/toss my towel, close to the portal, yet where it won't be seen from the road. Then I jump in, feet first, without bothering to check if Pete made it there before me again.

I get my answer as warm, strong arms encircle me before my downward momentum even slows. He spins us around, moving down the passageway with me still locked in his arms, his lips meeting mine in welcome. My blood boils from his scorching kiss, to the point where I imagine the water around us bubbling.

Pete finally releases me when we reach the cave bubble, allowing me to put on my still needed flippers. I finish wriggling my feet through the tight holes, when Pete hesitantly holds out my masciel towards me as well.

"Please?"

"Why?" I wonder out loud. "I don't need it to breathe."

"Yes, I'm aware. However, since every other human in Goroannocee can't breathe without theirs, it's probably a good idea for you to wear yours. Unless, of course, you'd like to be forcibly removed by the Sentries? I don't recommend it though." Even through the joke, I can read the seriousness of the issue by the tension around his eyes.

""Um, yeah. Let's avoid them." As I reach to take my masciel from his hand, securing it by tucking the gauzy material through the side of my bikini bottom, something else occurs to me. "Why aren't you a fish? I thought you aren't suppose to be in...in your natural form when you're out of your territory."

He has the decency to blush, since he's totally busted. "Well, I figure I'm already breaking so many rules by bringing you here, one more isn't going to matter. Also...once I kissed you..." He trails off, radiating embarrassment. "...well, I just didn't want to waste any of the little bit of time we get as...um, in fish form."

My blush matches his. Surprising myself more than him, I lean forward to show him how very happy I am about his admission, using only my lips.

We don't explore much, too busy enjoying being together. Many girls I know experience their first boyfriends by the sixth or seventh grade. I have a lot of making up to do. And by staying in or near the kelp forest, I don't need to worry about wearing my masciel. Knowing I don't need it, the thing is kind of a nuisance.

A perceptible shift in the light (with no sun?) makes me glance at my watch, and realize I'll need to be leaving soon. Pete notices my small distraction, echoing my regretful sigh.

"You want to go?"

"Want to, no. Need to, yes." I sigh dramatically. "It's team movie night tonight, and I promised I'd go." A flash of pain crosses his expression and I belatedly remember what happened the last time. "No! It's not what you think, really! Okay, Levi *tried* to ask me out alone. Then Kari Ann stepped right in and saved me. Before he knew what hit him, Levi's organizing movie night for the whole team, and *not* happy about it." I smile at the memory. "Kari Ann was awesome!"

Pete's mollified. His genuine smile makes me feel all rubbery.

Then I remember how all of this came up. "Unfortunately it means I do have to go soon, so I can get changed before Kari Ann picks me up."

"I understand, even if I am insanely jealous of your friend."

My jaw drops, my face a comedic mix of shock and amazement. "You're jealous…of *Kari Ann*?"

Pete chuckles, "Not in *that* way!" wrapping his warm arms around me and pulling me closer. "It's the *time* she gets to spend with you. It doesn't seem fair she gets you all week, and now this evening too."

I look away, feeling caught between a rock and a hard place. "Yeah, I know. It's just…I don't have a lot of friends, let alone close friends. I told you. And Kari Ann's friendship, it's like the most amazing gift, and…and I've sort of been neglecting her."

I feel my face sliding towards a mopey frown, so I angle my body to face away. He doesn't need to see me pouting.

Pete places his fingers under my chin, pulling my face back towards him. "Oh, my Doralis," I shiver, not at all cold, "I'm so sorry. I don't ever want to make you feel bad. Of *course* you should spend some time with your friend. I know we've spent all day together, I just miss you so much when you're gone."

Then he tilts my chin up, so he can more easily lean over, giving me the most tender of kisses. I wrap my arms around his neck and let myself get lost in it.

Soon enough, though, I really do need to go. Despite my feelings of loyalty towards Kari Ann, it's highly tempting to ditch her while I'm kissing Pete. He, however, is nice enough to bring it up before I do.

"Come," he takes my hand, pulling me towards the

mouth of the cave, "I know it's time for you to go, however I'd like to give you something first."

Give me something? What more can he give me? He's already given me a whole other world for crying out loud!

When we reach the air chamber, I stash my flippers and the useless masciel while he disappears briefly to retrieve my present.

Before I can get impatient, he's back. Holding out his hand to me, he's palming a shell. Not just any shell, either. This variety of clam lives deep in the ocean, its shell not something commonly seen or collected. Also, this particular shell is something more. The lacquered look, the softness yet resilience of the frilly deep pink clam, still inside yet unchanging, and of course the undeniable beauty of the piece. All of this tells me it's another of Pete's older sister's creations.

"Oh Pete! It's beautiful!" I exclaim, reaching for the precious container, eager to take a closer look.

"No, I mean…yes," he stammers nervously, "the shell is for you too. Your present is actually *inside*."

"Oh! There's more?" Holding the beautiful object now, I can't figure out how to open it. "A little help here?"

He laughs uncertainly. "Allow me."

Taking the shell and placing it flat on his hand, with one finger he gently strokes the petal pink ribbons once…twice…and on the third stroke, the top of the clam suddenly pops open, coming completely off the bottom layer with no hinge to keep it secured. While pretty amazing, it's what's inside the shell that takes my breath away.

There, nestled in the soft pink cushioning of the interior of the clam, is one of the prettiest bracelets I've ever seen.

Six large beads, made of some type of rough, uncut opaque white stone, are separated by large, flawless white pearls. Additionally, a second beaded string of tiny seed pearls and sparkling cut crystals, hangs down between each of the larger stones.

"I...I don't know what to say!" I gasp, totally overwhelmed by Pete's gift.

"Just say you'll wear it." He's flushing, his face luminous, enjoying my obvious pleasure.

"Of course!"

I lift the beautiful piece off of its velvety cushion, preparing to slip it over my hand and onto my wrist. It's a little big. I'll need to be careful not to let it slip off.

Pete reaches out a hand to stop me, chuckling again. "Actually Doralis, it's an anklet."

"Oh...*Oh*!" is all I can say, more than a little alarmed. How the heck am I supposed to get it on over my feet, which are gi-normous even without the flippers? I desperately looked for a clasp, coming up empty.

"Again, allow me," Pete comes to my rescue once more. He turns each stone a couple of times and the anklet magically falls apart in one place. "Is there a particular ankle preference?" he asks, placing the anklet around the limb I gesture to, somehow reconnecting it.

I lift my leg, pointing my toe and enjoying the sparkling beauty now residing near my foot. It fits my ankle like it's been made for me, seamlessly perfect once again.

"It's just so...beautiful!"

"I'd say a quality understatement," murmurs Pete.

Tearing my eyes away from my present, I see him eyeing my leg, not his gift.

"Ha, ha," Hastily I lower my leg, my heart stuttering.

"I'm so glad you like it." Putting his hands on my waist, he pulls me off of the shelf and into his arms with ease.

"I'd say a quality understatement," I parrot, then cut

off his reply with an enthusiastic kiss, determined to show him how seriously happy I really am.

***

By the time I get back to the house, there's only about a half an hour before Kari Ann is scheduled to come get me. No time and no real need to shower, I settle for fluffing my hair a bit with the dryer, putting on some clean shorts and a maroon tee shirt. Slipping on my ballet flats, I grab a light jacket and the purse with the lip-gloss, ready to go. Just in time, too. The doorbell rings as I make my way down the stairs.

"I found you!" Kari Ann exclaims as I open the door. She looks super cute in her miniskirt and jean jacket, and as perky as ever. "There's this GPS map system thingy in the car, which I never use, not even sure if it'd work this far north, and I found you on the first try! I'm so super glad I left early 'cause it still took longer than I thought to get here, and I'd really hate to be late to the theater. Whew!"

My sentiments exactly, I smile at her. When she's on a roll, she can talk *really* fast.

I'm turning to lock the door behind me (my parents out, of course) when Kari Ann's cry of "Whoa-ho-ho! Where the heck did you get *that*!" startles me so much I almost drop my keys. She's looking at my ankle, at my new…accessory.

"Oh, yeah, it's pretty huh?" I *love* my gift. It doesn't necessarily mean that I know what to tell others about it, though.

Too quick Kari Ann guesses.

"You got it from the mystery guy, didn't you?" she squeals. My hot red face almost matches my maroon shirt, plenty confirmation for her. "Nice! Looks like you landed one heck of a boyfriend! I can't wait to see Levi's face when he gets an eyeful of your new bling. And Crystal! Ha! She's going to implode with jealousy!"

Before I can respond, do much more than gulp really, she's heading for her black coupe. I hurry after, grateful for a friend who happens to be both sixteen and owns a form of transportation. I cautiously get into the passenger seat, expecting the third degree, relieved when she spares me. My relief is short lived.

We arrive at the theater in plenty of time, still the last ones there. The rest of the team is standing in a loose circle by the entrance, waiting for us, tickets already in hand.

We've barely crossed the street from the parking lot when Kari Ann pipes up "Hey guys! Check out Lee's new jewelry!" pointing at my ankle. At this point I'm seriously rethinking the shorts. My jeans cover my ankle.

Bryan and Daniel make appropriate noises of appreciation...appropriate for teen guys who couldn't care less.

Levi is the one who finally breaks down and asks the million-dollar question. "So where'd you get the new anklet Lee?"

I open my mouth to answer when Kari Ann beats me to the punch once again. "It's from her new *boyfriend*," she gushes. "He's really got great taste. Don't *you* think so Levi?" she continues.

Shut up already! I'm screaming in my mind. Outwardly I only stare at her as if she's sprouted another face.

She silently mouths *Trust me* before turning her attention back to Levi. "And really very thoughtful too. I can't imagine how a local guy could get something so pretty around here. Ordered it special from the net, I'd guess. Some serious *like*, if you know what I mean."

I don't know what she means, or maybe I just block the implication out. Levi seems to get it. I watch as he pauses thoughtfully before visibly pulling himself together with a shrug.

"Can't win 'em all," he simply states, turning to walk into the theater, followed closely by the other guys and Crystal, whose narrowed eyes are full of suspicion and pure venom.

Lovely.

I put my hands on my hips and look at Kari Ann.

She just holds up her hand, palm out, stopping my still forming tirade in my throat. "Just *trust* me. This will work out better than you know!"

I'm not so sure, withholding my planned chew-out for the time being. As it turns out, I never needed it. Once again, Kari Ann does a HUGE favor for her unwitting friend.

The evening turns out to be really fun. All the guys joking with us gals, and Levi treats me like nothing more than a good buddy again. The subject of my anklet and new boyfriend is totally dropped. The only one who seems irritated and preoccupied is Crystal. Not exactly a new thing for her.

We go out to eat after the show at the same place Levi and I tried before. I actually get to appreciate the diner's artistic flare and funky menu this time. It's the best night ever.

"Thank you Kari Ann." I put as much sincerity as I can into my voice. The evening is over and I'm leaning back through her car door before heading inside the rental.

"No problem, sweetie! I told you I got your back!" Trying to sound offhand, her eyes sparkle with pleasure. "Have a *great* weekend, Lee. See you on Monday!" she calls, driving out of the cul-de-sac.

I get ready for bed, wondering what I did to deserve such a perfect day. The whole day with Pete, his wonderful gift (besides his kisses) and the fun evening with my team, it's just…perfect!

Life can't get much better than this I think, as I quickly drift into sleep.

15

Mesclave

THE NEXT FEW weeks are a blur. I can't remember ever having been so happy in my entire life.

The weekends, which now include Friday nights, I spend with Pete. It's pure bliss. He's so knowledgeable about so many things, yet so totally oblivious to others. He can tell me about almost everything located in the water, freshwater or saltwater.

Then, like the mosquitoes, he's clueless about really random human stuff. He thinks shoelaces are for tying the shoes together, and a mohawk is some kind of flightless, grass eating bird. It's endearing, really, while also making me wonder what the heck they're teaching their people about humans in the Nocee school. Because, according to Pete, there really is a school for Nocee kids, where they learn about human culture…among other things. It kind of reminds me of my dad, too, how he gets American expressions not quite right, a habit I love so much.

The only disruptions to our days together are random appearances by Sentries on patrol. Their surprise pop-ups, while still terrifying in the extreme, expose another gift of mine, beyond the whole breathing under water thing. I can tell where things are under water – especially if they're moving, and from a much greater distance than anything Pete knew to be possible. I've always known where others were in the water around me. Who knew it meant something special?

We'd be touring the anemone fields, or the crop lands where they grow the edible underwater plants, or kissing near the kelp forest (blush), and I'd feel the water vibrate. The more it happens, the more accurate I get in being able to tell how many…creatures are coming, and from what direction. We always manage to hide before anything comes into sight, although there are a couple of close calls. Every time my heart hammers so wildly I'm sure it'll give us away, and my head pounds with pressure, my vision going dark. The next thing I know Pete's embracing me, kissing his reassurance they've passed, at which point nothing else matters.

My weekdays are spent with my teammates – now friends, with only one notable exception – and are almost as enjoyable as my weekends. As fun as anything can be without Pete anyway. We banter back and forth, hanging out in between workouts. I've never experienced this level of acceptance and camaraderie. I like it.

Coach Tim does his best to make each week more challenging, increasing our strength, speed and stamina. Despite the coach's best efforts, I'm still never as tired as I am after some of my days with Pete, who's stronger *and* faster than me. Talk about challenging!

Kari Ann is my best friend, more than ever now. Such a solid friendship is new to me, and so unbelievably welcome.

Thankfully, it looks like Levi's graciously decided to back off for good. He and Bryan are just good buddies to me now, no hurt feelings to be found. Everyone has to watch for sneak attacks though, unexpectedly landing one of us in the pool. Their adolescent sense of humor doesn't relent in the least.

The only person finding a problem with me these days is the only person who's *ever* had a problem with me here – Crystal.

One day before lunch she corners me in the locker room. Kari Ann's already left, needing to talk to Daniel about something, so I'm by myself.

"Who is he?" she demands, in her usual entitled acerbic way.

When Kari Ann asked me the same question, I didn't know what to say. I can't lie to *her*. Crystal, however, is a different story. Like I'm going to tell her anything, even if she asked nicely, which she definitely did *not*. I play dumb instead.

"What are you talking about?"

"You know very well what I'm talking about. Your new *boyfriend*." She says the word like she's trying to spit something nasty out of her mouth.

"Yeah, what about him?" I'm still not cooperating, long past the point where Crystal can intimidate me. Kari Ann's been a great influence.

"Who...Is...He?" she spits again, with as much venom and self-righteous assertion as she can muster. "He *can't* be local or I'd know him. I also know every guy worth having who's here for the summer. This is *my* town. So spit it out!"

"No," I answer simply, blithely smiling at her. "According to you, he must not be worth having, so I fail to see how it's any of your business." I smile again as I start to walk past.

She steps in front of me, firing daggers with her obsidian glare, blocking my way. Okay, no matter how much shorter than me she is, *that* is sort of intimidating.

"You listen to me, *girlie*," she starts, using the ugliest, nastiest tone I've heard from her yet. "*No one* gets away with humiliating me! In the pool, or otherwise! I *will* find out who he is."

"Ooooookay then," I reply, gingerly stepping around her. I briefly contemplate saying something witty like, *get a hobby Crystal*, but can't quite find the mojo to do it. I opt instead for the more cowardly. "Yeah, well, I gotta go." Not my most brilliant response. Edging past her, I practically sprint for the door.

Other than the one little altercation, life seems pretty close to perfect. I should have known it was too good to be true.

***

It's Sunday morning. Pete's given me his welcoming kiss, or twenty. While I could spend all of my time kissing Pete, he's careful to keep our romantic time limited. Short, but oh so sweet. I'm not sure why, or whose virtue he's trying to protect, but considering my hormones seem to make my brain take a hike every time his soft lips caress any part of me, I'm generally grateful…after my brain comes back on line anyway.

We're deciding on what to do today, the usual start to our mornings. What may be a boring pattern to anyone else is exhilarating when it involves spending time with Pete in Goroannocee.

Stopped in our usual private clearing, Pete looks a little nervous for some reason, his muscles twitching randomly. I never get enough of looking at his muscles, as perfect as they are, however this time they convey his discomfort.

"I want to show you where I live today." He looks at me from the corner of his eye, almost shyly.

"Really?" I'm so excited! I'm not exactly supposed to be here, which loosely translated meant I'd never get to meet any of his family. Or so I thought until today. I'm thrilled he likes me enough to take me, the idea warming me to my core.

These thoughts are cut short by his next words.

"Yeah. My family is at the Capital today, at an event where they sell some of their work. I don't create anything to sell yet, so I didn't need to go. My home is empty, and I know you've been dying to see it."

I smile at him, despite the slash of disappointment working its way through me. "I can't argue your reasoning, though I'm sort of bummed. I hoped to at least meet Kelpsie," I teasingly refer to his athletic younger sister, who makes his face light up when he talks about her.

"Sorry," he says, really meaning it. "But…we just can't."

"I know." I touch his cheek tenderly, making him look at me so he can see I really don't mind. "It's okay. Anything's okay…as long as I'm with you."

He smiles back, relieved. He's so beautiful, the situation so unreal. He still catches me off guard when he looks at me like he is now, his eyes smoldering with unspoken emotions, making my breath catch in my throat and removing my ability to respond.

"My sentiments exactly." Grabbing my hand, he kisses the back of it before powerfully kicking off with his tail. "Let's go!" he cries, towing me along behind him.

Once out of the kelp forest, we pause a moment, letting me get a feel of the area with my crazy acute senses to make sure we're alone. Once I confirm the all-clear, we head straight out, passing over a reef barrier and through a wild expanse of mixed coral, kelp, and a multitude of undersea life. After crossing over a second reef barrier, we're presented with a large section of what I now recognize to be Nocee cropland.

Staying low, we weave through the different aquatic plants. Some are saltwater varieties, others prefer freshwater, most don't exist at all in the human world…that I'm aware of anyway. The fact they all grow together, at the same time in the same crop field, doesn't strike Pete as odd at all. It's just one more item defying the laws of nature as I know them. No big deal.

Soon enough we're through the field and approaching a massive coral and rock formation. As we draw closer I notice some of the holes are bigger than others. They almost look like doors or windows, although there's nothing symmetrical about them, nothing like the rectangular openings I'm used to. I also notice the area surrounding the large formation is very pretty, in a more organized way than I've yet seen. Like underwater landscaping.

As Pete keeps leading me forward, understanding finally dawns on me. This is it...this is his home.

Not wanting to stay out in the open, he immediately pulls me off to the side and through one of the smaller openings. If I want another look at the outside, I'll need to get it as we leave.

"Here we are. This is where I live." His hand sweeps out in an arc, gesturing to the room in front of us.

I blink, taking in the space around me. It isn't what I expected. If an underwater garden could look modern, this would be it.

There is a sofa/chair-like set made of rock and almost completely covered with a blanket of fluffy jewel anemones. Nowhere are anemones so perfectly spaced, however. Not to mention, an experimental caress finds these emulations of the real living creatures are the perfect balance between firm and squishy soft, and they don't sting or grab.

Scattered around the room are tiers of tall, skinny cone coral with horizontal sections of round, tightly lacy gorgonian coral providing flat table space. Again, while incorporating extraordinarily realistic looking elements, they're far too perfect and round to pass for the real thing. Very cool though.

The floor looks like sand, shaped into wave patterns by the ocean's natural currents. It's solid, not loose, when I touch it experimentally. I wryly think it looks like major tripping hazard, if anyone actually walked on it.

The walls are the same stone looking substance as the outside of the building, though these are polished smooth. More like gleaming marble with streaks of white, silver and blue, than raw stone.

Finally my gaze lifts up towards the ceiling, coated completely with a mosaic pattern of pebbles. Some are lit up while others create shadows, the colors and design almost overwhelming my newly acute senses.

It's breathtaking, all of it…and sort of *smaller* than I expected.

"You don't all live in this one room, do you?" A dumb question, I'm sure.

"No, of course not!" he laughs. I deserve it, blushing anyway. "This is my room. We are in the family wing of the building."

"Building?" I'm confused again.

"Yes. Nocee building artisans, one of which included my grandfather, created this structure many years ago. As a rule, we try to emulate natural formations as much as possible, which is why being an artisan is such a highly sought after skill. It takes a lot of talent to make a purely functional item look completely of nature…and still work."

"No kidding." Drifting through the not-nature, I try to take it all in. Glancing over, Pete's expression is curiously wistful. My heart aches for him without knowing what for. "You must be very proud of your family's accomplishments."

"I am." I can hear the honesty in his reply, and maybe a trace of bitterness?

"Oh, right. What they do isn't exactly your bag." I think back over all of the amazing things he's shown me in the past several weeks. It's a long list, "But the memory stones, and light stones. Those are incredible! Why can't you to create those instead?"

He runs his fingers through his black hair, trying to

decide how to reply. "Because, other than the light stones, you can't *see* what my stuff does. Even though my gifts are rare, and very necessary to our way of life, they don't *legally* exist unless I receive testing and training. My family produces tangible wares, to see and be touched, using gifts almost as rare as mine. Why upset a family with proven gifts and status on the long shot one of them could pass the public test. Not happening." He shrugs, feigning indifference. I know better. "It's just the way things are here."

Reaching over I take his big hand in mine, giving it a squeeze. "Well, where *I* come from, what you can do is....well, *no one* can do what you can do! It's beyond special!" I add in a whisper, "...just like you."

He smiles, huge amounts of gratitude in his eyes, filling me with warmth. Cupping his free hand on the side of my face, his fingers thread their way through my floating hair to wrap around toward the back of my head. Gently pulling my head forward, my mush-muscled body unresisting while my heart staggers, he bends to kiss me.

"*PETOILE!* What de l'eau is going on here!"

The incensed voice comes from an open entryway to the rest of the...building.

I jerk my head out of Pete's gentle grip, completely startled, my hand flying to my face to check my masciel, which I'd fortunately remembered to put on. Kissing through the sheer material is strange, but we'd decided that no kelp forest cover meant no bare face for me. My respite of relief is short lived, and I'm torn between the terror of being caught—in a compromising position, no less—and the excitement of meeting a member of Pete's family. Fear wins once I take in the thunderous expression on the Nocee girl's face.

Pete darts in front of me, one hand held up in placation while not releasing me with his other hand, for which I'm really grateful. I grip his hand like it's a lifeline, as if letting go may mean the end of everything.

"Tura, let me explain..."

Tura? This must be the older sister he told me about, Turamiel. At least she shouldn't rat us out...will she?

"Explain? Explain! You're darn right you're going to explain, little brother! What kind of mess did you get yourself...and the rest of this family, into this time?"

Floating herself all the way into the room, hands on her hips, her wrath is willing to accept nothing less than full disclosure.

Despite the furious French and English jetting out of her mouth, I'm completely distracted by the jaw-dropping visage of the first Nocee girl I've ever seen. She's stunning! Just as beautiful as Pete, though in an obviously more feminine way, her coloring is wildly different. Pete's dominant colors are black and silver. While Turamiel's long flowing hair is the same sable shade as Pete's, there the resemblance ends. Her eyes are dark brown with flakes of gold visible from across the room, and not just the sparks flying from them. Her peachy pink skin is closer to the color of bright citrus than human skin, and under her perfectly straight nose are full and perfect lips, a darker shade of sunset coral. Her tail, the same espresso as her eyes, is patterned with shots of black, gold and swirls of apricot. Unlike Pete as well, she's wearing the most gorgeous and intricately beaded bikini–like top, covering her breasts. So much for the whole topless mermaid thing.

I'd probably blurt out something stupid about how pretty she is, if not for the whole obviously ticked off thing. Anger radiates from her in waves of fury...and fear. Me, of course, being the primary cause of all this drama, I'm surprised at how her glare barely flickers at me before netting her brother.

"*Well?*" It doesn't look like patience is one of her

virtues, something we have in common.

"Okay, okay! Calm down!" His sister's eyes blaze. Apparently she doesn't appreciate being told how to feel either. "Tura, this is Doralis. Doralis, this is my older sister Turamiel." She isn't mollified.

"I don't give a *tack* what her name is! *Whose* is she?"

Huh? Am I hearing right? What does she mean, whose?

"Mine! I mean...she's no one's, she's just here with me!"

Pete flounders, trying to sound defiant and really sucking at it.

"Ex*cuse* me?" Tura's flashing eyes narrow as she leans towards her brother, hands curling, nails wickedly long, as if she's going to take a swipe at him.

Backed into the proverbial corner, Pete quickly relents. "Well, I sort of...found a portal."

As Tura's eyes widen in shock, I can almost physically feel her fear. *What's the big deal? I thought they used lots of portals?*

Pete hurriedly continues. "Technically it's past the boundary, and only a window when I found it. I didn't think it needed to be reported. It looks out on a park with hardly any humans. I just went there once in a while to see the sky. Then...Doralis came."

Addressing me tenderly, my eyes lock with his and I can't help turning to mush inside. I should probably be wigging out, terrified of Pete's sister tossing me to the Sentries, but I'm not. Turamiel doesn't miss the look he gives me either, her eyes narrowing again, in speculation this time.

"At first we just talked," he continues. "Then...well, I wanted to be with her." He forces his gaze back to his sister, eyes sparkling with excitement. "You won't believe what we've discovered Tura! What she can do...!"

Cutting him off with a sweeping gesture of her tail, she stabs a finger towards my ankle. "So you gave her a *Mesclave* bracelet? What were you *thinking*? What am I saying, you're obviously *not* thinking! You don't have a *permit*! You don't even have a proper *wife* yet!"

"Maybe I *don't want* a 'proper' wife." Pete's deep voice sounds dangerously angry now, sending a shiver of fear running along my spine. He pulls himself together with visible effort. "Anyway, Lee is not my Mesclave. She's not staying."

"What?!" Tura gasps. "Then why did you bring her here in the first place? She can't *leave*! And there's no way she'd qualify as a Terremer. She's obviously not even a Halfling, Petoile! She has *both* of her parents!"

She lost me at Terra-something, but...oh, *wait*. How does she know about my parents?

"I *know*, Tura!" Pete retorts, almost desperately. "There *has* to be a connection though. You should see the way she swims. And Tura, she doesn't require the masciel to *breathe* here. She *has* to belong! We just need to find a way to prove it!"

Her voice is still menacing as she replies. "Well until you do, you'd better stay away from the studio. Unless, of course, you want to involve the rest of us in all of this...this idiocy!" After taking a deep, shaky breath, her face softens slightly and she reaches for Pete's hand, the one not holding mine, gathering it close. "As much as I love you, Petoile, I do *not* relish the idea of going before the Grand Council to explain the presence of an unauthorized human." Shooting me another dark look she adds, "One I do not care to be affiliated with in the first place." *Ouch.*

"It won't be necessary, Tura. I promise. I'll figure something out." His silky voice is firm as his eyes plead, almost begging her to understand.

She relents with a dismissive nod. "I'll tell our mother

you went to the outer reef to collect…*items,* for your work." She eyes him sharply. "You'd better return soon. I don't plan on making a career out of covering your tail, you know."

Pete nods, muscles relaxing with relief. "Fine, I'll see you later then."

Flicking her tail abruptly, she's quickly back out the way she came in, not even slightly acknowledging me. Suits me fine. I'm still in a state of shock after the argument I just witnessed anyway.

Pete, still grasping my hand, quickly propels us towards our escape. The landscape, usually so interesting to me, flashes by unseen. My mind is in turmoil.

"Wait! Just, wait!" I yank my hand from his grasp as soon we reach what I recognize as the outer reef, hurting my heart far more than my hand. I need some questions answered before I'll go any further.

My mind reels, too many questions and emotions jockeying for position. Where do I start? Opening my mouth to ask one, and they all decide to shoot out instead.

"How did your sister know about my *parents* if she doesn't even know who I am? And why would she even care about them? What's a Mesclave? And how is it related to my *anklet*? What's a Terre-whatever? A Halfling? What about the whole I *'can't leave'* thing? And what's the deal with you needing a *wife*? I mean, seriously! I think a marriage clause is a small detail you should probably mention before you freakin' *kiss* someone!.."

My voice is rising, more shrill with every question. Any higher and dolphins will understand me better than Pete. I'd probably keep babbling if not for the feather soft touch of his fingers on my lips, and the agonized expression on his face.

"I'm so sorry Lee. I should have explained more about our culture. I …I just liked you so much, and I didn't want to scare you away."

His touch threatens to distract me from my anger, fear, whichever, so I pull away to a sorta-safe distance. Folding my arms across my chest I glare at him, though not nearly as impressively as his sister, feeling my ragged breaths in my shuddering ribcage. As much as we've spoken over the past few weeks, it appears there are a lot of things…a lot of really *important* things, he never bothered bringing to my attention. I'm officially and totally freaked out, and it's taking all of my will not to show it.

"So get to scaring then, because I am not going anywhere until you explain what just happened back there."

He sighs, running his hand through his hair in a nervous gesture. "Well, to start with, Tura knows about your parents because seeing family history, to a point, is sort of a talent of hers. It comes in handy when bloodlines make all the difference in who you are, and are not, allowed to be with, let alone marry." He exhales again, like he's already exhausted. I don't budge.

"On that topic, I don't have a wife, fiancé, or even a girlfriend. Here or anywhere. Tradition says I should marry within five years of coming of age, two years ago for me. The 'proper wife' thing is sort of related to the other stuff." He pauses to take another deep breath of courage before continuing. I'm waiting for him to start making sense.

"Our people are close to yours for a reason. The…*purity* of our people requires regular…liaisons with humans. Without a consistent infusion, our…species, I suppose you can call it, um…alters. There are very strict rules about how much human needs to be in someone's blood, in order to…to *procreate* with another Nocee."

"How much are you?" I interrupt, not really wanting to know, yet morbidly curious.

"Full half. My sisters also, though they are both half sisters. We share the same mother, different fathers. Our

Nocee father raised us. He *is* our father, in every way that counts. Genetically speaking, however, he is not." He shrugs, seeing the shocked expression on my face. "It is the Nocee way."

What do you say when someone tells you they and their siblings are the products of, what sounds like, one night stands? "I...but..." I shake my head to clear it, trying another angle. "What about the other stuff then?"

"Yes, well as you know, most Nocee are Deusame. They maintain a fish shape and their natural form...what you'd call a merman or mermaid. Troisame develop an additional human form."

I nod, "Yeah, I remember."

"Well, a Terremer is a Nocee who travels to the human world. When Nocee men want to go to the human world to study, guard or...or to procreate, it's necessary for them to be Troisame in order to qualify for the proper portal permits. As I've mentioned before, the portal system is very well regulated. A Nocee woman wanting a baby doesn't need to perfect her third form. A lot of your mermaid and siren myths are the result of a certain amount of past...indiscretions? They're not exactly accurate, though there is some foundation in them."

"So let me see if I am understanding you correctly. Your mom married your dad, then went off and got herself knocked up by some random human guys?"

"Essentially...true." He looks embarrassed. "In our culture, marriage is not necessarily the result of love. It is a partnership between Nocee who's combined skill sets give them the best chance of being successful, productive contributors to society. That being said, my mother really cares for my Nocee father. He is her life partner."

"What about your biological dad? Do you even know who he is?" *Do you care?*

"Mama did once tell me about my human father,

although I never learned his real name. He was the love of her life. A French Canadian, she'd sworn to go back for him after I'd been born, and she did, hoping to bring him here with her. She never found him." He paused a moment, throwing me a meaningful look. "It broke her heart. It took her a long, long time to find the courage to try again, yet she wanted another child. It's why Kelpsie is so much younger than me."

"And your...stepfather? He's...okay with all this?"

Pete shrugs. "It is the Nocee way."

I gulp, not sure how well I'm processing all this information. It seems so...wrong. "And a Halfblood?"

"A Halfblood is what we call a child born of a Nocee and human...um, pairing, who takes after the human side. They're born with legs instead of a tail, and they can't breathe under water. Nocee women who've been...topside, usually give birth in air chambers, like the one we use in the cave, just in case."

"What happens to the Halfblood babies?" I ask, a little horrified, wondering if I really want to know the answer. Do they drown them?

"They get dropped off at orphanages or hospitals, and are usually adopted by human parents quickly. In general, they are very beautiful babies."

Whew!

Looking at Pete, his perfectly chiseled face and torso, the silvery perfection of his form, his sister just as gorgeous, if in a different way, it's really no surprise half-Nocee babies are beautiful. Yep, I can easily believe it. But it doesn't make giving up your baby just because they don't have a tail any less terrible.

"Okay, I understand about the babies." *I may not like it, but I understand it.* "So what about the Mesclave thing?"

"I'm getting there." He flushes as he speaks, his silvery skin tone sort of flashing and deepening at the same time.

247

"When a male achieves the level of Terremer and goes topside, he can choose whether or not to procreate.

"For example, the Sentries. Most of them who manage the third form pledge themselves to becoming guards. You'd probably be surprised at how many of your professional human sports players are Nocee guards. They travel across the country, working in different sports with different off seasons, keeping watch over situations that have the potential of becoming…problematic. It's worked out very well for us."

"Problematic." There's a loaded word. "Like what?" I ask, curious and suspicious both.

"Like human female pregnancies. While they are much more likely to result in Halflings, there's always the chance of the baby being a Nocee."

I can't help being intrigued now. "So what do they do if the baby is a Nocee?"

"Well, you know about the memory stuff I can do, right?"

"Yeah."

"Well what I do is really basic and unrefined compared what the masters can do. The school I want to attend is where they teach those born with the gift how to properly use it. I'm having to just figure it out for myself." He's getting off track, realizing it before I can start smoldering. "Anyway, the Nocee babies born to human mothers…let's just say the infant mortality rates are a bit less than your hospital records indicate."

"Wow." In a nutshell. More babies being taken from their mothers.

It's all so much to take in, none of it exactly endearing, and he still hasn't told me about my anklet. "And a Mesclave?" I practically growl, sure I'm not going to like this. He'd better get to the point…and quick.

"Okay, well…sometimes, when a Nocee goes to the

human world, he or she falls in love with a human." The look I receive leaves no questions about the truth of his statement. I flush hot, my skin tingling with pleasure. *Stop it!* I scold my misbehaving body. I really need to stay mad right now. Stay focused.

"They can bring the human back to Goroannocee, on two conditions. One, permission from the High Council is required. While not unusual, it's not exactly common practice either. The council generally just restricts the number to three."

"Restricts...to three..." *Are they building harems here?* He almost succeeds in distracting me. "And condition two?"

"Two, the human has to agree to...never go back."

My previously tingling skin now feels like a bucket of ice water's been dumped over my head, my blood running cold.

"Never go back? Like, *ever*? You mean stay in Goroannocee forever? Why?" I've been going back and forth this whole time. It's pretty easy. I don't understand.

"Too risky. They could reveal our existence to the other humans. A Nocee can go back and forth, because they'd never risk endangering themselves or our kind. A human? They may go someplace where we'd be unable to find them. It's far, far too risky."

"So? I mean, who's going to believe them?" I mentally picture the straightjacket and padded room again.

"If one or two people tell the tale, sure, of course no one will believe them. It's even happened. If more and more people start claiming the same thing, however, eventually someone will start to wonder if there's some truth to it all. Hence the myths, and why it became necessary to change our rules."

I put the pieces together in my mind, trying to form some conclusion. "So, a Mesclave is a human who can never go home, because they're married to a Nocee?"

I flush at the thought. Me married to Pete? It isn't precisely a bad thought…a tad early maybe.

"Um…not quite." He can't look at me.

My internal *uh-oh* meter spikes into the red zone. This is going to be bad, like tsunami bad.

"Nocee can't marry humans…no matter how much they care for them. Some Nocee marry into purely business relationships, and keep the Mesclave partners they truly love close to them. They're treated very well. Others…aren't so lucky."

My stomach feels like I just swallowed a 20 pound rock.

"So…so a Mesclave is like a concubine? Or some kind of a *slave*?" Things are clicking into place, the inevitable conclusions revealing an abyss of horror.

"Basically…yes."

Click, click, click. "And my anklet. It's not just a nice gift you thought I'd like, is it. It's really for telling other Nocee I…I'm someone's *property*?!"

"Well, yes but…" He reaches for me, he can see the wave of panic rising within, thinking he can comfort me somehow. It is *way* too late for that!

"Don't!" I quickly dodge, not willing to let him touch me after this last revelation, backing away, horrified. My romantic image of my relationship with Pete explosively shatters, the pieces raining down like shards of a broken mirror, reflecting my pain even as they cut deeper. Why did he do this to me? I thought he *loved* me!

I can't breathe. Air. I need air. I need out. *Gotta…get…outta…here!*

Turning away from him, I frantically strike out towards the cave. I've been here enough by now to be fairly confident in finding it on my own. Of course, no matter how fast I swim (and I am going flat out, enough to smoke anyone human) Pete easily keeps up with me.

"Please Doralis!" he keeps repeating. "Let me explain! It's not what you think!"

No. I won't let him explain. I can't. My brain can't make room for it. I'm too hurt and confused. I don't want to hear anything else he has to say.

I reach the cave, plunging in without hesitation. Pete's enchanted stones start glowing as soon as I cross the threshold. I follow them straight to the portal, not bothering to stop at the air bubble, knowing I could be easily trapped there.

Just as I see sky, Pete grabs my hand. While he's gentle enough not to hurt me, there's no getting out of his iron grasp.

"PLEASE! Doralis! *I love you!*" he pleads. His expression is pure anguish.

I almost react—his sincerity and radiating pain is undeniable—my emotional defenses quickly slamming a door on sympathy, or any other sentimental ties I may feel. I can't let him affect me. He's the betrayer here, not me.

"LET...GO...OF...ME!" Using all of my frail human strength, I yank my hand from his. "LEAVE ME ALONE!"

With a strong kick I launch myself through the portal, heedless of whether anyone is there to see me or not. I don't care. All I care about right now is getting away, away from the pain...and from Pete.

I stop barely long enough to yank off my flippers, hurling them back through the portal with as much strength as I can muster. Grabbing my stuff, emotions threatening to engulf me, I make a mad dash back to the colorless reality of the rental house. Dangerous, since I can't see through my tear filled eyes as I cross the street.

When I get to the house, my hands are shaking so badly I can hardly hold the key. Finally hearing the telltale click of the lock releasing, I fling myself against the door and hurtle up the stairs to my room. With just enough sense to shut and lock the door behind myself, I hurl myself onto the bed, tears flowing freely, horrified and humiliated beyond thought or reason. Nothing makes sense, the all-encompassing pain of betrayal smothering me.

At one point during my full-blown sob fest, I reposition myself, switching one tear soaked pillow for a drier one, and feel the Mesclave shackle shift on my ankle.

Furious at this symbol of false hopes, I roughly try to yank the anklet off. It won't budge. Oh yeah. Pete's the only one who knows the special trick to making the dang thing release. I glare at the once cherished, now traitorous object. How could Pete do this to me? He gave me this beautiful gift. A gift, I'd assumed, to symbolize how much he cared about me...*loved* me. In reality, in his world...it marked me as a slave. *His* slave.

My grip on the bracelet tightens as my anguish and despair descend ever deeper into a bottomless abyss, its crushing depths unreachable by the light or warmth of the day. I'm being flattened by it, by the memories of what I now see as the most horrible and complex ruse ever.

The skin on my palms gives in before the pearls and stones. What is this made with, steel cable? They cut into my palm, bringing me back to reality long enough to release my grip, desperately wishing I could just hurl it away from me. Maybe then I can forget all about Pete and his twisted, messed up world. Laying my head back down on the pillow, I succumb to the void of desolation.

Roslyn McFarland

16

Making promises

I IGNORE THE park and its puddle. I try to. Every day, I very carefully ride on the opposite side of the street when I pass, never even glancing its way. It doesn't help. Despite my precautions, I feel an almost tangible pull, can almost hear an imperceptible voice, calling me back.

Swim practice is a blur, details missed or obscured by the haze of melancholy I'm shrouded in. I spend my free time with the rest of the team, my halfhearted attempts to participate in the usual banter is pathetic at best.

The guys notice something's off, but they're guys, and not inclined to ask personal questions about anyone's emotional well being. Crystal notices too, smirking and sneering at me, delighting in my depression, happy to add to it if she can. And my parents...well, my mom's seminars are in full swing, so I don't really see either of them enough for anyone to notice anything.

The one person I should be counting on for support, caring and guidance, in this most tragic time of my young life...is oblivious.

Kari Ann's boyfriend came to visit the day after my tragic final departure from Goroannocee. With him here, she wouldn't notice a purple moose with neon spots acting as lifeguard. The only time I see her is in the water. She comes to practice barely on time, and is the first one out of the pool at the end of every session. Heck, she's practically dressed and ready by the time I even enter the locker room.

I can't fault her for not noticing my misery though. I remember what it felt like, the excitement and sense of expectation, the joy of seeing your boyfriend after being without him. After all, not very long ago I felt the same way. I envy her for it.

Ted's visit lasts a week. She's teary eyed and mopey the Monday after watching his flight back to Boston as it turned into an invisible speck on the horizon (she dramatically recounted the whole farewell scene to us at lunch).

By Tuesday some of her hyper-alertness is returning and she finally notices my pallid behavior. Dismissing the rest of the team to go about their business, she insists on a private lunch, just the two of us.

Once we're settled and our orders taken, she pounces.

"Spill! Okay, yes, I've been a bit distracted this past week. But I *know* when something's up. Details! Now! You are *not* getting away with the mopey little silent treatment with me!"

Crossing her arms in what I recognize to be her most stubborn pose, she pierces me with a look, her blue eyes flashing. For someone on the small side of petite, she can be kinda scary.

I trace an invisible pattern on the countertop with my finger, what's left of my emotions roiling, not looking at her. It's not like I've been *trying* to keep things from her, either then or now. There haven't exactly been a lot of opportunities to bring it up.

"Pete and I, um,…sort of argued," I finally admit, my voice weak and pathetic in my own ears. Talk about a total understatement, yet all I can think to say. *Pete planned to kidnap me and force me to be his concubine slave* just sounds a little harsh…and crazy.

"An argument? What about?"

"It doesn't really matter. I don't think I'm going to see

256

him again." My depression speaks volumes, all by itself.

"Oh honey! I'm *so* sorry!"

Her honest warmth and compassion is too much for me and I do something I swore never to do in public, ever again. My emotional walls crumble, breaking me down in the process, a massive sob ripping lose right there in the dingy little café.

Kari Ann leaps to my side of the table, hugging me, offering the comfort and support of her presence while shooing away any concerned or morbidly curious café staff that stop to check on us.

Absorbing particles of strength from her compassion, my tears slowly subside as I pull myself together. With a friend like her, I can live without Pete…without going to Goroannocee. It's what I'm telling myself anyway.

The next couple of days I'm closer to my old self than I've been in over a week. Closer…not the same. Maybe I'm simply getting better at faking it. There's a hollowness taking up residence in my ribcage, where my heart used to be. My life seemed so perfect such a short time ago, and I'm not sure if things ever will be fully right again. At the very least, I know I'll never be the same.

Levi correctly interprets my mood swing to mean I'm once again single, even though I still wear the anklet. I *cannot* get the darned thing off! The rusty bolt-cutters in the garage were totally ineffective. Trying to be my rebound guy, he makes a couple of attempts to flirt. With less than no reaction from me, he easily shrugs it off as a lost cause, which suits me fine. The last thing I need right now is another boyfriend…even if any other boy stood the remotest chance of competing with the last one.

The days drag on. As much as I avoid the park, the pull to go there throws everything else more and more out of wack. I'm a mental and verbal mute with my team. I can't even get it together enough to beat Crystal in our last mock-meet, which she gloatingly loves. Life is turning into little more than a series of robotic movements, cold and unfeeling. The world around me seems more grey and washed out than ever. I miss *real* color.

I can't deny it anymore…I want to go back. No, I *need* to go back.

Finally boiled down to the essence, there's no choice. I don't know whether I'm being drawn by Pete, or by Goroannocee itself. I don't know how to describe the intensity I feel, not willing to use the L word. It…or more to the point *he*, is a part of me now, and every day that missing piece gets louder and more insistent. It nags, nudges and impels me, making itself more of a pest by the hour. It's not going to leave me alone until I go back…unless I give up the piece of me completely. Just the thought of turning my back on it…on *him*…is far too painful to even think about.

Simply put, I'm not willing to give either of them up.

The days are slipping away, my summer almost gone. It's now or never.

***

Friday, late afternoon, we're changing in the locker room when I decide to confess to Kari Ann the decision I've made—as much as I can confide anyway.

"I'm going to go see Pete tomorrow," I mention casually, as I pull on my shorts, not looking at her.

She stops what she's doing immediately, turning towards me with her full attention, amped and ready for details.

"Really?! So you decided to forgive him? I'm so happy for you! I knew you weren't the type to hold a grudge." She leaps at me for a congratulatory hug. "You know, you never did tell me what got you so upset with him in the first place," she reminds me pointedly as she pulls away.

"Well, it doesn't really matter now," I evade. "I…I just

miss him. I decided it isn't a big enough deal to lose him over, you know?" I look at my friend, not bothering to disguise the emotions reflected through my eyes.

Her eyes soften. "Yeah, I know how it can be." She gives me a quick one-armed hug again before getting back to the business of packing up her things.

"So do you think he'll be there? You said he's an early riser, can you get up early enough to catch him?"

I grin, relieved she isn't making a big dramatic deal of the situation. "If I don't go out with you and the guys tonight I'll be fine. I'll never understand how people who get up so early for swim practice can turn into night owls on the weekend."

She laughs. "Just getting ready for college life!"

"That's two years away!"

"Practice makes perfect, right?" Laughing again as she swings her now packed swim bag up onto her shoulder, I follow suit and we head towards the exit.

We're almost at the door when I see Crystal. Glaring at me, per usual, there's something else in her expression, something calculating. I wonder if she's been eavesdropping on our conversation, dismissing the idea quickly. So what if she listened. It's not like I've said anything I shouldn't, right?

I blow off her negative energy and head for my waiting bike. There are way more important things to think about...like what the heck am I going to say to Pete when I see him. "I'm sorry I blew you off" and "I missed you" just doesn't seem like quite enough.

I'm so lost in my thoughts as I pedal away, I don't notice Crystal standing on the other side of the glass doors, watching me go.

***

Saturday morning I wake up, zinging full of nervous energy, at 0-freakin-early. I still haven't figured out what

I'll say to Pete...if he's even there.

He must be so hurt and mad at me for leaving the way I did. The fact I didn't return only makes it worse. For the first time since I made my decision to go back, I feel a real surge of fear he won't be waiting for me.

Putting on my bikini with trepidation, hoping it'll be needed, I pull on a tee shirt and shorts over the top. After fighting with my tangled hair for a while, I brush my teeth, pausing to study my reflection in the mirror for a moment. The person staring back looks terrified, pale with splotchy flushed cheeks. I firmly tell her to get a grip, but she's not buying it. Slipping on my shoes, I quietly make my way downstairs before I can freak myself out anymore.

I really don't feel like eating, my stomach already filled with a writhing mass of nerves, forcing down a piece of buttered cardboard toast anyway. If things go well, I'll regret skipping breakfast.

Scribbling a generic note for my sleeping parents, unable to count on Pete's wonder stones smoothing the way for me today, I leave the house. The walk to the park takes ages—at least it feels like it to me—the early morning fog making the landscape truly gray. I can barely see across the road. And it's so quiet, the normally audible sounds of my stumbling footsteps swallowed up by the repressive mist around me. Tense and slightly paranoid, I try not to take it as a bad sign. When I finally reach the portal, my nerves are hot pinpricks on my skin, firing with dread and anticipation.

"Pete?" I can't feel his presence. "PETE?" Nothing.

He's not here.

Of course not. What else did I expect? He tells me he loves me and I practically deck him—I think my fist may have grazed him as I ripped myself free from him. So what if he gave me a stupid masci-whatsit bracelet. He did it to keep me safe! I realize the truth of my thoughts, horrified, even as they come to me.

Oh dear lord. What have I done?

Tears brim in my eyes, sliding down my cheeks unbidden. For a moment I even let them, wallowing in self-pity and condemnation.

Knock it off Lee! I get myself in hand with a jolt, angrily wiping the traitorous moisture away. I will NOT let this be the end! *I need to fix this!* I've faked being brave a lot this summer. It's time for the real deal. Before I can think any more about it, I dive head first through the portal.

My flippers are on the tunnel floor, right where they landed after I hurled them through. Taking as little time as possible, I slip them on, swimming strongly through the familiar corridors within moments. The light from Pete's enchanted stones is dim, barely flickering enough to show me the way. He hasn't renewed their magic in a while.

Pain hits my stomach like a sucker punch, almost crippling, making my strokes uneven thrashing until I can get it together. It's not bad toast.

What have I done?

Unfortunately, I can't answer my own question, so I keep repeating it to myself, over and over again—*What have I done? What have I done? What have I done?...* Maybe if I say it enough I'll find an answer to let me off the hook and relieve my tremendous guilt.

Not likely.

I check the air bubble first, sort of on the way. No Pete. Grabbing my masciel off of the stone ledge, just in case I need it, I hurry on my way. Every moment I can't find him is more excruciating than the next.

Making it to the cave entrance, I start pushing my way through the kelp to the clearing. I'm sure I know the way...pretty sure anyway. It doesn't matter. I *won't* let some overgrown sea-lawn stop me now!

The kelp starts to thin and I know I've made it.

Pausing to assess out of habit, I think there's something in the clearing. I can't be sure. If there is someone, they aren't moving much. Very carefully, I pull back the remaining piece of surfboard-sized seaweed, peeking through.

"*Pete!*"

He's resting on the sandy floor with his back to me, his hands occupied with something. Hearing his name, he whirls around in a blindingly fast move. He's so beautiful it hurts to look at him, the embodiment of everything I've ever wanted and many things I never knew I needed, in one supremely perfect package. But it isn't my hurt I'm worried about right now.

Scrambling through the closing gap of greenery, the array of emotions flashing across his face stop me mid stroke as I rush towards him. Pain, *lots* of pain, dominates his features. My stomach gets sucker punched again, leaving me breathless. Confusion, guilt and the smallest kernel of happiness, or hope flicker in his eyes, quickly extinguished.

My hands unconsciously reach for him, desperate to touch him, hold him close, sooth his pain. "What have I done?"

"You?" He's shocked, his voice strangled with emotion. "You didn't do a thing Doralis! I'm the villain, the one who wasn't honest with you. I didn't tell you the ramifications of what coming here meant. I put you in *danger*. You're right to leave me…" Turning away from me, clutching one hand into a fist, grasping his bowed head in the other, his face is a mask of pure torture.

I can't take it.

"No!" Dropping my mask, I close the distance between us within one heartbeat. Folding my arms around his strong back as I'd imagined so many times, I hold him to me. "I'm the one who was wrong. I should have asked more questions in the beginning, *listened* when you tried to explain to me. I should have stayed…"

He still won't look at me, his whole body trembling beneath my embrace, his fist clenching harder around the object in his hand.

I take a deep breath. There's nothing left to say, except…the one thing I never said. The one thing I avoided even contemplating, too scared to admit even to myself.

"There's so many thing I should have done or said. I should have told you, I…I love you. I *love* you, Pete. And I'm so sorry it took me this long to figure out."

Finally he looks at me, his silver eyes probing mine, trying to find the truth, or the lie, behind my words. I stare right back, releasing all the love I've hidden into my eyes, willing him to believe me. After what feels like an agonizingly long time, a seed of hope finally forms. Then joy blossoms, wild and beautiful, lighting his face like the sun emerging from the clouds. Before I can blink he's spun back around, crushing me to him, his face hidden in my hair billowing around us.

"Oh Doralis, my Doralis…" he murmurs, his voice never sounding sweeter.

I clutch him to me as well, emotions threatening to overwhelm me after finally admitting to them. When he kisses me, it's like truly coming home. My world is complete.

We stay there for a long time—embracing, kissing, enjoying the unreality of simply being together. What feels like seconds is probably pushing an hour. I don't care. I could stay here for days.

He finally releases me, enough to pull back and see my face. His arms still encircle my waist, his body pressed against mine, refusing to lose all contact. His expression is earnest.

"My Doralis, will you promise me something?"

"What?" I gasp, my mind still caught in a whirl of

physical and emotional sensations.

"Please, my Doralis, promise never to leave me again. Not in such a way." I don't need to imagine his anguish, exhibited as it is in his eyes. He tightens his grip on me. "I…I couldn't bear it. Not again."

Amazingly, I understand what he's asking. Not to stay with him in Goroannocee forever, which would be a pretty stupid request after our little misunderstanding, and Pete is anything but stupid. No, he's asking me…to be his girlfriend I suppose, although there's a lot more to it. Since I can't imagine wanting anything or anyone more than him, it's an easy promise to make.

"I will go back Pete…which you know…" I hold his exquisite face in my hands, looking deeply into his eyes to better make my point. "…but I will always be *yours*…heart and soul. I promise." I pull his face down to meet mine, sealing my promise with another kiss.

He puts his one free hand on my cheek, the other still around my waist and clutching the unknown object, which finally gets to me. I break off mid kiss.

"Okay, *what* is in your hand? You've got some kind of death grip on it or something!"

The shiny happiness in his eyes dulls a bit as he looks away from me in embarrassment, not answering right away. Bringing his fist up, he holds it out to me, opening his hand.

There, nestled on his palm is a small, smoky gray stone. The black aura of negativity surrounding it makes me cringe away without thinking.

"What is it?" I'm not sure if I really want to know.

"An…experiment, sort of." He's still not looking me in the eye. I wait impatiently for him to explain.

Finally meeting my gaze, his expression is pained and pleading. "I…I couldn't deal with the knowledge of what happened. Knowing how much I loved you, and how much you...hated me, for what I'd done."

I repress the urge to tell him I never hated him. Something tells me to keep my mouth shut, not interrupt.

"After you didn't come back, I didn't know what to do. You were out of my reach. Gone, forever." He looks at the stone in his palm. "So...I made this."

The stone appears more evil to me than ever. I need to know. "What does it do?"

"It's an eraser. When activated, it will erase the memories of the next person it comes into contact with. Very specific memories. It will only erase thoughts of...you." He takes a deep shuddering breath, running his hand through his hair in agitation. "And to think, I planned to use it this morning."

My blood runs cold at the thought of the power he was describing, of Pete forgetting all about me. What if I'd come too late and he didn't know me? What if I never experienced his love again? Horrified pain envelopes me. It's too unthinkable, so I push it away, mentally stomping it out of existence.

Then another thought occurs to me. I back up a bit, using my arms to maneuver myself away. A rock to make someone forget me? What if *I'm* the one it touches? I sure as heck do *not* want to find out!

"So get rid of it!" my voice, an octave or so higher than normal, reflects my rising anxiety. It's all I can do not to smack his hand away.

"I can't." Looking up at me he seems to realize I'm freaking out, because he closes his fist on the offensive object, hurrying to explain. "See, it's got some of my energy inside it...my magic, as you understand it. If I leave it here, someone else could find it. Anyone affiliated with the Nocee Council or the Portal Masters could read it to find its maker."

"So what do we do?" My voice shaking, I continue to

back away slowly, scared—scared of the stone, scared of someone finding it, and almost a little scared of Pete, for being able to make such a monstrous thing in the first place.

"I can drain it, though it will take some time and I can't do it here. I'll need my shop. Don't worry," he adds, very obviously slipping the piece of anti-Lee into a small pouch he's wearing belted to his waist. "It's safe. It's not activated. It will never hurt you...*I* will never hurt you." Reaching for me, he cradles my face in his warm strong hands. "And I will make a promise to you, my Doralis. I promise to love you forever. I will cherish every single memory of you I possess, and never think to make such a stone ever again."

He kisses me, sealing his promise this time. If my eyes weren't already filled with water, I think I'd be crying...from happiness. How do Nocee cry, anyway?

The rest of the morning is spent in pure enjoyment—of each other and the beauty of Goroannocee. My hollow chest is filled to bursting with euphoria. Already the most wonderful place in existence for me, everything is better, brighter and more alive, like releasing my emotional block also somehow released some other kind of block as well.

Already extremely aware of my underwater environment, I'm hyperaware now. I can sense movement *within* schools of small fish. I can see every spectrum and shade of color clearly. None of the reef and anemone garden inhabitants are camouflaged well enough to hide from me. It's fantastic! I laugh delightedly at each new discovery, none of it striking me as weirder than anything else down here.

Pete, already aware of my unusual skills, just shakes his head and laughs along with me. "I always knew you were special," he whispers in my ear at one point, following it up with a kiss. I could wish for this to last forever...sort of.

We're in the anemone garden, laughing stupidly and holding hands, when I feel a certain vibration in the water. My own personal warning signal, I know someone else is approaching. Focusing, I can tell it's a very light someone, not the large bodies of Sentries who sometimes come our way...as if there's only one small person.

I clutch Pete's arm to get his attention, looking in the direction the sensation is coming from. The kelp forest?

Shoot! It's blocking our exit!

Pete immediately understands, pushing me behind himself in an effort to shield me. We're in the middle of a flat-ish area of the garden, where there's literally nowhere to hide. I peek around his shoulder, terrified, yet morbidly curious to see what danger's coming for us. My alarm bells are banging wildly out of control.

A moment later a small figure emerges from the kelp.

It's another human, no question about it. The whole bi-ped thing is an immediate giveaway. She's wearing a masciel and flippers of the Nocee, but something's off. Something about her, about how she moves, tugs at my brain, urging me to acknowledge it. I look closer, easier with the clarity of the water and how much better my vision seems to be getting, despite the long distance.

The first thing I notice is her lack of a Mesclave bracelet. My recent drama notwithstanding, I know it's a pretty big deal. What are the odds of another Nocee bringing in an unauthorized human? Not a bet I'd be willing to take.

Then I notice her swimsuit—a navy and purple Speedo which looks vaguely recognizable. Her hair is long and dark, almost black, and so familiar. When she turns in my direction, I can finally see her eyes—piercing dark brown and immediately recognizable, in spite of the mask covering the rest of her face.

"HOLY CHOWDER! That's *CRYSTAL!*"

17

Queen B

PETE SWEARS IN French, probably unaware I understand what he's saying.

Thanks for the colorful education, Dad. The sarcastic thought flits briefly across my mind before Pete pulls me towards a part of the garden with more cover. Okay, more accurately, he just about yanks my arm out of the socket trying to get me to a hiding place. Once there we position ourselves behind a large boulder covered in pale orange and white anemones, like a giant creamsicle.

Crystal hasn't noticed us yet. What would we say she did? *Welcome to the neighborhood* somehow doesn't quite cover it.

A. This isn't exactly your average neighborhood, and

B. She isn't *welcome.*

Anyway, remembering my first trip here, she's probably plenty distracted enough to give us some time to think.

"How...did...*she*...get here?!" I'm terrified of what her presence might mean, not just for me, for Pete. It's freezing me in place, my limbs slowly losing all sensation as the fear takes over, traveling towards my core, my hyper-beating heart. What I want is to be pissed off. I'm trying, really! This is *my* magical place! I just can't seem to convince my body.

"It's quite obvious." Pete replies, calmer now, just a razor's edge of the anger I can't seem to find. His eyes never leave Crystal's form as it slowly moves along the edge of the kelp forest in the distance. "She followed you somehow, and my lighted trail led her to the air cave." *At least it isn't* all *my fault.* "I never removed the spare masciels and fins, so she probably helped herself. Then she managed to find her way out." He pauses for a moment, thinking. "It would be impressive, if not so inconvenient and possibly dangerous…for you especially." He looks at me, anger and frustration at war with the growing concern for my safety.

"Yeah, well, Crystal may be a lot of things, but stupid isn't one of them." I respond, robotically honest. The enormity of her presence here is starting to register, weighing down my frozen form with fear, anger, resentment, hostility and a plethora of other, equally unhealthy emotions. This cannot end well.

"The real question is, what are we going to do?"

Is he asking me? *Me?* The idiot who apparently led the problem here in the first place? "I don't know. I *don't…know!*" My mind one moment as stuck as a fish in a net, catches the nearest emotional runaway train.

Breaking through the frost in my limbs, I curl forward, holding my head in my hands, willing my brain to work better as I try to keep my skull from exploding. I'm done, *so* done. Put a fork in me.

Between the emotional upheaval of reuniting with Pete (the good, the bad, and the yummy) and my worst nightmare of *Crystal* intruding upon my shiny-happy-feel-good fantasy, all we need are some jumbo sharks and my nemesis Belinda Schneider showing up to round out this terror-ific day. Heck, let's throw in some killer jellyfish, while we're at it. My perfect happiness, barely realized, ruined by my perfect nightmare. The train has just gone off the tracks and I'm dangerously close to losing it. My eyes squeeze shut as I wish for a pair of ruby slippers. *There's no place like home… send* Crystal *there.*

I'm checking into a padded room for sure after this. It's all too much. I start shaking, the water around me rippling with my progressively worsening tremors, my grasp on reality starting to slip away...

Suddenly strong arms are wrapping around me, a muscular tail winding around my legs, and I'm utterly enveloped by the warm protective embrace of Pete's soft skin and iron muscles. "Shhhh," he murmurs quietly in my ear. "It's going to be all right, Doralis. You'll see. We'll figure this out. Together." His hold tightens fractionally, reinforcing his words.

With great effort, I open my terror-filled eyes to meet his—liquid quicksilver, so full of affection. It's like he's pouring his love directly inside me, my heart swelling in response, my shaking subsiding. We'll work this out...we have to. I only just now realize what I'd be losing, and I will *not* let it happen.

Keeping a firm hold on me, satisfied I'm somewhat stable...for now anyway, Pete turns his attention back to the problem at hand. In silence we watch as Crystal moves further along the line of the forest...in the direction of the guard barracks!

"Maybe we should go talk to her," Pete murmurs thoughtfully.

"Maybe *you* should go talk to her." I growl, unable to repress the bitterness in my voice. "She's despised me since the first day I arrived."

"You're not giving me a lot of incentive to help her you know." He smiles down at me, his eyes tight.

"Sorry, just saying it like it is."

He reaches over, unhooking the mask I now wear for show, freeing my face. Cupping my face in his hands, he leans down slowly, letting his lips touch mine softly, so softly. My already racing heart practically leaps out of my chest with an explosion of sensations. I lean in, trying to deepen the kiss, wanting to forget everything else in this moment but the feel of him. Pete is more conscientious, however, gently but firmly pulling away.

"I'll take care of this…for you."

I need to blink a few times before I realize he's gone. Peeking around the boulder, trying my best to see through the waving tentacles of the anemone, I watch as Pete approaches Crystal cautiously. While I can't quite hear what they're saying, I can read their body language easily enough.

Pete's telling Crystal he isn't going to hurt her, his hands up in a gesture of peace. Crystal looks surprised and a little taken aback by my gorgeous merman, everything but scared. Figures.

Don't even think *it Crystal…He's* mine*!*

Now he's explaining how he knows who she is and how it isn't safe for her to be here. Being told to leave, Crystal's back straightens and her chin comes up defiantly. Big surprise there. She probably thinks she has every bit as much right to be here as I do.

Pete's trying to reason with her now. I told him it wasn't going to work. He reaches for her, touching her arm imploringly.

A flash of jealousy strikes me…hard, like a bolt of green lightning. Suddenly I'd be very happy to introduce Crystal to a hammerhead or great white shark. Before I can think of a way to lure them to her though, she's yanked her arm away from Pete, telling him off before kicking away.

Pete balls his fists in frustration for a moment, watching her go, calming himself before turning to swim back to me.

"That…*girl* is impossible!"

"Hmph!" It's all I can manage without an *I told you so.*

"Uh! I think she'd get along quite well with the barracuda clan. Maybe I should arrange an introduction."

A small giggle escapes me, though there's a manic edge to the sound. Pete looks over at me like I'm nuts, so I answer his unspoken question. "I was actually just thinking she might like to get to know some of the sharks."

He smiles briefly.

The bit of black humor out of my system, I continue, serious again. "Look, I know there are people like her all over the place. Nothing should surprise me at this point, but she's just so...so *vile!* I wish I'd never met her."

Pete puts his arm around me comfortingly for a moment, before suddenly jerking away. "That's it!"

"Excuse me?" As if I'm not confused enough.

"I don't know if there's time." He's mumbling to himself as he grabs my hand again, towing me quickly towards the kelp forest. "...it'd be better if I could use my workroom. Definitely no time to go there..."

"Pete! What are you talking about? Clue me in, I'm freaking out here!"

He reaches into his pouch and pulls out the ugly gray pebble, holding it out towards me on his palm.

"We've got this!"

"Yeah?" I back away, increasing my distance from the anti-me rock. "So?"

"So...we can use it on Crystal! You just said you wished you'd never met her. Well, after I hit her with this, *you won't have*...as far as she's concerned anyway!"

"Yeah, so what do you need time for?" *Still anxious here, Pete!*

"Well, I carry a couple of stones designed to help the guards forget us, in case we were ever unable to avoid them."

"Okay." Totally lost now. "I thought we're talking about making Crystal forget? How many of those things do you have, anyway?"

"We are. The other stones are in case the guards see us

before they see her. What I need time for is to fabricate some memory of how Crystal got here. She can't come from Prince George. According to official records, there's no portal there." His smile is bright with excitement as he speaks. He seems pretty convinced this will work. I'm not so sure.

"Can you do that? Just a little tweak and voila, one specific set of memories gone? Replaced by...what, a wrong turn on a surfboard?"

"Well, I *think* so." He looks a little less sure now though. "I've never tried to fabricate a memory from scratch, only modify. So, maybe? I can use some memory she has stored..." He's mumbling to himself again, his eyes far away. I need to bring him back.

"Pete! Focus!"

"What?...Oh yeah! I think I've got it. I just need a little bit of time to do the tweaking." His face gets thoughtful again. "We'll need to distract her...and we definitely need to get her *away* from the guard barracks."

I'm hit by a sudden inspiration. "I think I can handle it."

"How?" His skepticism borders on insulting.

"Easy. I just tell her she's not supposed to go somewhere. She won't be able to resist going where I don't want her to be." Duh, look around.

"Huh. Makes a lot of sense. It might actually work."

"Thanks," I reply sarcastically. "We can't all be creative magical geniuses you know. Every once in a while one of us mundane boring types does come up with a good idea."

He leans towards me, cupping my face in both of his hands this time.

"You are anything but mundane and boring, my Doralis." His voice is the sweetest of music, and his eyes mesmerize me. I'm entranced, just like seeing him for the first time.

He kisses me again then, soft and loving, possessive and urgent at the same time. One hand moves to cup the back of my head, while the other drifts to my waist, pulling me close. His lips part, the sweetness of his tongue tracing my teeth before caressing mine. My mind and body light up like a torch of desire. The water around us should be boiling. A confusion of senses and I know only one thing for certain.

I will never, *ever* love anyone the way I love Pete. Never.

He releases me all too soon.

"Back to business." His voice is husky with emotion. I could easily say the heck with Crystal, brushing her off so I can fall back into his arms, but I know he's right. Pulling away from me, the hand on my neck traces its way down to take my hand, so very, *very* distracting, and not helping my willpower at all.

"Let's go."

"Wait!" I pull him to a stop with some effort. "Where am I supposed to take her?"

"Oh, right." His brows come together in concentration. "How about the transition between the inner and outer barriers? The one with the large cleft in the reef? It's closer to my home than I'd like, but we can't let her be discovered anywhere near the kelp forest...just in case this doesn't work right."

"Okay. How much time do you need?"

"As much as you can give me. I've never done this particular spell before. I don't know how long it will take."

Great. Simply nodding, I square my shoulders, gathering every last bit of bravado I have left to muster. "Okay then, I'll see you soon." I pull him to me for a quick parting kiss. "I love you," I whisper, starting forward before I can lose it...again.

Heading for Crystal, who's only a vague shape in the distance now, I can see she's way too close to the Sentries' domicile for comfort. Pete pointed them out to me once, from the safety of a highly concealed vantage point. Trying my best to keep close to any kind of cover, the need to reach her before we're seen propels me forward at an almost reckless pace.

"Hey! Crystal!" I call, as soon as I'm close enough for her to hear.

She turns, her eyes growing wide when she sees me, before narrowing again into their usual condescending slits.

"So Lee, this is the little secret you've been keeping. Very interesting." She folds her arms over her chest, waiting for me to explain, or something.

"Not my place to say anything." I shrug, attempting nonchalance. What I'm going to attempt next will be even harder. "I'm pretty sure *you* weren't invited though, Crystal. You should probably go back, you know, to where you can fool at least *some* of the guys."

I think my weak try at being nasty may be working for a minute, Crystal is shaking like she's fighting the urge to pummel me, then she notices something I forgot about.

"Where's your mask, Lee? How are you *breathing*? Talk about a superfreak!" She's trying to turn the tables back on me. I can't let her. I need to keep her off balance.

"What can I say, I'm gifted. Unlike some people, who *obviously* don't belong here. Go *home* Crystal. Or keep going that way, by all means. I'm sure you'll get along great with the sea slugs. You are related after all." I'm laying it on thick and making stuff up as fast as I can. I need to get her to follow me, without her knowing it's what I want. Anyway, it doesn't really matter. If we're successful, she won't remember a thing. If we get caught before Pete can fix Crystal's memory, I'm totally hosed anyway.

Leaning forward, I jab a finger at her at her chest. "Just back off, *girlie*." I throw her own choice words back in her face. "*I'm* the Queen B here."

With that I turn and arrogantly kick my fins, narrowly missing her head, before zooming off in the direction of Pete's home. Inside I'm terrified, and utterly appalled at how capable I am of being just as snarky mean as Crystal…no matter how necessary. It's vital I don't let her see me waver though, so I keep going.

My senses tell me, after being frozen in shock for a moment, Crystal's decided to follow me.

Whew!

Taking a roundabout path, gradually spiraling closer and closer to the destination I discussed with Pete, I'm careful to go at a pace to push Crystal, yet still followable. I don't look at her once, or otherwise do anything obvious to alert her I know she's behind me. A zig here, zag there, I wonder how long I should stall. Suddenly the water stirs in front of me. I stop dead.

Oh no! Sentries!

Flipping around and heading back towards Crystal, I grab her hand to haul her along with me before she's even realizes what's happening. There's no point in hiding how much stronger a swimmer I am anymore—it isn't even a blip on the importance meter at this point.

Where can we hide?! I think desperately.

Slowing to get my bearings, trying to decide if I know where to go, Crystal manages to find her voice again.

"What do you think you're doing!" she exclaims, as she tries to yank her wrist out of my grip. I hold on tight and keep going. She has no idea how important it is we get out of here…unseen. "Answer me, you little skank! And LET…GO!" She's yelling at the top of her lungs now. Idiot. She may as well be waving a red banner reading 'Come get me! I'm over here!'.

I spot a tall patch of some sort of plant life. I'd know what it is if I'd paid more attention to Pete's lessons and less to his body. Praying it'll be enough to conceal us, I plunge in, yanking Crystal along behind me. Spinning quickly around, I clamp my hand over her mouth before she can say anything else, lowering my head close to hers. Looking into her angry eyes, I try to convey how very serious the situation is, without raising my voice above a whisper.

"Listen! We *have* to hide and be quiet now. The Sentries are coming and, to put it simply, if they catch you, you will *never* see the light of day again! Get it?!"

Her eyes are hard, glaring at me with utter loathing, but she jerks her chin down in a brief nod. As I said before, she's spoiled, not stupid. I slowly remove my hand from over her mouth.

"Some Queen B," she spits, quietly nasty at least. "More like a pathetic fraud."

Ouch. That hits the mark all right. No matter the source, no matter how much I *know* I'm right this time, the accusation contains a stinging kernel of truth to it.

There's no time to dwell. The vibrations in the water are stronger now. Ignoring Crystals' words and keeping my mouth firmly closed, I touch her arm to get her attention before pointing out the reason for our concealment.

She haughtily glares at me again before looking in the direction I gesture, peering through the greenery to try and see out. When her body stiffens, going perfectly still, I know what she's seeing. I take a deep breath, peaking out to confirm the horror for myself.

Five Sentries are drifting towards us. A barracuda and three sharks, joined by a stingray this time. I shake with fear. Pressing my palms to my head, I will them to go away. Our little patch of green is so thin. Maybe, if I pray hard enough, they'll somehow miss us. My reasoning is totally flawed, yet I cling to it anyway.

Where's Pete? I need him! I miss him so much! I need his warm hands, holding and comforting me. Need his strong presence, keeping me safe.

But Pete isn't here right now. It's just me and the B, who's even more ridiculously clueless than I am down here. I focus on trying to be as still as possible, aiming my thoughts at the Sentries, building a mental wall between them and us. The pressure builds. They're less than thirty feet away from us. My vision is blurring and I think my head is going to split with strain before they can catch us. Fifteen feet.

The barracuda in the lead suddenly starts, rearing up like he's been stung by some kind of underwater bee. Agitated, he turns, thrashing his powerful tail and smacking one of the smaller sharks. We hear the solid whap as the larger animal takes the blow without question. Satisfied he's meted out justice, the barracuda leads the group in a new direction...away from our hiding place.

Expelling a huge sigh of relief, I wait until everything stills completely before emerging from our improvised sanctuary. Crystal's right behind me, her bad mood intact, despite the recent fright.

New movement makes me turn, just in time to be knocked back, and just as quickly caught as I'm enveloped in Pete's arms.

"Doralis! You're safe!" He crushes me to him. "I saw the Sentries. They came so close...I don't know how they missed you. I'm so grateful they did!" He bends his head to kiss me, evaporating my fears and filling me with warmth and calm once more.

An irritated "Ahem" breaks into my little bubble of happiness, bringing us both back to the unpleasant reality.

"So *this* is the mystery boyfriend, huh Lee? No wonder you kept him a secret. Don't want him showing up on the national circus tour now do we." She smiles, nastily. "Leave it to a freak like you to find a mythological freak for a boyfriend."

Right, I know pure bull when I hear it, and Crystal's words reek of jealousy. However, Pete's stiffening beside me says she may have hit one mark. I can feel the pure anger rippling off of him in waves.

Uh oh...

Releasing me just enough to loom over Crystal, his muscled form is truly massive in comparison to hers. If it were raining, she'd be dry as a bone, though I wouldn't trust an umbrella who looks at me like I should be pushing up daisies. Her eye twitches, just a little, as she holds her ground. Grudgingly impressive.

"That...is...*quite*...enough," Pete's musical voice rings with authority, his already huge body swelling impossibly in size, his corded muscles straining against his skin.

I can see Crystal fighting not to cringe before him. Her resolve wins, barely, and she shoots back, "Oh yeah? What exactly are you going to do about it...f-freak."

Yeah, not so tough when you're trying to talk down an über-hottie from another world who's more than twice your size, are ya? I think smugly.

"Me? *I'm* not going to do anything," Pete responds, an undercurrent of something dangerous in his tone. "The Sentries aren't far, however, and I'm sure they'll be happy to take care of you for me. I don't recommend calling *them* names, however. You see...*you* are the freak down here." His smile is not a nice one. "You're *human*." He practically spat out the word. "You carry absolutely no power down here. And, unlike my Doralis, there is no one to speak for you. There are multiple forms of slavery practiced here. Did you know that? Though a small, poorly behaved thing like you would hold little value to any decent owner. While

282

I'm not sure what the Grand Council will decide to do with you, I'm quite certain it won't be something you'd consider pleasant." He pauses dramatically. "Well, if they don't just let the Sentries keep you."

Crystal recoils. I don't know if she believes his words or just the intensity emanating from his eyes and body. Either way, she's speechless for the moment.

For that matter, so am I.

Roslyn McFarland

18

Getting Back

"LET'S GO," PETE snarls.

Gently holding my hand, he pushes Crystal ahead of us. I'm sure she thinks he's being pretty rough, though I can see how careful he is not to push her too hard.

"Where are we going?" I whisper to him, still a little shaky after his speech. I know he meant every word of it.

"Somewhere safe, where I can think things through for a minute."

Makes sense to me, only I don't know if there *is* somewhere safe here for two unauthorized humans. The only place I can think of is our little clearing in the kelp forest, and we certainly can't go there. Not to mention, I'm not sure how long Crystal will remain cowed and unresisting.

As if reading my thoughts, Crystal turns and attempts to plant herself in front of Pete—not so easily done in the water.

"Where are we going?" she demands. The same question I just asked, in a much snottier tone. Her fists are clenched and she's glaring at Pete, daring him to do something about it.

Pete lets go of my hand, crossing his arms across his broad muscular chest, flexing his biceps a bit as he does so, his form magnificently huge. He's so beautiful, my breath catches in my throat. He isn't about to let Crystal get to him, not here on his turf…so to speak.

She trembles a bit, otherwise holding his gaze.

"We're going somewhere the Sentries will hopefully not check today. It will give us a chance to think of how to get you…" he waves dismissively at her "…safely home. Not my first choice, of course, but my Doralis insisted." Turning his head to give me a smile, he winks at me with the eye she can't see.

"What's there to discuss?" she shoots back, not willing to acknowledge her current safety is in any way due to my generosity. "How does *Lee* go back and forth? If *she* can do it, there certainly shouldn't be any problem for me." She overcompensates, saying my name like it's something super nasty.

Pete bristles at both her obvious distaste for me, and her arrogance. She's not helping herself. As much as I dislike her, I don't really want to see her as shark bait. Pete looks pretty capable of tearing her into little pieces of chum all by himself right now.

"Look here, you two legged little *snit!*" Obviously, nice is over. "If you possessed *half* the talents of Doralis, we wouldn't be having these problems. If you could do even a *fifth* of what she can, you may well have been *invited* here yourself. The truth is, you *can't*. No talent. No grace. Certainly no tact. Not even close. And you most definitely aren't welcome here. You…are…a…*pest*, who has chosen to inflict herself on us. So get over yourself and do as you're told. You *may* just get out of here alive." Then he pushes her forward again, a little harder this time. She soars through the water like she's been ejected from a cannon.

"Um, wow…" I unintentionally whisper.

Taking my hand again, he makes sure Crystal gets an eyeful as he lovingly kisses it, making it perfectly clear where his preferences lie before carefully towing me forward. My face is on fire after hearing myself described in such a way, though now's not the best time to raise any objections. We can talk about his irrational picture of me later.

Not used to being treated this way, and not picking up what's being put down, Crystal snarls back at us. "You guys are perfect for each other. You're both completely delusional. Good luck dating while fish boy hangs in his tank at the traveling freak show. I am *so* outta here!" She spins around and starts swimming. I don't know where she's going, so she can't possibly know either.

"What are we supposed to do now? It's bad enough when she isn't actively trying screw things up!" I look up at Pete's face, shocked and a little scared at this most recent turn of events. He's glaring after Crystal, muttering something like "...talk about delusional...."

Taking a deep breath, Pete calms himself with difficulty. "It will be fine, Doralis," he reassures me, staring into my eyes, intense sincerity radiating from his. I can't look away from the molten silver. "She's going in the general direction I wanted to go anyway. We'll simply follow her, until she either figures there aren't any other options down here, or we think of something else to do. Whichever comes first."

He'd probably be more convincing if I couldn't read the stress in every line of his body. Well, if he can fake it for me, I can fake it for him. "No problem. We can handle this. We'll do it together." The only part of which I really mean is the last bit.

It looks like he wants to believe me though because his smile gets more honest. He nods agreement and we turn to follow Crystal. She can't be far. She isn't very fast...comparatively anyway.

We're in the dip between the two major reef-like walls Pete and I crossed to get to his house. This area is more…wild, I guess. Less manicured looking than the anemone gardens and coral fields we've visited anyway. Staying in the dip means more cover. It also means I have no idea where we're going.

"Where does this lead?" I ask in a low voice. Sound travels unbelievably underwater…especially if you're as sensitive to it as I am. I don't think Crystal can hear as well as I can here, though I'm not prepared to take any chances.

"In general…towards Goroannocee City. These walls don't keep much out, not in the water. They're more of a visual reminder of the city's borders. It's not a circle, more triangular, and the main population center of the city is located near one of the narrowest points between the walls. If we keep going the way we are, we'll be able to see the city soon."

This doesn't make much sense to me, strategically speaking. Then again, what do I know? Who do the Nocee defend against? I obviously play too much Risk and Stratego with my parents.

As if he conjured it, the city begins to slowly emerge before us. All of my silly speculations fly out of my head as I view the central home of Pete's underwater people for the first time.

"Well?" Exited to hear what I think, no doubt.

"It's…not what I expected," is about all I can muster for the moment.

The city is mountainous. No, it *is* a mountain…literally. I've seen it from a distance, when looking out at the landscape from near the kelp forest, never thinking anything of it. It's like seeing Mount Hood from Portland on a clear day, though apparently a lot more populated. Up close it's a great big, *humongously* large, treeless, snow-less, piece of rock…with a bunch of relatively smaller pieces scattered around its base. It sort resembles pictures I've seen of Ayers Rock in Australia…

only with a lean, like the tower in Italy.

I know Nocee like the whole natural thing, but...
seriously? Someone actually *made* that?

As we swim closer, I start to make out dark spots on
the previously blank surface, some much larger than others.
It finally clicks in my brain, what they are. Doorways, like
the one in Pete's house. There must be *thousands* of them!
And I can only see one small section. This place must be
huge!

We move closer still. I begin to make out the tiniest of
forms, swimming to and fro from the various doorways,
when a horrific thought strikes me. *If I can see* them, *won't
they be able to see* me?

The same terrifying idea occurs to Pete and we're
suddenly diving for cover together, taking refuge behind
the questionable screen of a large yet lacey gorgonian coral.
I pray Nocee eyesight isn't any better than mine.

"What do we do?!" I hiss at Pete, my voice shrunken
to a terrified squeak.

Pete's thinking hard, his eyes forward, looking at the
place where we most recently saw Crystal's stolen flippers
disappear. My heart's hammering wildly in my chest.
Everything seemed like such a lark with just the two of us
against the world...his world.

Hang out with Pete (*my very real pleasure*), breathe
without a mask (*no problem*), act brave around Pete's sister
(*sure thing*), berate Crystal (*piece of retaliatory cake*), ditch
the Sentries (*there were only five of them*)...

Now this?

I'm faced with the irrefutable evidence of thousands, if
not millions, of these strange Nocee mer-people—right
over this wall in fact—and I'm not supposed to be here.
What will they do to me? Will I be allowed to go home—to
Prince George anyway? Will I ever be allowed to come
back? And then the worst thought of all.

What will they do to Pete *if they catch us?*

No. Uh-uh. I shut my brain down before it can come up with any really creative answers. I can't allow my mind to go there, and I certainly can't allow it to happen…for real. Pete is way more important to me than any pathetic need to cave into my fears and hide.

I tug on his arm to get his attention. He looks down at me, stressed, a questioning expression on his face. "We're in this together," I whisper, targeting him with my eyes, meaning it with every fiber of my being.

He squeezes my hand. "Yeah, we are." Bending, he kisses my fingers. "Come on. Let's go get Crystal."

We slip out from behind the huge coral and, hugging the walls, increase our pace as we attempt to catch up to her. The massive bulk of the capitol looms higher and higher above us as we close the distance.

"There she is," Pete whispers.

I see her too. Her usual façade of haughtiness is gone. She looks confused and scared. I can understand how she feels. If she hasn't been so…well, so *rude*, to me and then to Pete, I might even feel sorry for her.

Pete's poised to zoom in and grab her when the water vibrates, hard, yet again. We've reached Crystal, but we're out of time to do anything about it. The Sentries are back.

And from the rate of speed at which they're closing the distance, they know something's here. There's no time to get Crystal and hide, not when they're still in their faster fish forms, and moving so swiftly.

We are so completely fubar.

Pete reacts swiftly. Pulling me into the center of a small-ish clump of waving water-grass, he deftly wraps some of the grasses around both of our bodies. Leaving us with a certain amount of maneuverability, we're both much better camouflaged now. It's not doing anything for Crystal though.

I'm terrified. Not for Crystal, not totally anyway, but for what she might say. My instincts are in full flight mode, only Pete's arm around my waist and the grass he wrapped around the rest of me keep me from bolting...like now.

We see the Sentries come into view. It's the same five Crystal and I managed to evade earlier. Crystal sees them too, turning and trying to swim as fast as she can away from them...towards us.

!!!!!

Unfortunately, she's already been spotted. They're coming after her...fast.

The barracuda leader's form begins to shimmer. His front fins start to morph and lengthen, the top half of him growing and changing, expanding into a broader chest, narrowing at the neck and head. His lower half morphs too, keeping in proportion with the rest of his body. His coloring stays the same sort of muddy beige, reflected in his newly sprouted hair and tail, with his torso lightening to a more sallow skin tone. His eyes are a dark yellow. While he isn't quite as big and broad as Pete—and nowhere near as good looking—he still retains the lighting fast, with a big dose of nasty, look about him. He's easily just as dangerous in this form as in the other.

And he didn't slow a bit during the transformation. The reason behind this becomes only too clear, as he calls out to Crystal in a harsh voice.

"Arête humain! ...Stop human!"

Of course Crystal doesn't stop. She only looks back at the Sentry, proving she did in fact hear and understand him, before trying to swim faster.

Stupid! Stupid! Stupid!

Then again, what else would I have done, if the roles were reversed? Oh yeah, I wouldn't be dumb enough to *be there* in the first place, having accepted help when offered!

My attention is riveted on the chase, however short it

will be. I don't notice Pete's body tensing next to me, preparing for…something. As Crystal comes barreling past our hiding spot, Pete's arm flicks out towards her, lightning fast. Understanding dawns on me, though I never see the small rock leaving his hand, striking her. She's too preoccupied to notice as well.

The pressure in the water created by the Sentries' onwards rush is almost palpable. I can't help myself, shifting back, trying to put as much space between me and the hundreds of sharp teeth as possible, while staying within the confines of roughly textured plant material. The leaves wrapped around me shift too, and I feel a slice across my left thigh as the abrasive edge breaks skin. While not especially deep, the cut immediately starts bleeding, with at least three predators acutely sensitive to the smell of blood in the water bearing down on us. *Oh no!*

I look to Pete, eyes wide and terrified. Once I catch his gaze, I glance down to the source of our problem and back again, silently informing him of the dangerous turn in our circumstances. Looking down, he stares at my leg in horror, like it's been lopped off instead of sporting a shallow cut. When he finally brings his gaze back to meet mine, the anguish in his expression seals our fate. I knew it. There's no way they'll miss us this time.

A moment later the Sentries are shooting past us, intent on their prey. The hammerhead slows for a moment, looking with interest at the waving grass where we hide. It must have caught my scent. Holding my breath, my tears mingle with my blood in the water as I futilely try to stem the flow with pressure from my hand. It's all my fault. Pete will be caught, *punished*. At the very least, I know I'll never see him again. Noooo!

I keep my eyes locked on the hammerhead, desperately willing him to miss us, willing him to dismiss the smell of my blood, to attribute any movement to the grass itself...not something *inside* the grass. Time stops, everything but the oncoming shark dims into the blackness surrounding my vision. I wait for the rush, the slashing of sharp teeth, while still pushing back against the idea with all my might.

The menacing hammerhead abruptly stops, or is stopped. He looks like he ran into an invisible wall, his body crumpling before he can straighten back out, and we're witnessing it, as if from the clear side of a two way mirror. Shaking it's head—Male? Female? I'm not up on my fish anatomy—it can't seem to make sense of what just happened. Neither can I, for that matter. Not the brightest of the bunch, though, it gives a predatory sort of shrug and turns back towards the pursuit...which by now is over. I don't have time to wonder at our amazing luck—either that or this particular hammerhead is extremely off his game and ready for retirement—as Crystal's plight immediately recaptures my attention.

The two bigger sharks are in their Nocee forms, their change unseen by me while my terrified gaze had been locked on the hammerhead. They're gi-normous. Way bigger than Pete, with gray hair and tails, rough white skin, and black, pitiless eyes.

Between them, they hold a struggling Crystal, not bothering to be gentle. She's kicking furiously, screaming profanities, trying to remove chunks of flesh with her teeth, to no avail. All of her efforts are about as effective as a newborn kitten against a Rottweiler.

"Where do you come from?" the barracuda leader is asking...interrogating, his voice rough and ufriendly. "Who do you belong to? Who brought you here?!"

Crystal's eyes are wide with terror. "I...I don't know!!!" she cries. "I don't know what I'm doing here and I don't know who or...*what* you are." She pulls herself together, going on the offensive. "Look, I don't really *care* either! So how about telling your goons to get their big muscle-brained hands OFF me, you pasty faced...*fuh-reak!*" True to form, terrified or not, she still has to open her big fat mouth and let the arrogance flow.

Oh Crystal...

The barracuda man's eyes narrow, his mouth curving in a small, evil smile, revealing his sharp teeth, far scarier than a frown would be.

"We'll see about what you know and don't know...*human*. For now you are an unauthorized trespasser, and will be dealt with accordingly."

He smiles again, making a small jerky gesture to the others, as he turns back towards the city. Taking a more direct route, up and over the reef, he avoids passing our hiding place again. The others follow with Crystal, still a helpless captive, struggling between the two titans.

Oh no! Oh no! Oh no!... What do we do!!! My panicked thoughts scream.

"Yes!"

Pete's triumphant whisper breaks my train of thought.

"Wh-what?!" I hiss back, deliberating for a moment on his sanity.

"It worked!" Still whispering, he's exuberant.

"What are you talking about? What worked?!" I'll give him about twenty seconds to explain before completely melting down again. This is so far outside my comfort zone it's...well, in a different universe!

"The stone! The memory stone! I hit her with it as she passed us, and it worked!"

"Oh." My voice quavers as I remember the little rock meant for Pete to forget about me. "What did it...*do* to her?"

Pete hears the tremor in my voice. Quickly turning, he carefully extricates me from the sharper-than-it-looked grass before winding both of his strong arms around me, comforting me with his embrace as he explains. My skin lights on fire wherever the warmth of his silky soft skin touches mine, yet my insides are still ice cold with lingering fear.

"She's forgotten all about you, my love, as if you'd never met. I also managed to adjust the stone, not much, but just enough so she has forgotten the past few hours, including how she got here. I couldn't insert a new memory, unfortunately. Much too complicated and I needed to hurry."

"So...she can't tell them about me...or you?" As my mind catches up, my insides start to thaw in the warmth of relief.

"That was the general idea, wasn't it?" He's teasing me, his voice so gentle I don't take it badly.

"Yeah. I guess so." Feeling a few shades better, I reached my arms around him, hugging him back. "Couldn't do anything about the personality though, huh?"

"Not this time. I'll be better prepared next time."

We're both delirious from the rush of our near escape, I guess.

"So now what?"

A shadow of some emotion flits over his features. Though he controls his expression quickly, he can't fool me.

Uh oh.

"Well, first, let's get out of here...go someplace where we can really talk. Even if the Sentries don't come back this way, we're still much too close to the city and its population for comfort."

"Well, when you put it that way..." I keep my voice light. Despite some seeds of cold sprouting in my stomach again, I can put on just as good a show as he can.

Without another word, we finish disentangling ourselves from the concealing grass. Pete take a moment to inspect my leg, the sensation of his fingers sending zings of electricity through my entire body. Satisfied that I'm not mortally wounded, and the bleeding has stopped, he puts an arm around my waist, one hand apparently not enough. Extending my senses as far as they'll go, listening ever so carefully for the slightest tremor meaning unwanted company, I confirm to Pete that we're in the clear.

Making our way back to the now familiar kelp forest takes a really long time. Never sensing or see another patrol, Pete isn't taking any chances. He won't let me move from the vicinity of one piece of cover until he's located the next. It's very cloak and dagger, almost comical, if his reasoning isn't so dangerously serious.

Reaching our goal, we plunge in, straight to "our" clearing. I'm utterly exhausted. I feel like I've been up for days. Who knew intense periods of fear could drain you so completely, both emotionally and physically?

I settle down on my usual rock, waiting for Pete to tell me what's on his mind. I know there's something he needs to say. I also know, being with him, I can wait…as long as I need to.

"Doralis, you need to leave."

"Yeah, I know. It's been a really long day. I wonder what time it…"

"No," he cuts me off, "you don't understand. What I mean is, you need to leave…and not return." His voice breaks on the last part, mirroring the breakage I can feel going on inside of me. As if made of glass, jagged fissures explode through the center of my chest as if hit by a hammer.

No, I must be hearing him wrong. "Pete, what are you saying? I…I can't come back?…*ever?*"

"No, not forever, my Doralis." He's not very convincing. "But…the Sentries. They will be on high alert now. There's been a major breach and they'll be turning over every rock and plant to try and find it…how *she* got here. We can't take the risk…*I* can't take the risk…not with you…" His hands ball into fists as he throws his head back, letting out an anguished sound, reflecting his anger and frustration. "That…that girl! That awful, awful girl! Why? Why did she need to come? Why did this happen? *Why*?!"

He whips away from me then, gripping his hair like he's going to yank it out by the roots, the muscles on his arms bulging, his tail thrashing while his torso curls in on himself.

I want to go to him. However, those little seeds of ice in my stomach sprouted, taking over the rest of my body and making me immobile in the process. I can't think about Crystal, can't make myself care or be worried about what her fate might be. I'm too wrapped up in mine, as my dreams are cruelly yanked away by the receding tides of fate.

Leaving Pete…possibly forever? I just got him back! I couldn't let him go when it was *my* decision. How am I possibly going to deal with this *now*?

His tail whips again, inadvertently turning him in the water, allowing me to get a look at his tortured face. My once proud, supremely strong merman, is collapsing in on himself, falling apart like a confectionary castle in the rain. Pulling out fingernails one by one probably feels more pleasant. This is…*wrong*.

I push myself off of the rock, lunging towards him and doing my best to envelop his massive form with my suddenly too small arms.

"Shhhhh, Pete…shhhhhh…" There's nothing better I can say, so I hold him, taking my turn at trying to comfort him. As I desperately cling to him with every ounce of my frail human strength, my emotions swell, a sinkhole of love and pain and inevitable loss, enveloping us both, bound as we are by our shared grief.

Slowly, ever so slowly, he relaxes within my embrace, getting a hold of himself and his emotions. He lets his arms fall, and suddenly we're embracing each other. I cling to him desperately now, not knowing when I'll ever get the chance to do this again.

"Yes, you are right, my Doralis. We will be together again." He sounds stronger, more sure of himself than ever now.

"Yes," I whisper, totally unconvinced myself.

There's no time for long farewell scenes. The Sentries have probably already started their search, combing the area, checking every nook and cranny, and being especially vigilant. We start back to the cave, holding hands, Pete remaining in his natural form.

"I can tell there's a LOT you still haven't told me." I'm trying to lighten the mood while in reality really trying not to think about what's coming.

"There is," he admits. "I guess you'll just need to wait until we see each other again to learn more," he tries to joke back, the attempt a wasted one.

"You promise?" I choke, unable to hide or contain my own grief anymore. "We will see each other again?"

"Of course we will." His voice is confident and soothing—I'm not sure which of us he's trying to convince—and just as filled with emotion as mine. His music is melancholy.

"Promise me," I whisper, not a question, a request this time.

"Don't worry, we will find each other again. I'm sure of it." His conviction is stronger, yet still missing something.

"You didn't promise."

We've almost reached the portal now. He pauses, taking my face between his big warm hands, holding me as gently as if I'm the most fragile of blown glass, gazing into my eyes. I let myself drown in his liquid silver pools.

"I promise. I *will* find you, my Doralis." His voice rings with truth...with love. It's like the sweetest caress and the strongest of promises combined.

I believe him.

He bends down, his lips touching mine in the most tender of farewells. I kiss him back with the gentlest of pressures. I don't dare put any more vigor into it than I am now. My already grieving heart can't take it.

Pulling away from him, I turn towards the portal. I need to leave now...or I never will. Kicking off my fins, I drive myself up and through. Back, to a deserted playground, to the stench of a place I'll never call home. For this, I leave a far better place. Most especially, I'm leaving the only person who'll ever truly matter to me. There's something so ridiculously wrong with this picture.

Standing there, my wet feet making mud out of the dust, I feel new drips on my face. Looking up at the cloudless blue sky, I wonder how it could be raining.

Oh.

The fresh drops are mine. Collapsing to my knees, it feels like my soul is being torn in half. Maybe part of me isn't leaving, staying in Goroannocee with Pete. I certainly don't know how I'll ever feel whole again, not without him. I have to hold onto his promise, *my* promise to myself. This *will not* be the end. Our story isn't done yet.

I gaze down at Pete through my moisture-filled eyes, so much harder to see through than water.

"I love you, my Doralis." His music whispers to me, as he flicks something towards the portal. "Always..."

Through the tears, now flowing freely, I see him shimmer and change. My beautiful merman is morphing into a fish before my very eyes. It's the first time he's shown me his transformation. Will it be the last?

Then I watch as my beautiful Angelfish drifts away, water swirling around him, muddied and obscuring. The ache in my chest sharpening, the fissures grows wider and deeper as he fades from view.

Then he's gone.

And the puddle...our puddle, is simply a dirty, shallow, mud filled hole once again.

Epilogue

Whatever Happened To...

"HEY LEE!"

I look up from my book. It's our last week here and I'm outside leaning against a tree, disinterestedly killing time before the afternoon session. Things fell back into their usual pattern these last couple of weeks. Only I'm different, not as affected by the world around me, missing real life and color. And it wasn't my choice this time.

Levi's trotting towards me, a huge smile on his face, "Did you hear the news about Crystal?"

"No," I respond cautiously. It's not like I can gossip using my version of what happened to her.

"They found her down in So Cal!" He burst out. "That's Southern California by the way, for those less informed."

"I *know* what So Cal means you big nimrod. I'm from Oregon, remember? It happens to be located right above California, on the same coastline." I retort back acidly, a little too anxious to act as thrilled as he'd like for this choice piece of news.

"Yeah right!" He's a little breathless, a lot oblivious. "Well the word is she met some guy online and he talked her into coming down to visit. I guess when she got there the ice queen didn't thaw out enough to impress him or something, because he totally ditched her. He left her stranded at a *mall*! Totally classic! Can you *believe* it!" Levi's practically giddy with glee. She must have done a serious number on him the previous summer.

Despite our mutual dislike of Crystal, though, I breathe a sigh of relief. Pete promised she'd be returned safely. She didn't know anything at all, an easy fix, and her bad attitude would actually work in her favor. No Nocee in their right mind would want to deal with that on a daily basis. They'd take the easy way out and assume she took a wrong turn snorkeling.

While I believed Pete, not knowing what actually happened to her has worried me more than I'd like to admit.

Now, as I listen to Levi, crowing about Crystal's brush with karma, I feel a little twinge of guilt. I know what really happened. I know the truth behind her random disappearance, the story behind this major of major embarrassments, being found dumped in some random suburban mall.

It's just a twinge though.

Sentries

SNEAK PEEK
AT AT ANOTHER STORY BY

Roslyn McFarland

THE PARADISI CHRONICLES

LIGHT
THE
WAY:
LOVES LIGHT BOOK ONE

Chapter 1

LIFTER

Neyve

THE EARTH SPUN miles below, a somewhat tarnished marble in the sky. Looking out through the inches-thick clear windowpanes of the Solix Sky Elevator, the glimpses of space were surreal. No sign of floods, famine, and imminent threat of nuclear war from this vantage point. Neyve Colgan shook her head, wondering how a group of uber-elite astronaut wanna-be's thought they could avoid the tragedies inherently caused by basic human nature by relocating to another planetary system.

For three days, Neyve had been pent up in this metal box on the move, which really messed with her sense of time. Despite the Solix Sky Elevator being one of the coolest pieces of technology out there, it could still bore the pants off any teenager. Melancholy already, her brain spun through topic after unanswerable topic. Like why Uncle Dugal, her only remaining family member, didn't warn her. Before arranging for her passage up the elevator to the

309

Nautilus-11 Space Station, he'd made this trip a number of times Working on cutting edge ship technology and frequent trips above the planet were simple perks of being a top engineer, she supposed.

Thinking of that presented the next question. Why bring her up now? She questioned the universe, fingering the aged pendant on its chain resting at the hollow of her throat. Why not two years ago? Mirco and I could still be together . . .

Soaring through the air, strong arms circled her waist, holding her tight, keeping her safe. Neyve distinctly remembered the sharp slap of high velocity winds tempered by soft lips kissing her neck. They careened through the sky in the power-para-glider, bodies pressed close, the constricting ground hundreds of feet away. Barely teens, living for the moment, loving for an eternity.

With effort she tried to wrench her mind away from the train of memories to nowhere. Yeah, not working so well.

What if Mirco never left?

What if she'd been able to go with him?

Memories of her lost love came with too many painful pieces of baggage, so she switched tracks.

What if mom and dad were still alive? The flood that swept away their hotel wasn't the first environmental disaster to claim thousands of lives, nor would it be the last. The global downward spiral added a string of new tragedies every year. An inescapable situation for most.

But what if the opportunity to leave Earth actually existed for her?

Finally, a question worth thinking about.

On the whole her life circled a sucktacular drain, not fully flushed yet moving in the general direction. An all too common condition nowadays. Rationed food, mostly from a Nutrition Actualizer and totally tasteless, added nothing to a person's daily experience. Palpable fear of the terrorist factions becoming their own governmental superpowers. You could practically countdown to when some psycho hit a button and blew everybody up. Yeah, there's something to look forward to. At seventeen, Neyve knew she'd never see adulthood.

As one of the million suddenly parentless children worldwide, thanks to a parade of natural disasters and routine terrorist attacks, Neyve often heard how lucky she'd been as a toddler to be taken in by her uncle, one of the corp of engineers they called Reachers, The planet's most prestigious group accessible to the non-elite, where skill determined membership—not birth. Yet Uncle D's justifiable pride in his position covered a core of arrogance and secrecy.

Neyve could blame his furtive behavior for igniting her passively rebellious side. She didn't like being left in the dark. Or maybe her basic nature propelled her toward any and all activities considered thrilling and brave, like high-speed parasailing, great white shark dives with nothing but a small re-breather and a bag of chum, or powerblade skating through Deathtrap Alley. Brave or stupid, she obviously didn't need him or his secrets. Or so she told herself.

Especially since he was about to leave her too.

"Gah!" Pushing off from the chair she'd been lounging in, she forced her body into motion. A change in scenery might help her get out of her own head before the carloads of what-ifs completely derailed her.

"Sir, can you tell me our ETA?" Neyve asked the nearest adult, a dark-skinned man clothed in a red Reacher uniform and aviator cap. The ginormous man towered over her, at least a couple feet taller and easily twice her size. Hard to miss.

Starting, the man glanced down at her. "About two

hours or so," he said. "You can see there through the fenestella"—he pointed up through the porthole at the massive docking station looming large above them—"that we've just about made it to Solix Sky Station."

"Oh, okay. Thank you." A couple of hours. No problem.

Soon enough, she'd be taking the shuttle to the space station, actually stepping into a world previously only imagined. While surely worth waiting for, and incredibly exciting under different circumstances, she couldn't escape reality. Soon enough, she'd be returning to an empty home on an unstable planet, with everyone she loved moving on with their own lives a wormhole away.

"I don't think I've seen you before," the dark man said. "You're not a Reacher's child, are you?"

"Yes. Well, no." Oh bugger. She'd been purposefully avoiding attention from Reachers or other personnel, her trip to the station not exactly on the up and up. Ask a simple question . . . "He's my uncle, really. Dugal Colgan?"

Neyve felt the heat in her cheeks give away her discomfort.

"Ah, Colgan. Of course. He's one of my most brilliant bio-engineers. He brought the biome labs online aboard the SS *Challenge* back in '92. His niece, you say? Why aren't you already aboard the ship and in your cryo-bed?"

"I'm not going to New Eden. I guess Uncle D called me up to say a final goodbye or something. He didn't tell me the details."

Technically true. Any theories of why he'd send for her now, though many and varied, rated as fiction. Still, Neyve couldn't help but wonder why didn't he do it two years ago. She and Mirco could have shared a proper goodbye instead of the lack of closure brought by a heart-shattering vid call.

"Do you mind if I see your spacepass?"

Bobshite, seriously? Neyve held her hand out so tall, dark and snoopy could see the credentials and ticket digitally printed on her wrist comm, a less fancy version than the UiComms the Reachers used but nicer than most in her neighborhood could afford. She hoped he didn't notice the slight tremor she couldn't quite control.

He scanned her screen.

FORENAME: NEYVE
SURNAME: COLGAN
CLEARED: SOLIX LIFTPORT, SOLIX SKY
DOCKING STATION, NAUTILUS-11 SPACE
STATION

See? Same last name and legitimate spacepass. Can I go now?

Her mental pleas went unanswered, however, as he maintained his grip on her arm and scrolled down with his thumb.

REASON FOR TRAVEL: 1-DAY BEREAVEMENT
PASS.
UNAUTHORIZED FOR TRANSPORT: SS
CHALLENGE.

"Ah, I see. I understand you've lost a family member."

I did? Who else is left? Oh. Clarity. The bunk line her uncle used to get the pass. What could be such a big deal for him to risk deceiving everyone, especially those Reachers he revered, putting in peril a job he'd built his life around?

The Reacher closely scrutinized her face, waiting for a response.

Neyve nodded. "I suppose that's why he'd like me to come up to see him. He's my last relative," she added, no intention of elaborating despite the man waiting expectantly.

"I completely understand," he finally caved. He probably hoped the offered beaming smile would put her at ease. If anything the squirrels in her stomach picked up their pace. "I'm sure Colgan will be glad to see you one last time. I'm sorry for your loss."

"Thank you," she replied, finally extricating herself from the uncomfortable conversation and heading for the opposite window. Neyve needed to put space between her and Mr. Too-Many-Questions.

The reinforced glass felt warm against her forehead as Neyve watched the Earth recede further and further away. Earth, ocean, and clouds all visible to her at this height, she thought she spotted the beginning of sunset a half a world away.

Adults were conversing behind her, their current topic somewhat racier than appropriate for the general public. Unintentionally eavesdropping, she half-listened to the conversation as it moved on to hushpuppies, catfish, Buenos Ares nightclubs, and moussaka, highlights of the things each crewmember would miss when boarding the Challenge to leave the Earth for the final time. Neyve sourly wondered if she might make her uncle's list.

"I've asked Kasen to disable the comms in the room."

The changed timbre and urgency of the woman's words were enough to jolt Neyve out of her melancholy reverie.

"What's the news?" a male voice asked.

"Tavian Hunt just sent me an encrypted message."

While Neyve didn't know this person, like at all, the name elicited a pause from the voice replying.

"Is the SS Challenge's Cav Drive down?"

Another pause.

"Well, no, not yet. It will be soon," the woman replied,

her tone mixing trepidation and triumph in equal shares. "But that's the good news."

Unable to fight her escalating curiosity, Neyve shifted her position slightly, the warmth on her forehead transferring to the back of her head. Grey eyes slit, her view somewhat obscured by long lashes and her black hair falling in a curtain to half-cover her abysmally pale face, she glanced sideways toward the speaker.

More Reachers. Their distinctive uniforms matched the gear hanging in her uncle's closet. Correction: the clothes he used to hang in his closet, before he packed them up for the last time.

"Out with it, Vida," the man attached to the voice prompted as the woman, Vida, exhaled raggedly.

"Just start from the beginning." The big dark-skinned man she'd spoken to earlier joined the crowd, silent as the night. Ninja skills? Nah. He didn't strike Neyve as the kind of guy who got ignored.

"Yes, better to start there. Yesterday Tav heard a rumor that Challenge Command has been bringing people up in the Tolux Sky Elevator lifters at a steady clip for about three weeks."

"Did he say who they are? I've heard rumors about increased spacecraft activity between the Tolux Sky Elevator and Nautilus-11 in the last couple of weeks. I assumed it was Founder business. I wondered about it but—" Jumbo ninja man frowned.

"We'll mutiny before they get away with that."

The other man's bold statement pulled Neyve away from her wandering thoughts and back to the present. Mutiny? Whoa! This conversation suddenly became much more serious, one she should probably not be listening in on.

"Vida, did Tavian say anything about how they planned to get us off the ship?" the big guy responded, lines of intense concentration etching his brow.

"Tav didn't say, but they'll have a plan. Most likely a ruse. They know we wouldn't go willingly," the Reacher scoffed.

Though the Founders held the power and controlled the resources, everyone knew you didn't mess with the Reachers. Not only were they the brains of the operation, they provided most of the muscle—didn't they? For her uncle's safety, Neyve fervently hoped so.

Her heart rate began to creep up its pace, responding to the anxiety of a situation she should know nothing about. Yet, glancing around the relatively open space, she could not find a less-than-obvious way out. Remaining as still as possible, she fervently hoped they were wrong. Or at the very least moved the conversation elsewhere.

" . . . But that would have taken them months if not years in the planning, which would mean the betrayal goes all the way back to our original contract with the Founding Families."

Neyve's stomach soured, her fingers again finding the pendant at her throat at their own volition. Her boyfriend Mirco—okay, ex-boyfriend by circumstance—flaunted his Abramov surname like a badge. A member of one of the big ten Founding families, they controlled . . . well, just about everything on modern-day Earth. No one thought Neyve should be with him, the upscale guy slumming it with the wild child girl, especially his family. Despite a predisposition to dislike those people in general, Neyve knew her Mirco. No way he'd ever be involved in anything so . . . so wrong. Feeling offended for him, she raised her gaze. Now brazenly observing, she quickly caught back up to the conversation.

"Don't ask. Plausible deniability is a priceless commodity," the woman, Vida, ominously suggested. "All you need to know is that I'll have Tavian Hunt take care of it, since he's already aboard the SS Challenge. In fact, I'll Ui him now."

"Disabling the drive would buy us time," the big man conceded as he watch the womans fingers flash over her comm unit. "But to what end?"

"So you can come up with a brilliant plan to save us all."

Neyve didn't need saving. Without a slot on the dang ship, her fate extended as far as the first missile strike down on the ground. When a person knows they're going down with their destabilizing planet, the whiney-baby discussion of a bunch of adults being protective over their first class seats becomes less than entertaining.

Tough luck. You might be stuck here with me.

"Ah," the big black man said, avoiding the gaze of the other Reachers who so nicely dumped such a load on him. His penetrating stare eventually landed on Neyve.

Staring directly back, she wordlessly dared him to respond. Go ahead, her flashing grey eyes taunted. Explain how you'll save them "all" in front of the girl you know will be left behind.

Breaking off first, the man collected the attention of his compatriots with a single look, angling his head in Neyve's direction.

With all eyes on Neyve now, her eavesdropping career screeched to a halt. Neyve schooled her features into a mask of passive indifference, giving her pendant a final rub before nonchalantly pushing off the glass to get up. Ever-so-casually moving past the group of Reachers, a challenge considering the distinct lack of gravity at this point, she made her way toward her sleep rack to collect her meager possessions.

Less than two hours to go now. Whatever plans they were making or revolutions they were planning, it definitely fell into the none-of-her-business-and-heck-with-them-anyway category.

And it most assuredly didn't involve her.

Chapter 2

ICE-BOUND

Neyve

AT SOLIX SKY Docking Station, Neyve waited in the holding room, impatient for the hatch to the docking station to open. Passengers disembarking from the elevator were required to levitate themselves up to the next level, like a people sized flutter of butterflies.

Finally clearing the crowd, Neyve used the lack of gravity to shoot up through the hatch and into the tube leading to the station, streamlining her body for optimal speed. What a rush. The best part of the trip as far as she was concerned.

With her I.D. scanned and validated by the guards, she headed for the docking station's transporter bay by sliding along the east wing of the main concourse, using handholds and footholds to propel herself through gravity-less space. While her stomach wasn't exactly in her throat, it didn't feel like it resided in its usual place either. Sort of like the sensation of that first big drop on a roller coaster, only no landing and upward arc to alleviate the physical displacement here.

The hairs on the back her neck rose from more than the micro-G as Neyve became aware of a man, seriously good looking in a dark and broody sort of way, watching her. Obviously too old for her, Mr. Hottie Pants's attention moved from flattering to creepy in a nanosecond. Turning his head to say something to the two thugs behind him, he moved in her direction.

Hulks one and two weren't alone. The guy she'd talked to in the lifter stood unhappily sandwiched between them. Wait. Didn't she hear one guy call him Solomon? As in Reach? As in the guy pretty much responsible for building all the spaceships up here and why they called his crew Reachers? He came as close to royalty as any blue-blood born out of the elite could get.

Before she could wonder further about the odd situation with Solomon Reach and the double-thug strong-arm maneuver, the creepy older guy took her entire attention.

"I'd like to ask you a few questions, Miss," he asked in some type of thick Euro-accent.

Taking the whole bad boy thing a bit too far, he grabbed the handhold directly in front of Neyve's path, cutting her off from the flow of the passengers down the concourse.

"What about?" she responded, feeling less intimidated than annoyed.

"Two hours ago, you witnessed a conversation that took place in Lifter 2 between Reacher crewmembers. Do you recall it?" The guy walked a fine line between smooth and oily, his accented voice lulling, but with a mysterious edge she didn't trust.

"I guess. There were some Reachers talking about something. They weren't talking to me. I don't remember seeing you there, though," she accused.

"I wasn't," he said, not explaining further.

Neyve didn't possess the patience for this weirdness. "Okay, great. Nice talking to you," she threw out for politeness sake, trying to make a break for it. If she could weave by him, she'd cake-easy lose him in the crowd.

"Ah, no. I have more questions." He blocked her again, slipping a booted foot into a foothold and this time physically pushing her up against the bulkhead. Quite a trick in micro-grav.

"About what? I don't know the Reachers. I don't know you. I need to go meet my uncle on the Nautilus. Please move." Internal alarm bells rang like crazy throughout her body; Neyve mentally prepared to defend herself.

He moved in menacingly. "What did you overhear them say? I saw you lean closer to them. What did they say?" He enunciated the words, the underlying demand for an answer manifest.

This guy needed to back the heck off. And maybe pop a breath mint.

"Nothing. They were just talking about some people going up in the Tolux Sky Elevator. So what? An elevator is an elevator."

Unfortunately, the glint in his eye told her she probably said something she shouldn't have. Something inside chided her for being even a little bit accomodating.

Aw, spark nuts.

"Thank you, Miss. You've been very helpful."

"Don't mention it. Seriously," she snarked, already pulling away from him. "Wackjob," she mumbled under her breath, deftly moving into the flow of the crowd and leaving the drama behind her.

Were these the kind of people her ex Mirco dealt with all the time? No wonder he hadn't fought harder for her to come with him—probably trying to protect her.

Warmed by her reasoning, she continued toward the shuttle gates, mentally following Uncle D's directions. He'd insisted on her memorizing every step, drilling her until it felt like the info would be permanently etched into her brain. Did he not want her asking for directions or something?

For her trip to Nautilus-11, the mega space station currently docking the SS *Challenge,* she boarded the communal Nautilus Bus with the other passengers missing a badge or position of power. Getting bumped from behind she threw a scowl at the pushy oversized woman, before plopping down into her seat, as much as she could plop in micro-G anyway.

I bet Mirco's family never rode coach, she mused, spying a sleek private transport leaving a neighboring dock, expected to arrive a good hour ahead of her own ride. Being one of the Top Ten Founding Families had its privileges.

After finally arriving at the main station more than 24 hours later and making her way through the checkpoint, Neyve waited for her turn in the grav flux chamber. A fifteen-minute turn in there and she'd be back in the world of gravity. She looked forward to being able to walk upright again.

"Neyve, girl!"

Uncle Dugal crushed her in a bear hug before she'd made it five steps out. Despite the inability to breathe, she couldn't be happier to see him.

"Uncle D!" she exclaimed, hugging him back.

"Have a good trip? Break any inter-spacial hearts on the ride up?"

"Oh please," she rolled her eyes, "You know nobody's good enough for me." Not since Mirco, her mental voice sounded. A topic she'd never bring up, though, playing her role in the uncle-niece-posturing game.

"Of course not, but that doesn't mean they won't be tryin'," he winked, slinging an arm around her shoulders and escorting her onto the Central Lift.

Down in the main station central esplanade, offices were mixed with retail stores selling snacks and travel knick knacks, with the restaurants rounding out the commercial spaces.

"Okay tour guide, where is it you want to take me?" she asked, following Uncle Dugal through the spiraling chamber.

"The SS *Challenge*," he hedged, casting a furtive glance around as they approached a large gate guarded by two men. A nearby sign labeled it as the Cryo Hatch.

"What? Really? Am I even allowed to board the ship?"

"Shh!" he hissed.

Somewhat concerned at this uncharacteristic behavior, Neyve let him pull her aside and away from possible prying ears. Across the hall a pretty girl greeted a man cradling a bandaged hand. Solomon Reach again?

The guards noticed him too.

"Hey, I thought Graversen had detained him," one of the guards said, loud enough to be easily heard.

"Should we intercept?" the other guard asked, elbowing the first guy forward.

Uncle Dugal recaptured Neyve's attention before she could hear the rest.

"No, technically you have no clearance," he whispered urgently, eyes shining with an intensity she'd never seen before. "Listen to me carefully, Neyve. You've got nobody else now. Just me. And I am not about to leave my niece, my only family, to die by herself on a time-bomb planet. I love you, Neyve girl, and I am going to find you a place on this ship."

"But . . . but how? The security up here is crazy tight and I'm not listed as a passenger. There's no way," she insisted. Though warmed by his professed emotion, unusual for the tougher-than-nails engineer, anxiety skittered through her nervous system.

"Don't worry about the details. We just need to get you past this checkpoint."

Over his shoulder Neyve saw the guards begin their move toward Solomon and the other Reacher woman. Stepping in front of them, the woman started animatedly peppering them with questions. When one tried to push past her, she cut him off again. The twitchy guard started to pull his stun gun from its holster.

"Oh no," Neyve breathed, nodding toward the altercation to alert her uncle.

The woman protested loudly. "What are you doing, Georgie? Pulling a gun on me?" she demanded, pushing the gun's barrel away from her.

"Here's our chance, Neyve girl," Uncle Dugal hissed. "Let's go!"

The guard not intimately involved in the fray spotted their attempt to slip by and waved them over, dark eyes narrowing with suspicion. "Hey, old man. I haven't checked you in yet. Wait in the holding area."

"Oh, sir, I have my pass right here," her uncle responded, theatrically opening his vid screen on his wrist tech and scrolling though random pages. In the same breath, he whispered to Neyve, "Go now! Get on board." He shoved her forward toward the hatch. "I'll follow you."

"What do you mean?" Neyve asked, her voice an octave higher than usual. Instead of doing as he said, she stumbled to a halt, unwilling to go anywhere without him.

On the other side of the docking module the scuffle between the Reacher woman and the guard she called 'Georgie' heated up. Trying to keep the gun out of her face, her elbow connected with his chin as she grasped for purchase on the weapon.

The gun flashed, its wild beam of energy squarely striking her uncle in the chest. Thrown back a foot with a grunt of pain, he franticly clutched at Neyve's arm, shocked eyes meeting hers. She desperately grasped his hand, hoping to arrest his fall, a scream escaping her throat. Squeezing Neyve's hand once, his grip slackened as he crumpled to the ground, eyes wide and sightless.

"Uncle Dugal! Oh my god. What did you do?" she shrieked, crashing to her knees and hysterically grabbing fistfuls of Uncle D's shirt as she accused the guard.

'Georgie' stood frozen as he took in the sight of the dead man. "It was only set to moderate stun, I swear," he breathed, the words barely audible.

"He has a bum heart, you moron!" she cried, her attention on the body of her final family member. "Uncle D, can you hear me?" she begged, grasping his shoulders and shaking hard. Finally realizing her efforts were useless, she collapsed onto his still chest, her sobs echoing though the docking module.

"Aw, cripes," the closer guard swore, black eyes cold, uncaring but for the glint of irritation. "What's a guy with a bum heart doing here? He should have been screened out of the selection process."

"Who knows?" 'Georgie' replied, regaining some semblance of calm. . "Must be useful enough to the Reachers to risk the trip," he sneered, flashing yellowed crooked teeth.

"So now what do we do?" asked the first guard.

The murderous guard shrugged, taking a look around the foyer as he holstered his weapon. The nasty teeth flashed again as the guard grimaced.

Solomon and the pretty woman managed to disappear in the commotion.

Approaching Neyve, all concern for loosing the killing shot appeared to have disappeared as he asked, "What's your name, girl?"

"Neyve," she sniffled, regaining her voice as she sat up. "Neyve Colgan."

"Yeah? Who's he? And what are you doing here?" the other guard queried, black eyes flat and menacing.

"Dugal Colgan. My uncle." Neyve wiped her eyes, grief and anger almost overwhelming her. Survival instincts kicked in, honed by years of life-threatening stunts, as she willed herself to get a grip. She needed her mind to work right now. sniff "He was supposed to be boarding the ship, leaving me on this crummy planet alone. He is—was—my only family." sniff "We were saying goodbye." sniff

Uncle D lost his life trying to get me on board that ship, her brain said. Make it happen. Her heart wanted to collapse in a puddle and never move again.

"Both Colgans, huh?" Dark-eyed guard threw the nasty-toothed murderer guard a look, which he shrugged off. "Well, girlie. Looks like this is your lucky day. Let's get you to your cryo-bed, shall we?" Grasping her arm, he none-too-gently pulled Neyve to her feet.

She wanted to punch him in the throat. "Lucky day," indeed. She'd put some luck in his day, she thought darkly, longing for a chance at payback. Not today, unfortunately. Holding back took everything left in her, though she made sure to memorize their faces. Maybe she could find him again after they got to New Eden.

"That," the dark-eyed guard told his gnarl-mouthed partner, referring to her uncle's body, "is your problem. Deal with it."

Looking at the loving man who took such good care of her, Neyve felt the last piece of her heart disintegrate, only the shell of the girl she used to be remaining, Physically dragging her away, the black-eyed guard led her through a maze of corridors.

"One for cryo," the guard announced, throwing her at

the cryo tech as they entered the cryogenics facility.

The main cryogenic bed storage facility took up most of the space of the ship's Cryo Deck. While the containers were grouped for easier tracking purposes, individual beds were pulled and taken to separate, smaller chambers for loading, unloading, and servicing purposes. The room the guard brought Neyve to, about the size of an elementary school classroom, could comfortably hold up to twenty horizontal cryo-beds at a time.

Neyve slumped against the plain white wall in a haze of shock, the space around her vacant of everything but a sole staffer, her fingers tapping on the oversized wall console.

"Name's Colgan."

"Colgan. On the list. She's late but I'll take her," the busy woman confirmed, barely glancing at the log.

"Perfect. I'm outta here." And the guard left without a backward glance.

"Take off your clothes and put on the required bodywear, please. Changing closet to your left," the tech directed, turning back to the monitoring and stabilizing of the cryo-beds already in use, which Neyve's entrance interrupted.

Numbly doing as instructed, Neyve slipped on the one-piece metallic bodysuit without a word.

"Fine," the woman said, acknowledging Neyve's return to the main room.

Coding in a series of commands generated a virtual control table, this one specific to the cryo-beds. A see-through mosaic of light, the buttons and screens were as touch sensitive as a physical device.

Stepping up to the newly formed table, using what seemed to Neyve to be a complex series of instructions, the tech selected and deployed a single bed from the storage unit, efficiently opening and prepping it for occupancy.

"Step in," she instructed.

Mutely, heart and soul already frozen by shock and grief, Neyve climbed in. As she lay back into the strange container already half-full of water, a sheet of thermal material automatically rose, covering her head to toe. Temp dropping too quickly to measure, her tears mingled with the water as it fully engulfed her.

ACKNOWLEDGMENTS

When I started this journey, I had no idea that instead of a run around the neighborhood I was signing up for a multinational, multi-leg marathon. So many people helped and inspired me on this journey, it's hard to list them all. But I'll try!

THANK YOU to...

My husband. The man who has been by my side through more trials than most men I know would bear, and still supporting me through this process on so many levels. I love you.

My sister-in-law, Keturah McFarland. My original beta reader, she spent months enduring endless cliffhangers, waiting patiently for each chapter as they came, then rereading my MS numerous times. Also my pre-teen beta reader Willow R., a literary phenom. Look for her work in another decade.

My best friend KariAnn Assur. Sister of my heart, and lifelong inspiration, she also carved out a significant portion of her very precious and limited time to act as my editor. And before you skeptics-against-friends-and-family-editors scoff and turn up your noses, she's not only brilliant but professionally qualified.

My friends and family, biological and otherwise, who give their love and opinions in equal measure. I also have to thank those that unwittingly let me borrow their names and/or descriptions for otherwise purely fictional use. You know who you are. And if you don't like how you're portrayed, it's obviously someone else.

My author friends—especially Robin Deley, Brian Tashima, and Nancy Scanlon—met at various writers conferences and writing groups, which I attended in the effort to better wrap my head around an industry and craft far more complicated than it first appeared. They've all been instrumental in providing information and inspiration in their own way. This category includes Author Salon, a website for writers trying to perfect their craft, where tough love gains new meaning. I never would have pushed through and made certain changes to my text without my team's feedback.

And last but never, ever, least. I thank God.

ABOUT THE AUTHOR

Roslyn McFarland is the author of "See No Sea" (currently available in both e-book and paperback formats, audiobook to follow soon) and it's follow up "Hear No Sea", the short story "Soldier Boy" (originally released in the Fall of 2014 Northwest Independent Writers Association Anthology), and "Light the Way" (Loves Light book one of the Paradisi Chronicles, Book two to follow shortly). All are nice clean Young Adult Romances.

In 2006 she was struck down by health problems, which progressed into full immobility over the course of six and a half years, undiagnosed. Going out of her mind via the enormous worry-frustration-pain-boredom combo she shouldered, Roslyn's solution and salvation came in the form of writing, as she expelled a childhood recurring dream onto paper. The completion of her first novel coincided with a diagnosis of Lyme Disease. Treatment and a cure quickly following cleared the way for editing and preparation for publication. God works in mysterious ways.

Roslyn currently lives in Oregon with her husband, two extraordinarily active and strong willed little girls (karma) and a house full of fur kids (cats and dogs, and one goldfish still hanging in there).

She's already outlining new books she hopes to release within the next year, amassing a lengthy list of future series ideas. Roslyn hopes to be able to continue turning dreams into reality for many years to come.

45415491R00192

Made in the USA
San Bernardino, CA
08 February 2017